W9-BGG-089

Circus World

Captain Bostany swore that if she perspired any harder her boots would overflow.

Kahn picked up a sheaf of papers from his desk. "As mission sociological officer, Captain Bostany, perhaps you would be kind enough to tell me why the Momus military mission has the worst disciplinary rate in the Quadrant."

"Yessir. The positive soci . . ."

"Skip the parameters and the poop loops. Cut the crap, Captain. Why is this group of top-rate soldiers turning into a bunch of juvenile delinquents?"

"Sir, uh. . . . The personnel. . . . They want to go to the circus, Sir!"

Berkley books by Barry B. Longyear

CIRCUS WORLD
MANIFEST DESTINY

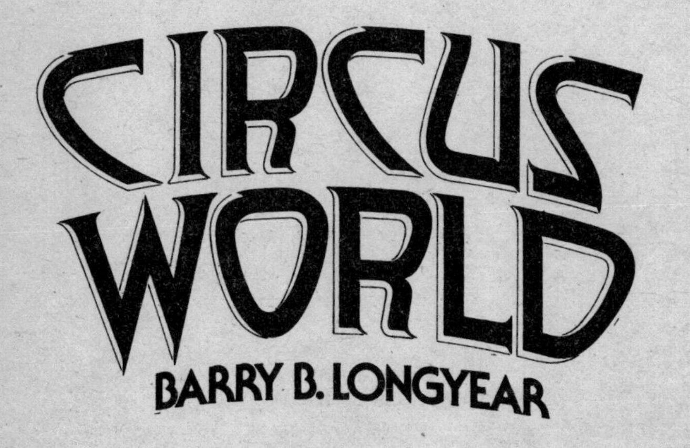

BERKLEY BOOKS, NEW YORK

CIRCUS WORLD

A Berkley Book / published by arrangement with the author

PRINTING HISTORY
Berkley edition / January 1981

All rights reserved.
Copyright © 1981 by Barry B. Longyear.
"The Tryouts," copyright © 1978 by Davis Publications, Inc.
"The Magician's Apprentice," copyright © 1978 by Davis Publications, Inc.
"The Second Law," copyright © 1978 by Davis Publications, Inc.
"Proud Rider," copyright © 1978 by Davis Publications, Inc.
"Dueling Clowns," copyright © 1979 by Davis Publications, Inc.
"The Quest," copyright © 1979 by Davis Publications, Inc.
"Priest of the *Baraboo*," copyright © 1979 by Davis Publications, Inc.
Cover illustration by John Rush.
This book may not be reproduced in whole or in part, by mimeograph or any other means, without permission.
For information address: Berkley Publishing Corporation,
200 Madison Avenue, New York, New York 10016.

ISBN: 0-425-04709-1

A BERKLEY BOOK ® TM 757,375

PRINTED IN THE UNITED STATES OF AMERICA

DEDICATION

Book dedications are an inadequate but cheap way of attempting to pay off debts. "The Tryouts" was the first story I ever sold. With the interest of George H. Scithers in the story's premise, and the pitiful bit of leverage of my first sale, I proposed to George a series of stories that would constitute an episodic novel. In the process of purchasing these, and other stories, George had placed into *Isaac Asimov's Science Fiction Magazine*'s inventory approximately 150,000 words worth of my stories before "The Tryouts" appeared in the November–December 1978 issue of *IA's sfm*. This kind of commitment doesn't come cheap, and is not done without risk. But it happens. New writers take note. Therefore, to the man who bought them, and to the man who paid for them, *Circus World* is gratefully dedicated to:

George H. Scithers
Editor, *Isaac Asimov's*
Science Fiction Magazine

and

Joel Davis
President & Publisher, Davis Publications, Inc.

Contents

The Tryouts

The stranger sat cross-legged on the sand staring at the vent from which the natural fire of the planet Momus illuminated the small wayside depression on the road to Tarzak. His black hood was pulled forward leaving only twin dancing flames reflected from unblinking eyes as evidence of a face. As a light breeze rose from the desert, bringing the heavy smell of sulphur from the fire, a portly figure dressed in grey robe and apron stepped between the rocks into the firelight. He raised his hand and motioned toward a place near the flames.

"The fire is free," answered the black-hooded stranger. The newcomer squatted next to the flames, pulled a wad of dough from his pack and placed it on a rock close to the fire. In moments the sweet smell of cobit bread drove the odor of sulphur from the depression.

"Care you for some cobit, stranger?"

"For half, two movills. No more."

"Two? Why, it would distress me no more to hand out my bread for nothing."

"In which case, I would gladly take all."

"Three."

"Two."

The man in grey broke the cobit and handed half to the black-robed stranger who handed back two copper beads. The bargaining hadn't been in earnest; only enough to satisfy custom. Finishing his cobit first, the one in grey tapped himself on his chest. "I am Aarel the mason. Have you news?" Aarel jingled his money pouch. The one in black shook his head. "But, you wear the newsteller's black."

"True, Aarel, but I apprentice only. However, my master will be along directly."

"What fortune! A master newsteller at the fire! Is he known?"

"No."

Aarel shrugged. "I am not one to discourage youth. Is this his first news?"

"No, but only small ones until now. His news tonight will play Tarzak, he thinks."

Aarel raised an eyebrow. "Tarzak? I hope his is the enthusiasm of experience rather than youth."

"My very words, Aarel."

They sat in silence watching the flames until two other men, wearing the tan robes of merchants, entered the circle of firelight.

"Ho, Aarel!" called the taller of the two.

"Parak," the mason answered, then, nodding at Parak's companion, "Jum."

Parak pointed at the fire. "It costs nothing, join us," said Aarel.

The merchants squatted close to the flames, each placing wads of cobit dough on the hot rocks. After some social bargaining and exchange, the four travelers sat munching cobit. Parak produced a wine flask, they bargained further, then passed around the flask while Parak pocketed his movills.

"It has been a weary trek from the Deeplands." He cocked his head toward the black-robed stranger and asked Aarel, "Has he news?"

"His master has news he believes will play Tarzak, and he should be here soon."

"Tarzak, eh?" Parak rubbed his hands together in anticipation. "Has the apprentice introduced it?"

"No."

At that moment they all turned to see another black-hooded figure enter the firelight and gesture toward the flames. "No copper for the flames, newsteller," said Parak. "Are you the master of this apprentice?"

"Yes. I am Boosthit of the Farransetti newstellers." Boosthit seated himself by the flames and cooked cobit, which, after rapid and impatient bargaining, was quickly gulped by the eager travelers. The master newsteller finished his cobit and brushed the crumbs from his robe. Turning to the travelers, he asked, "Is news to your liking tonight?"

Aarel squinted and tossed his purse in the air and caught it. "I can meet a good price for good news, Boosthit. But, I admit, your name is unfamiliar to me. We get few Farransetti this way."

"I agree," said Parak. "Could you tell us a little about it to enable us to judge the fairness of your price?"

Boosthit held up his hand, palm outward, and shook his head. "The Farransetti do not introduce."

"Why so?" asked Jum.

"We believe small glimpses of the whole are devoid of the grace of logical construction."

Aarel shrugged and held up his palms. "How, then, do we judge the price?"

"What would you pay for excellent news?"

The mason and the two merchants thought deeply.

"Twenty movills," answered Aarel, "but only for excellent news."

"I would pay twenty-five," said Parak. "That is a fair price in Tarzak for excellent."

"I agree," said Jum, "twenty-five."

Aarel wagged a finger at the merchants. "But, friends, we are not in Tarzak. Do we not deserve credit for trudging out here on the road to hear Boosthit's news?"

Parak smiled. "You are a bandit, Aarel. The newsteller has trudged just as far to tell us the news, and we would be on the road in any event."

Aarel shrugged. "Very well, twenty-five movills."

Boosthit nodded. "Hear me then. I will give my news at that price in advance, but no money back."

"But, what if . . . ?"

"I must finish my offer, Aarel. Twenty-five movills apiece in advance, or hold onto your coppers and pay me double that price at the conclusion of my news, if you judge it to be excellent."

Aarel's mouth opened in amazement. "It is an honor to meet a newsteller capable of making such an offer." Parak and Jum nodded in agreement. "We will hold our coppers."

Boosthit arranged his robe, closed his eyes and began. "This news is of Lord Ashly Allenby, special ambassador to Momus from the Ninth Quadrant Federation of Habitable Planets. His mission: one of grave importance to his government, and to the people of the planet Momus. His journey: one of great heroics and high comedy."

"A peculiar opening," said Aarel, "but it captures the attention. The hint of serious events relating to Momus is the true hook, am I correct?"

"I agree, Aarel," said Parak, "and what could it be that interests the Federation in Momus? We have no trade for them, and we refuse to serve them. What could Lord Allenby's mission be? Jum?"

"It is the promise of comedy that intrigues me, but, nonetheless, the opening captures the attention. I had heard the Farransetti were experimenting with openings devoid of prayers and tributes, and many think this radical. But, having heard such an opening tonight, I approve."

Boosthit waited a moment, then continued. "On Earth, the ancient parent planet, high within the tall, gleaming spires of the Federation complex, Lord Allenby was called to meet with the Council of Seven.

"'Allenby,' said the council president, 'you are made special ambassador to Momus, with all of the rights and privileges of an ambassador of the first rank.'

"'I am most honored,' replied Allenby. Lord Allenby stood fair tall as he accepted his charge, his pleasant features composed and dignified, his uniform uncluttered and tasteful."

Jum held up a hand. "Boosthit, is that the extent of the hero's description?"

"Yes."

Aarel scratched his chin. "We are used to lengthier descriptions. Is there a reason for this brevity?"

"Perhaps," Parak interrupted, "it is to let us fill in the description ourselves. Would a mistaken image affect the truth of your news, Boosthit?"

"No."

Aarel frowned. "That is radical, no doubt." He closed his eyes. "But, I can see an image. Yes, I can see him."

"And I," said Jum.

"And I," said Parak.

Boosthit cleared his throat. "Allenby was confused, since a planet of Momus's stature hardly rates an ambassador of the first rank." Aarel, Parak and Jum nodded.

"This is true," said Parak. "What could the Council of Seven have in mind to make such an appointment?" Aarel and Jum shook their heads.

"Allenby asked the reason for this," continued Boosthit, "and this is the president's answer: 'Momus lies just upon the boundary of the Ninth and Tenth quadrants. In actuality, it is closer to the main population centers of the Tenth than it is to ours. We have learned that the Tenth Quadrant Federation plans to occupy Momus to use as a forward base from which to launch their invasion of the entire Ninth Quadrant.'"

Aarel, Parak and Jum gasped. "But Momus has no defense against a military force," said Parak.

"This is grave indeed," said Aarel.

"But," said Jum, "what, then, could the mission be?"

"Lord Allenby asked this question, also," said Boosthit. "The president told Allenby that his mission was to establish relations between the Ninth Federation and Momus for the purpose of mutual defense against the coming invasion."

"A worthy mission," remarked Aarel. "I think sufficient to motivate the hero. What do you say Parak?"

"It would appear so. Do you agree Jum?"

Jum rubbed the bridge of his nose. "Allenby is only told of the threat. In the actuality, not the telling, is the real threat, and, therefore, sufficient motivation. I shall reserve judgment."

Boosthit waited until it was silent enough to hear the hissing of the flames. "Lord Allenby could not prepare for his mission; there was no time. He had to make all possible speed to Momus to warn us of the threat, which was difficult since there are no regular routes to Momus. A Federation cruiser brought Allenby as far as the Capella system, but had to turn back because of power problems. Stranded on Capella's fifth planet, awaiting passage on a freighter reported to be heading in this direction, Lord Allenby's baggage was stolen, as well as his money and his Federation transportation pass."

Aarel shook his head. "All he could do, then, would be to wait for the return of the Federation cruiser, is this not true?"

"It would appear so," answered Parak. "A sad day for Momus, except there's something wrong. Jum?"

"Indeed there is, Parak. Such news would be pointless and futile. No newsteller, Faransetti or otherwise, would bother with such a tale, much less inflict us with it. Perhaps the hero is made of stern stuff and will complete his mission?"

"But how?" Parak shook his head. "He cannot travel without money or his pass."

Boosthit smiled. "Lord Allenby, not the kind to be defeated by chance circumstance, set himself the task of continuing his journey. At the Federation consulate, he demanded transportation; but the consul, in turn, required verification of Allenby's mission before he would authorize the release of a ship or money. Allenby was furious, since it would take many weeks for verification to come from Earth; but the consul was within his rights and could not be swayed.

"Allenby haunted the spaceport, the consulate and even exporting establishments trying to get transportation, but was unsuccessful until he caught wind of an opening on a freighter for a cargo handler. Selling his uniform and medals, he purchased ordinary clothing and secured able-bodied spacer papers from the Federation consulate. Then he signed on with the *Starwind*, which was scheduled to pass near Momus on its way to trade with the Tenth Quadrant."

"I think I see his plan," said Aarel. "It is daring, but it is also dishonest."

Parak shook his head. "The mission outweighs the act, Aarel. Besides, the Federation would pay for the stolen lifeboat, would it not?"

"Perhaps. What say you, Jum?"

"I will relent on the motivation; I think it is sufficient."

Boosthit leaned toward the fire, spreading his arms. "As you guessed, Lord Allenby took a lifeboat from the freighter as it passed abreast of Momus, but the range was not ideal. After covering the distance, establishing an orbit for pickup was out of the question. He decided to break atmosphere and go for a hard landing as soon as he arrived. To do otherwise would cost both his life and the mission, as he was low on air.

"He had hoped to assume manual control after achieving flight, in order to put down near a large city, but he lost consciousness before reaching our outer atmosphere. As chance would have it, however, the boat's automatic system put Allenby down near Kuumic on the edge of the Great Desert. He wandered the desert for two days until he chanced to meet Garok the cobit gatherer."

"Hah!" Aarel exclaimed. "I know Garok—the thief."

"I have heard of him," said Parak. "A spirited bargainer, Garok."

"Allenby said to Garok, 'Say, fellow, can you point me in the direction of Tarzak?'" Boosthit smiled and suppressed a chuckle. "Garok tapped his purse and said, 'What is this information worth to you, stranger?'

"Allenby, coming from a rich world where such information is as free as the fire, was very confused. 'You demand payment for such a thing? Absurd!'

"Garok began walking away, but thinking better of it, came back and explained. 'What I say now, stranger, has no value to me and I let you have it for free. I know where Tarzak lies, and you do not.'

"'So much,' said Allenby 'could be deduced from my question.'

"'That's why it is of no value. But, the direction of Tarzak is of value to you, is it not?'

"'Of course.'

"'Then, it is of value to me.' Again, Garok tapped his purse. Lord Allenby had little left over from the sale of his uniform, and he felt in his pocket for the scraps of paper they use for money."

Aarel grabbed his ribs and laughed until he gasped for air. Parak and Jum shook their heads and chuckled.

"Allenby held out one of the scraps at Garok, who took it and examined it closely. 'What is this?'

"'Money. That's what you wanted, isn't it?'

"Garok handed the scrap back, and said, 'Stranger, how long have you been in the desert? The paper itself might have a value, except for its being covered with ink.' Garok opened his purse and brought forth a single moville. 'This is money, stranger.'

"'Well, then, fellow, where can I get my money converted into yours?' Garok tapped his purse. Allenby was perplexed. 'You would charge for that information, too?'

"'Is the information of value?'

"'Yes, but . . .' Garok kept tapping his purse. As he turned to leave, Allenby had one remaining try. 'Tell me, fellow, would you accept something of value in exchange for the information?'

"'Barter?'

"'Yes.'

"Garok rubbed his chin, then fingered a fold of Lord Allenby's utility suit. 'This would do.'

"Allenby was outraged. 'Not that! I landed here in a ship's lifeboat. Would that have value to you?' And, Garok was interested. The boat's fuel and supplies were exhausted, and the ship itself was inoperable, but the furnishings were intact as well as the wiring and other materials. Garok made an offer of one hundred movills, and Allenby accepted."

Aarel snorted. "I said Garok was a thief. I wouldn't have parted with it for less than four hundred. Parak?"

"I was thinking the same thing, although my price would have been higher. Jum, does this make our hero a fool?"

"I think not. The boat had served its purpose and no longer had any value to Lord Allenby. Besides, if I was stuck in Kuumic and didn't know the direction to Tarzak, I might have even taken a lesser amount." Aarel and Parak pondered Jum's remarks, then nodded.

"Garok counted out a hundred movills," continued Boosthit, "and handed them to Allenby. Allenby took two of the coppers and handed them back to Garok. 'Now, can you tell me the way to Tarzak?' Garok pointed the direction and reached into his own purse to pay for Allenby's information concerning the location of the lifeboat.

"'Where is the lifeboat, stranger?' Allenby didn't notice Garok's hand in his purse, and he truthfully pointed the way to the lifeboat. Garok assumed, since no payment was demanded, that the information was worthless. Therefore, he turned in the opposite direction and struck out to find and take possession of his new purchase. It is said that Garok still wanders Momus looking for his lifeboat, and if he maintains his direction, he will eventually find it."

"No more, Boosthit," gasped Aarel. Parak and Jum rolled in the sand laughing. "No more! Let us rest!"

After more cobit and wine, Aarel rose to present and resolve a complicated stonecutting problem in pantomime, followed by Parak's mummery of a wedding ceremony he had supplied with gifts at a price that drew admiration from the travelers. Jum recited a comic poem concerning his efforts to marry the daughter of a cheese merchant. Exchanges were made, and silence settled around the fire as they waited expectantly for Boosthit to continue his news.

"Lord Allenby's journey to Tarzak was one of privation and hardship, not knowing that just under his feet fat cobit roots slept, waiting to be milked. Instead, he visited the fires along the road, buying cobit from other travelers, until he ran out of movills."

"Boosthit, had this Allenby no act?" Parak frowned and shook his head. "Had he nothing of value?"

"He had the news of his mission, Parak, but this he kept to himself."

"Why?" asked Aarel.

"Why, indeed?" asked Jum.

"It is curious, but it is the custom among Allenby's people to play information of that sort only before governments. He was waiting until reaching Tarzak," Boosthit laughed, "to play it before *our* government!" The travelers laughed and shook their heads. "Yes, it was not until he hired himself out to a priest as a beast of burden in exchange for cobit and information that he learned Momus has no government."

"A sorry fellow," said Aarel, chuckling.

Parak nodded. "Yes, and can such a character be the hero around which excellent news transpires? I fear for your fee, Boosthit."

Jum held up his hand. "You are too hasty, Parak. Think. Would any of us do better, or as well, on ancient Earth, Allenby's planet? As Boosthit said, the information is for no charge, but I have heard that the fire is not! Would we appear any less foolish if someone asked us coppers for fire?"

"But, Jum, is it not part of the diplomat's skill to be versed on where he is sent?"

"Only recall Boosthit's opening, Parak." Jum closed his eyes. "In the second part covering Allenby's trip to Momus: 'Lord Allenby could not prepare for his mission; there was no time.'"

"Ah, yes," said Parak, "I stand corrected."

"And I," agreed Aarel.

Boosthit nodded and smiled. "Allenby carried the priest's pack and paraphernalia, and the priest told him of our freedom. From the priest, and from other travelers along the road, he learned that for Momus as a planet to agree to something, half of each town must petition for a meeting, then half of all the towns must vote and agree, for this is the law.

"Allenby remarked to the priest, 'Momus doesn't have many laws, does it?'

"'Only one,' answered the priest, 'which is our law for making laws. It suffices.'

"Lord Allenby, coming from a planet which has millions of laws, was perplexed. 'If Momus needed a new law,' he asked the priest, 'how would one go about it?'

"'To move the people in each town to petition for a meeting, the law must be something the people want. Before they can want it, they must be aware of it.'

"Allenby nodded at this wisdom, and said, 'Since I have yet to see so much as a wheeled vehicle in my travels on Momus, I don't suppose the planet sports anything resembling mass broadcasting media."

Boosthit laughed with the other travelers. "'Ever since the first settlers of Momus were stranded here, we have communicated with art,' said the priest to Allenby. 'It was many Earth years before the skies of Momus saw another starship, and by then we were numerous, satisfied with our lot, and with our customs.'

"'And mass media, I take it, is not art.'

"'I suppose it could have been,' answered the priest, 'except no one knew how to build a radio. In any event, it was not their way.'

"Allenby's doubts concerning the success of his mission grew. 'The original settlers of Momus,' he said to the priest, 'what were their occupations?'

"'Why, there were many. Acrobats, mimes, storytellers, clowns, razzle-dazzle operators . . .'

"'It was a circus ship?'

"'Not just a circus ship,' answered the priest, 'but O'Hara's Greatest Shows, the finest collection of artists and games in the entire quadrant.'"

Boosthit allowed the travelers a moment of silent prayer. When they raised their heads, Aarel rubbed his chin and thought deeply. "I do not understand, Boosthit, why the hero needs a new law. It would seem sufficient for the Ninth Federation to occupy Momus itself without fanfare. This would serve their objective, and we would be powerless to stop them."

"And," said Parak, "once Momus learned of the threat from the Tenth Quadrant, we would not object."

"The law does seem unnecessary," Jum concluded.

Boosthit held up his hands. "It is complicated, friends, but I shall explain. There is the Great Law of the Ninth Federation, which is actually a collection of many laws. It decrees that the protection of the federation cannot be extended to a planet that has not asked for it. Because of our one law for making laws, Momus is considered a governed society. If the Ninth Federation occupied Momus without our consent, the Tenth Federation would coinsider that an invasion, because of *their* laws. This, too, would violate even greater laws that govern all the quadrants . . ."

Parak held his hands over his ears. "It is clear to me why our ancestors chose to remain on Momus!"

"That is true," Aarel agreed. "Would it not be easier for the Ninth and Tenth Quadrants to change their laws?"

"Impossible," answered Jum. "The objectives of the two quadrants differ. They could not agree. Boosthit, this means that the hero must resolve his mission with the laws that already exist?"

"That is true."

"Which also means he must move the people of Momus to pass another law."

"True, as well, Jum. Allenby asked the priest how this could be done, and the priest told him to wait. 'We will sit at the fire this night, and you shall see how. I have heard a newsteller, Lett of the Dofstaffl, will entertain.'

"That night, Lord Allenby saw the work of his first newsteller. Lett performed well and fattened his purse. Afterward, Allenby asked the priest, 'Is this how the news is communicated?'

"'Yes.'

"'Doesn't it strike you as a trifle inefficient?'

"'Bah! Art is not to be judged by efficiency!'

"'But, what if there were news that should be communicated to all of the people quickly?'

"'You weary me with your endless questions! What kind of news could it be that would be of such immediacy?'

"'I have such news,' answered Allenby. 'Would you listen to it?'

"The priest took his things from Allenby. 'Stranger,' he said, 'your price of endless answers to endless questions to carry my things is high enough. But, to sit and listen to a frustrated newsteller? You take me for a fool!' With that, the priest left Allenby by the fire and hurried off into the night."

Aarel looked into the fire and frowned. "I see the hero's problem, Boosthit, for even I would have acted as did the priest. I would not have listened."

"Nor I," said Parak. "Even though he has news of importance, I would not have listened."

Jum rubbed his hands together, then pointed at his fellow travelers. "The hero is the thing of importance here. Lord Allenby, an ambassador of the first rank, reduced to a beast of burden in an attempt at accomplishing his mission. Will he continue his struggle to bring his news to the people of Momus, or will he be defeated letting Momus fall to the evil designs of the Tenth Federation?" They turned toward Boosthit and saw that he had pulled his hood over his eyes. Bowing their heads, they moaned softly.

"For three nights, Lord Allenby stayed at the fire, trying to tell his news, meeting with failure with each new group of travelers. After failing on the fourth night, Allenby was defeated. He bartered his wedding ring for a card trick from a wandering magician, and using this trick he kept himself in movills until he reached Tarzak, where he planned to find transportation to Earth.

"While awaiting the rare ship that comes to Momus, Allenby purchased two more card tricks and an illusion. With these he paid for his town lodgings, meals and clothing, and began saving for his passage back to Earth. It was during this period that Lord Allenby chanced to hear of Vyson of the Dofstaffl newstellers, playing his news at the Great Square in Tarzak." Boosthit removed the hood from his eyes.

Aarel smiled. "Will the great Vyson inspire Allenby?"

"I heard Vyson play the burning of Tarzak years ago," said Parak. "I was inspired to petition in the town to form the fire company."

"Yes," said Jum, "I heard just an apprentice licensed to repeat Vyson's news, and was inspired to petition for a fire company in my town of Miira. Yes, that was good news."

"Indeed," said Boosthit, "Allenby was inspired, but not by Vyson's news, which concerned the second eruption of the Arcadia Volcano. What caught Allenby's attention was the number of newstellers and apprentice newstellers among the listeners. After Vyson finished, the newstellers gathered around to bid for licenses to repeat his news. I was among those attempting to get through the listeners in order to bid, when I was stopped by Lord Allenby.

"'Unhand me, trickster,' I said, for he wore the black and scarlet of the magicians. 'I must get to the bidding.' He released me, but try as I might, I could not get close to Vyson before he closed the bidding. Times had not gone well with me and I was desperate for news that I could take on the road. With this opportunity lost, I turned to look for the trickster to vent my anger. I found him standing behind me. 'See what you've done? News that played in Tarzak, but I can't repeat it because you made me miss the bidding.'

"Allenby pointed at the newstellers clustered around Vyson. 'They will repeat Vyson's news?'

"'Of course.'

"'But the people of Tarzak have already heard it.'

"'They won't repeat it in Tarzak, fool. They will take it on the road and play it in other towns. Some newstellers will issue second licenses to unknown and apprentice newstellers. In days, Arcadia's eruption will be all over Momus.'

"'Can't you get one of those second licenses?'

"I admit I was exasperated with this nitwit trickster, and told him so, for even children know there are no coppers in a second license. 'I am a master newsteller, trickster. I do not second license, nor do I pick up fireside gossip and play it for news. My news must have played Tarzak!'

"'News that plays Tarzak will spread, then?'

"'Of course. You tire me; go away.'

"Allenby stood there a moment, watching the clamor of newstellers running off with their new licenses, then he turned back to me. 'Newsteller,' he said, 'how much would you charge to hear my story—a story that will play Tarzak, if done properly.'

"I laughed. 'Trickster, there are not enough coppers on Momus to entice me to endure your amateur efforts.' He tossed his purse at me, and when I caught it, I could feel the weight of over five hundred movills in it. As I said, I had been on desperate times. 'Very well,' I said, tucking the purse into my belt, 'but be brief.'

"Allenby told me his tale, and it was raw, clumsy and presented in bad order. But, I saw in it the potential for greatness—possibly news that would play Tarzak.

"'Can you play this in Tarzak now?' he asked me.

"'Of course not. It must be worked on, polished, and then taken on the road to see how it plays. If we do well on the road, then we may try Tarzak.' Allenby rubbed his eyes, sighed, and nodded.

Aarel, his eyes wide, turned toward the apprentice newsteller. "But, then . . ."

"Yes, friends," said Boosthit, "I would like to present Lord Ashly Allenby, special ambassador to Momus from the Ninth Quadrant Federation of Habitable Planets."

The apprentice stood and pushed the robe back from his face. "Oh, excellent, Boosthit!" Aarel exclaimed.

"Yes, excellent, indeed!" said Parak. Allenby turned to Jum.

"And you?"

"Oh, yes. Excellent, most excellent."

Allenby reached within his newsteller's robe and withdrew an empty sack. "In which case, friends, that will be fifty coppers apiece."

As they trudged through the dark on the road toward Tarzak, Allenby said to Boosthit, "We were judged excellent and brought twice the price. I think we are ready for Tarzak. I don't see why we should play any more fires."

"There are still a few things that need to be worked out, Allenby. Your escape in the lifeboat was too easily guessed. I'll have to rework that."

"Humph!" They walked along in silence for a piece, then Allenby spoke. "Boosthit."

"Yes?"

"Since we will be on the road a bit longer, perhaps there is something we could do about my presentation as a comic character. Don't you think if the news were a little more serious . . ."

"Bah!" Boosthit strode ahead, raising angry puffs of dust from the road. "Everybody wants to be a critic," he shouted at the night. "Everybody!"

The Magician's Apprentice

Yudo and his two brothers stood looking at their grain field. Green only the day before, it now lay brown and withered. Yudo nodded. "It is the power of Rogor. Your tongue angered him, Arum."

"Bah!" Arum bent over and pulled up a handful of the brown plants, then held them over his head. "Rogor! Since the circus ship brought our ancestors to Momus, we have served no man . . ."

"Arum!" Yudo held up his hands and looked with horror at his brother Lase.

Lase stood next to Arum and grabbed his arm. "Would you bring down more of this upon us?"

Arum shook off his brother's hand. Throwing the withered plants on the ground, Arum turned to his two brothers. "A fine pair you make. Look at you shaking in your sandals."

Lase wrung his hands, looked to Yudo, then back at Arum. "We are barkers by tradition, Arum. Perhaps we should go to Tarzak and be barkers again."

Arum shook his head. "As I said, a fine pair." He held out his arms, indicating the fields belonging to the three. "After all our work you would have us fetch and carry pitches for others?" Arum put his hands on his hips. "We are men of property. No carnival trickster will change that . . ."

Lase and Yudo watched as Arum grabbed at his own face and his red and purple striped robe burst into flames. In seconds, Arum lay dead, his body burned beyond recognition. Then, it disappeared.

"Arum!" Yudo took a step toward the spot where his brother had been standing, but stopped as a figure clad in black and scarlet appeared on the spot. Its face was hidden by a hood. "Rogor!"

The figure pointed at Lase. "Arum offended me. Do you believe as he believed?"

Lase clasped his hands together and bowed. "No, Great Rogor. Spare me."

"Lase, you would do my bidding?"

"Yes, Great Rogor."

"Then, go to all the towns in Emerald Valley and tell them to go to Ris. They are to wait there until I appear."

"Yes, Great Rogor."

"Then, go." Lase looked at Yudo, back at Rogor, then began running across the field toward Ikona. Rogor turned toward Yudo. "For you, barker, I have an important task. Go to the fountain in Ikona. Your instructions are there." Yudo closed his eyes and nodded. When he opened them, Rogor was gone.

Eight days later, far to the south in Tarzak, a young girl looked nervously at a great magician's door. Its black and scarlet curtain hung motionless in the noon sun, while the reflection from the whitewashed adobe hurt her eyes. Making her decision, she clenched her fists, held her arms straight at her sides and marched through the door. Inside, she found herself standing next to a tall, sad-faced barker. He was dusty and smelled of the road. At the back of the small room, a tiny old man in black-and-scarlet robe sat on a low stool, supporting himself by gripping a heavy, gnarled staff. The old man nodded at the barker.

"A moment, Yudo, while I find out who my hasty visitor is." The old man raised his eyebrows at the girl.

"Fyx, I am Crisal. I, I didn't know you had company."

"I suppose, Crisal, it would have been too much trouble to call to the house. Never mind, little fortune teller. What brings you?"

"Fyx, I would be a magician."

The old magician looked the girl over from the top of her unkempt tangle of red hair to her dusty bare feet. "First, you are a girl; second, you are obviously of the fortune tellers; third, you are rude. Why should I apprentice you to the magician's trade?"

"First, Fyx, women have been magicians before. Myra of Kuumic played the Great Square here in Tarzak only yesterday."

The old man nodded. "Rare, but it has been done. But, Myra is the daughter of a magician. Explain that blue robe you wear—at least I think it's blue under all that dirt."

"I am of the Tarzak fortune tellers. My mother is Salina. I told her as I tell you, I *choose* to be a magician. I have completed my apprenticeship; no one can force me to be a fortune teller." Crisal folded her arms, her nose in the air.

"Salina, eh?" Fyx scratched his head, then rubbed his chin. "You say you told this to Salina?"

"Aye."

"And what did the Great Salina say to you?"

"She said my life was my own and to do with it what I choose."

The corners of Fyx's mouth went down as his eyebrows went up. "She did? And your father, Eeren?"

Crisal frowned. "He was not understanding."

"I see. Now, about the third thing: your rudeness. Not even my own sons addressed me simply as 'Fyx.'"

Crisal cocked her head to one side. "You insist?"

The old man nodded. "Try it once."

The girl bowed, loading her voice with sarcasm scraped from the floor. "*Great* Fyx."

"I see your respect would be more of a burden to both of us than your rudeness. And, now for the important part. Why should I take you on?"

Crisal smiled. "I know how you do your trick of the missing card."

The old man nodded, smiled and pointed to a cushion next to his table. "Sit there, Crisal, and we will talk later. I don't want to hold up my visitor's business any longer." Walking in front of the barker, Crisal approached the table and sat on the designated cushion.

The barker bowed. "Great Fyx, is this something to say in front of the child?" Yudo pointed at Crisal.

Fyx looked at her, then turned back to the barker. "The little beast is my apprentice, Yudo. She is held under my vow of confidence, which is something she *will* respect!" Fyx turned back to the girl. Crisal nodded, and smiled.

Yudo shrugged. "As you say, Great Fyx. Will you come to Ikona?" Cirsal saw fear in the barker's eyes, but it was not fear of Fyx.

"And you say the fee is twenty thousand movills?"

"In advance." Yudo pointed at the stack of bags on the floor.

Fyx nodded. "A handsome sum. We were interrupted before you said what I must do for it."

"Ikona is a farming village, Great Fyx, and our crops die..."

Fyx held up his hand. "Save your coppers, Yudo. I am a magician, not a farmer."

"The crops die, Great Fyx, because of a magician. Rogor the Black One."

"Rogor... I have heard of this one, but he calls himself a sorcerer, not a magician."

Yudo bowed his head. "You all call upon the same dark spirits. Ikona has no place else to turn for help." The barker reached into his robe and brought forth an envelope. "The Dark One made this appear at the fountain in Ikona. It is addressed to you."

Fyx opened the envelope and squinted at the sheet of paper inside. Lifting his head, he turned to Crisal. "Fortune tellers do not read, do they?"

"I do."

Fyx held out the letter. The girl stood and walked to the old magician and took the letter. "Read it aloud."

Crisal held the paper to the light and began: "To Fyx, ancient and worthless patriarch of the Tarzak Magicians, Greetings. A fool from Ikona will ask you to come and do battle with me in my Deepland kingdom. He is a fool because he asks you; you are the bigger fool if you accept.

"Stay in the city, carnival trickster, and stay safe. In the Deeplands, I rule without challenge, for I have the power of Momus at my hands." Crisal looked at Fyx. "It is signed 'ROGOR' in a strange way."

"Strange how?"

"In a cross; look."

Fyx looked at the bottom of the sheet and saw the signature in bold letters:

```
  R
  O
ROGOR
  O
  R
```

"What does it mean, Fyx?"

The magician frowned. "It is a palindrome—a word that reads the same frontwards or backwards. Other than that, it means nothing."

Yudo shook his head. "Great Fyx, it is the Dark One's sign. Show disrespect to it in Ikona, and your crops die. You then must pay Rogor to leave you be."

Fyx looked at a dark spot on the ceiling. ". . . ancient and worthless patriarch . . ." He turned his gaze on the barker. "Yudo, you fool, a bigger fool accepts your offer. Tell that to Rogor."

"I cannot. No one knows where Rogor lives."

Fyx shrugged. "How then am I supposed to do battle with the fumble-fingered Dark One."

Yudo trembled. "Please, Great Fyx. Express your discourtesies after I have left." The barker bowed and backed out through the door. Fyx looked into Crisal's eyes.

"In the barker's eyes, what did you see?"

"Fear. As though Rogor could reach down and pluck him from your house if he chose."

The old magician nodded. Standing, he hobbled over to a chest, opened it and pulled out a black and scarlet robe. He handed it to the girl. "Wash, then put this on. There is a pool in back of the house. We will leave before light tomorrow for the Deeplands."

The next evening at the midway fire to Tieras, Crisal lifted her weary head from the sand and looked over her aching feet at the old magician. Fyx tested the many wads of cobit he had baking around the fire, and finding one done to his satisfaction, he put it into Crisal's sack. "There, that should keep us to Miira when they're all done." The girl let her head fall back to the sand.

"Fyx, aren't you tired? We've been walking all day."

The magician cackled. "So, apprentice, you are ready to end the day, are you?"

"You aren't?"

"I would be a poor master, Crisal, if I failed to give you your lessons."

"Lessons?"

Fyx nodded and dropped the remaining cobit cakes into the sack. "Sit up."

Crisal pushed herself up and sat cross-legged in front of the magician. Before her was a rock, and on the rock was a feather. Fyx sat across the rock from her. "What must I do?"

"Turn the feather over without your fingers. Touch it only with your mind."

Crisal frowned. "I don't understand."

"Look." Fyx pointed at the feather and turned it over as easily as if he had used his fingers. Again, he turned it back. "As a fortune teller's apprentice, you were taught to see as the fortune tellers see, with an extra pair of eyes. Now you must learn to use your extra pair of hands."

Crisal stared at the feather. "This is not a trick?"

"No. It is something you must learn, however, before you can do the better tricks and illusions. Try it."

Crisal fixed her eyes on the white feather, held her breath, grunted, went bug-eyed and began growing blue in the face. It didn't move. Letting her breath out, she shook her head. "It didn't move."

"Pick it up and feel it; rub it against your face. Your mind doesn't know what it's trying to do yet, and you must teach it." Cirsal picked up the feather and felt its smoothness with her fingers and with her face. "Place it on the rock and try again."

The girl put down the feather, looked at it through almost closed eyes and imagined tiny hands reaching under and gripping the feather's edge. With her mind she felt resistance as though she were attempting to lift a great rock plate. Heaving against the weight, she strained until she slumped forward letting out her breath. The feather lifted and fluttered to the sand. "Did I . . . ?"

"No, child. You blew it off the rock. But, I saw it rock before it took flight. You have done well for your first try."

Crisal shook her head. "It seemed so heavy."

The old magician placed the feather back on the rock. "If you had never walked before, your body would seem an unbearable weight to your legs. With practice you will gain strength."

She frowned at the feather, then placed her finger on it holding it tight against the rock. Fyx smiled a toothless grin and pointed again at the feather. Crisal jumped as she felt it pulled from beneath her finger. "It *is* no trick then!"

"No trick."

"Fyx, is this one of those dark spirits Yudo said you and Rogor call upon?"

The old man picked up the feather and tucked it in Crisal's robe. "Child, the power you call upon to move the feather is your own. Only you can say if it is dark. Prepare for sleep. I want to make Tieras by nightfall tomorrow."

Fyx turned back to the fire, while Crisal scooped holes in the sand for her hip and shoulder. As she settled in, resting her head against her hand, she saw the magician looking into the fire much as her mother would look for secrets in a glass sphere. The old man's eyes showed fear, but more than that, they showed sadness. About to ask a question of him, he turned and looked into her eyes. Crisal's mind grew cloudy, then blank.

The next evening, as they reached the outskirts of the desert town of Tieras, Crisal watched as the occasional farmer or workman would put their chores aside to stand and bow toward them. Fyx would return the greeting with no more than a curt nod, which was more communication than Crisal had had with him since leaving the fire. During their walk, her fortune teller's eyes revealed little of the future, but much about her master's apprehension. Each step toward Ikona seemed to deepen the creases in the old magician's face.

"Will we stop here, Fyx?"

Fyx looked at her as though realizing for the first time that the girl had been walking beside him all day. "What was that?"

"It is toward night, and we are in Tieras. Where will we stop?"

Fyx looked around, then nodded. "Yes, we have made good time. Have you kin here?"

Crisal nodded. "My aunt, Diamind, lives here with her brother Lorca. Should we sleep under a roof tonight?"

Fyx pointed at the dark clouds gathering in the west. "One does not need the eyes of a fortune teller to divine the meaning of that."

The girl frowned. "I'm not sure we would be welcome, Fyx. Diamind is my father's sister, and they think much the same."

"About you becoming a magician?"

"Aye. Surely the Great Fyx must have an admiring trickster in Tieras that can be imposed upon."

"Perhaps." As they crossed a small stone bridge spanning a muddy creek, Fyx pointed his stick toward a dark, narrow alley. They turned from the bridge into the alley and could barely walk side by side from the closeness of the walls. Reaching a black and scarlet striped curtain, Fyx stopped and pounded his stick against the wall. "Ho, the house! This is Fyx and an apprentice. Are you there Vassik?"

The curtain opened exposing an old woman dressed in the scarlet and black cuffs of a magician's assistant. "Fyx, is it you?"

"Aye, Bianice. Is Vassik in? Is he well?"

"Please, enter." Fyx and Crisal followed the old woman into her table room. Seated on a cushion before the table was, what seemed to Crisal, the oldest man alive. "Vassik, it is Fyx and an apprentice."

The ancient's face broke into smiles. "Fyx? Fyx, is it?"

"Aye, Vassik. This is my new apprentice, Crisal." Fyx shoved the girl toward the old man.

"Crisal? Come here, child." Crisal stood next to the old man while he gently passed his hands over her face and body. "Fyx, your eyes are worse than mine. This is a girl!"

"My apprentice, all the same, Vassik. How much would you charge for the use of your roof tonight?"

Vassik shook his head. "For you, Fyx, a special rate. Tell me of what brings you to Tieras. Sit, sit."

Crisal and Fyx lowered themselves to cushions at Vassik's table. Bianice left the room and returned with hot cake, cheese and wine, then seated herself next to Vassik.

"We go to the Deeplands, Ikona."

"Ah, yes."

"You have heard of their troubles then?"

"I'm blind, not deaf, Fyx. Black Rogor is feared even this far south. What have you to do with him?"

"Ikona has hired me to rid them of the sorcerer."

Vassik nodded, then rubbed his chin. "How do you plan to do this?"

"I have no plan, Vassik. I only have my knowledge that whatever powers he has do not come from the beyond."

"Well said, but I don't hear as much conviction as there should be. Do you have doubts?"

Fyx shrugged. "Not all is known, and it has been many years since Rogor and I last met."

Vassik waved a hand at Bianice. "Take Fyx's apprentice out to the kitchen to help bring in the food. We would talk alone." The old man dropped two copper movills on the table.

Bianice rose and Crisal looked at Fyx, who nodded at her. The girl stood and followed the magician's assistant out of the room. When they stood on the other side of the curtain, Bianice grabbed Crisal's arm. "Girl, why do you wear the black-and-scarlet?"

"To be a magician." The girl tried to free her arm but couldn't. "It's not as if you are paying for this information."

"Fyx uses you for his own ends, child. Do you know what you are getting into?"

"How do you know so much about my master?"

Bianice snorted out a laugh. "Just as you are apprenticed to Fyx, many years ago Vassik was Fyx's master."

Crisal shrugged. "What has that to do with me, or with our mission in the Deeplands?"

Bianice shook her head. "Vassik had three apprentices then: Fyx Dorstan and Amanche. Of the three apprentices, Dorstan was the best and soon became the special pride of Vassik. But, Dorstan died and the blame fell on Amanche. He was exiled into the desert and from the company of man. You see, Fyx, Amanche and Dorstan were brothers."

"I still don't see . . ."

"Oh, child! Amanche *is* Rogor! You child are a film of vapor waiting to be caught between a sledge and anvil."

As the sun broke over the horizon the next morning, its rays stole across the chilly desert, reflected from the river alongside the road to Porse and warmed the brush and trees beginning on the opposite side of the road. The low hills upon which they grew signaled the start of the incline that would become the Snake Mountains soon after Crisal and her master left Miira. Trudging behind Fyx, Crisal noticed neither the scenery nor the scent of the rain-washed air. She watched only the back of the old man and his stick, plodding steadily toward Porse.

"Fyx." The magician continued as though he hadn't heard. Crisal moved beside him and looked him in the face. "Fyx, is Rogor your brother?"

Fyx looked at her then returned his attention to the road. "It is none of your concern."

"Oh, none of my concern, is it? Then, why am I here?"

"It was your choice."

Crisal fell back and shifted her sack to her other shoulder. After a few more moments of walking, she reached within her robe and withdrew a clear glass marble. Holding it in her left hand in a manner to catch the sun's rays, she stared deep within the tiny sphere. Raw, random patterns in her mind associated, abstracted and drew conclusions, but with little information and Crisal's inexperience, the future was hidden. The past, however, was clear. Fyx had no desire for an apprentice; Fyx wanted Crisal's eyes—the eyes of a fortune teller. Again she moved beside the old man.

"Fyx."

The magician shook his head. "What is it now, pest?"

"What will happen when we reach Ikona?"

"I'm no fortune teller, Crisal. Haven't you consulted your ball?"

Crisal frowned. "Have you eyes in the back of your head, old man?"

Fyx cackled. "No, child, no. But, I can turn my head without moving my hood."

Crisal smiled, then shook her head. "I see nothing past our present footsteps, Fyx. My glass did tell me you wanted me for your eyes, and not as an apprentice. Explain."

Fyx frowned, darted a glance at the girl, then looked ahead. Then, looking down, he cackled. "Your eyes see guilt in me?"

"Aye. That, and fear and sadness."

The magician nodded. "Rogor, the one called black and dark, he is my brother, Amanche. I learned this years ago from the Great Tayla."

"She is my mother's mother, which you knew."

"Aye, that is true. You also know of my brother Dorstan's death?"

"Bianice mentioned it."

Fyx nodded. "Dorstan was better than any of us. The exercise with the feather, the first time he lifted it from the table and held it for half a minute." Crisal saw Fyx's eyes moisten. "He was quick and all of us knew he would be a master before either I or Amanche perfected our simplest drills. Amanche was jealous with an envy and hatred that knew no bounds. Then one day, Dorstan was found dead."

"How?"

Fyx shrugged. "Amanche told Vassik that Dorstan had challenged him and that his magic was the more powerful of the two. He expected praise, but Vassik threw him before the town of Tieras for judgment. He was exiled to the desert.

Tayla the fortune teller heard the story once and concluded that Dorstan had been poisoned."

"There was no magic, then?"

Fyx stopped and faced Crisal. "Child, there is no magic. This one who calls himself Rogor did not use magical powers against my brother Dorstan, because no such powers exist!"

Crisal's face wrinkled in confusion. "But, Fyx, I myself have heard you call upon spirits in performance . . ."

"The act, child. The act. Ever since chance brought our ancestors to Momus on the circus ship *Baraboo*, magicians have had but one trade: to entertain. We do the possible and make it appear to be the impossible. As part of the illusion that we do magic, we burn incense, call upon mythical beings and spirits, mutter nonsense incantations, roll our eyes, wave wands—all to create an aura of mystery. We take that doubt that rests in all of us, that things may not be as they appear, magnify it, and walk home with our purses full of movills."

"But, what about the feather? This is not magic?"

"No more than your fortune teller's eyes. When you see the future, do you use magic?"

"Of course not. Things in motion take certain paths. If you know the path up to the present, it takes no magic to see where a thing will go in the future."

The old man nodded. "But, child, this power of the fortune tellers seems to be magic to those who do not understand it."

Crisal nodded. "Only the fortune tellers have this power. But what powers do magicians have?"

Fyx shook his head. "Many have the powers of magicians and fortune tellers, child, but only few train their powers. You are of the fortune tellers, yet you rocked the feather. I can see enough of the future to have sense enough to step out of the path of a falling rock. A trained magician can confuse the minds of others, or even put them to sleep as I did to you our first night on the road."

Crisal frowned. "I can get to sleep under my own power, Fyx. That does not explain the feather."

"With the magician's extra pair of hands, objects can be moved. The best card tricks are aided in that manner. Someday you will be able to put pictures in the minds of others or make time seem to pass very slowly for them. You will be practicing your trade, but others will think it magic."

Crisal nodded and they continued their walk down the road. "A few things are explained then, Fyx. Are there other powers?"

"You shall learn of them in good time."

Crisal turned her head toward the old man. "The fear I read in your face—is it that Rogor plays upon your own doubts of dark powers?"

Fyx nodded. "I cannot reconcile what I know with what I feel. Rogor is never seen and no one knows the location of his lair. Yet, he destroys entire crops at will and is said to cause illness and death by wishing it. Are there dark powers that serve Rogor? I cannot prove that there aren't."

"But, the guilt, Fyx; why do I see guilt?"

"You are of the Tarzak fortune tellers, Crisal. That I should become an agent to you betraying your tradition . . ."

"That's not it! You think me stupid because I am young."

Fyx cackled and shook his head. "My apologies, little beast." He reached into his robe and dropped a movill into Crisal's hand.

"You think one is enough?"

"Look upon it as the balance of the respect you owe me."

Crisal dropped the copper into her purse and looked sideways at the old magician. "I haven't forgotten my question."

"I suspected as much."

"Well?"

Fyx's face became serious, and his pace slowed, then stopped. "Crisal, I do not know what I am going to meet in Ikona. I have my tricks and illusions, but they don't tell me how Rogor kills by wishing. I need a fortune teller's eyes to see the things I cannot. But . . ."

"But, you fear throwing a child into a battle between you and your brother." Fyx nodded. Crisal walked a few steps, and then turned back to face the old man. "I see something else, Fyx."

"And?"

"I see you arranging this with my mother, Salina. Yes—and Eeren, my loving father, providing the proper amount of disapproval to insure my choice—hah! My choice. Bianice spoke the truth. I am used."

Fyx shrugged. "Eeren and Salina are my friends, and

they know of Rogor. You were selected from among all their apprentices as the best..."

"You would try flattery?"

"It is only the truth, Crisal."

Crisal dropped the sack of cakes on the road and kicked it. "I am my own person, Fyx. I dance at the ends of no one's string. Find yourself another pair of eyes." She turned toward Tieras, stomped past the old magician, not looking back.

Around the first bend in the road, Crisal stopped, found a suitable rock, and sat down. Salina must think me still a child, she thought, and Fyx thinks me a fool. And my father! His mock outrage that a fortune teller would want to become a magician. Unheard of! Disgrace! Bah! Crisal stood and kicked the nearest rock, sending it skittering across the road.

She turned to the darkening skies. "If the old trickster needed a fortune teller, why did he not hire a master? Why this game about me being a magician's apprentice?"

She pulled the feather from her robe and fondled it. This is what I want more than anything else on Momus: to be a magician. I don't want to sit in dark little rooms peering into futures and planning lives. To stand before the crowd, amazing them with my tricks—that is what I want. But, is this too all sham?

She dropped the feather on the sand, reached her imaginary hands under its edge and heaved with all her might. The feather rocked, rocked again, then turned over. She sat, looking at the feather for a moment, then picked it up and got to her feet. The road was deserted in all directions. She looked to the blackening sky. "Did I do that, Fyx? Are you still playing with me?" Only wind mixed with a sprinkle of rain answered her.

Crisal looked down the road toward Tieras, and from there, to Tarzak, where she still might be apprenticed to some lesser magician. Perhaps she could follow the fortune teller's trade. Turning to look at the bend in the road toward Porse, she knew that on the other side of the bend, the greatest magician on Momus waited for her to make up her mind. Rounding the bend, she saw Fyx standing where she left him, holding out the sack of provisions.

"We must hurry, Crisal. I fear we are in for a soaking."

Crisal walked up to the magician and took the sack without stopping. As she strode ahead she wondered if she would ever know what she would do before someone else did.

After reaching Porse that evening, they found all curtains closed to them. The uniform excuse was "Rogor would see." The two walked through the deserted-looking town until they came to the square. In the half light of the stars peering through the parting clouds, they saw an upright figure in the center of the square, head and shoulders slumped over. As they came closer, they could see his feet did not touch the ground.

Fyx held Crisal back. "Stay here child, while I investigate."

"What is it?"

"It is not for your eyes, Crisal."

"I thought my fortune teller's eyes were the reason for my company. I cannot see if I do not have information."

Fyx nodded. "Then come, but be prepared. He has been impaled."

Only close to the corpse did the dim light reveal the red and purple stripes of a barker. Crisal froze as Fyx walked around to view the dead man's face.

"Is it the barker who came to your house?"

"Yes, it is Yudo."

Crisal walked slowly around the grisly scarescrow and looked up into a face blessed with death. She heard a noise behind her and started. The old magician was storming around the square swinging his stick around and over his head. "Up slime!" he called, his voice strong and bitter. "Off of your sleeping cushions, cowards! I Fyx of the Tarzak magicians will reduce this town to rubble unless my questions are answered satisfactorily! Up slime, up!" Crisal watched as the ancient magician went from door to door pounding on the walls, shouting his oaths. No one dared enter the square.

Fyx stood silent for a full minute, then reached within his robe. "Very well, cowards of Porse let your town be no more!" The magician waved his hand at the nearest house which immediately burst into flame. Screams from within curdled Crisal's blood. From the next house a man in clown's orange ran to Fyx and fell on his knees.

"Great Fyx, I beg you! Please spare us. We had no choice."

"This?" Fyx pointed at Yudo's motionless body. "You had no choice for this?"

"Great Fyx," the clown blubbered, "the Dark One was here!"

"Rogor? This is his doing?"

"Yes, Great Fyx. Look." The clown pointed to the wall at the far side of the square. In the flickering light of the burning building, Fyx could read:

WELCOME

R
O
ROGOR
O
R

Fyx walked to the wall, studied it, then returned to the center of the square, next to the corpse. "Clown, come here!"

The clown scurried to the magician's feet, hardly rising from his own knees to get there. "Yes, Great Fyx?"

Fyx aimed his stick at the dead barker. "Who did this?"

"Great Fyx must understand, Rogor . . ."

"I must understand nothing!" Fyx delivered the clown a kick in the ribs sending him sprawling in the mud. "Who committed this outrage?"

"Rogor made us do it, Great Fyx. Those who didn't do the work were forced to watch."

"Forced? Did he have an army at your yellow backs?"

"He . . . he has great powers. We were afraid . . ."

"Afraid? And for this you denied the protection of your town to a traveler? Bah! Not only that, you do another's murdering!"

"Great Fyx, the Dark One has fearful powers . . ."

"Bah! By the grey beard of Momus, I'll show you fearful powers!" Fyx kicked the clown again, waved his hand at the corpse and suddenly the square was filled with a blinding light. Crisal peeked through her fingers to see Yudo's body at the center of a roaring pyre of white and blue flames that reached up into the night sky. In seconds, the stake supporting the body burned through. "Clown, drive the curs that people this town into the square."

"Great Fyx, what if they will not come?"

Fyx raised his arms and screamed. "If they do not come, I will roast them in their homes!"

The clown scurried off, and one by one, the people of Porse edged into the square, shielding their eyes from the light of the pyre, and from the sight of Fyx. The magician walked around the pyre, looking at the townspeople. By the time the flames had been reduced to glowing embers, Yudo was but ashes, and the people were assembled. Fyx bent over and lifted a handful of embers and held them over his head.

"You will take these ashes and mix them with the mud from this square. Hear me, scum of Porse?"

The people bowed their heads. "Yes, Great Fyx."

"Take the mixture and paint your houses with it. From this day hence, that shall be the color of Porse. Live with your shame and be faithful to it, for if I should ever pass this way again and find as much as a white fence post, Porse shall cease to exist." Fyx searched the crowd until he saw the clown. "You!"

The clown ran from the crowd and kneeled at Fyx's feet. "Yes, Great Fyx."

"Show me the ones who drove the stake into the barker and planted him."

"But, we had no . . ."

"Show me, or in the blink of an eye you shall be nothing but ashes!"

The clown bowed, got to his feet and walked around the square. As he passed by, six men separated from the crowd and approached Fyx with cowed heads. His task completed, the clown stood with the others. "I am one of them."

"Then, stand for your shame!" Fyx marked the forehead of each with his thumb leaving an ugly blue "M." "Now, into the desert with you, and never let the sight of good men fall upon you." The seven men looked around the square at their neighbors, bowed their heads and walked from the square. As they reached the edge, the crowd parted, not daring even to look. Fyx tossed his handful of embers, now dead, on the remains of Yudo's pyre.

Crisal watched the old magician turn in her direction and walk toward her, his eyes burning with an emotion she could not read. Standing before her, he lifted the hand that had held the embers. It was dirty, but unburned. He placed it on her shoulder. "Come, child. This is no town for anyone to rest in, for they will have none of it from now until their shame is washed away."

Fyx took the street leading to the high road to Miira, the crowd parted, and Crisal followed, trying to decide in her own mind whether what she felt for Fyx was fear or love.

Through the night, Fyx marched toward Miira town as if possessed. Crisal stumbled along behind, marveling at the old man's strength. Twice, rain and wind whipped them, causing the already muddy road to grow slick as grease with dark, forbidding pools. Unmindful of the mud or the pools, Fyx strode through both as though he were on a hard, dusty street in Tarzak. As the second rain stopped, a dim grey dawn fought against the black clouds. Fyx stopped and turned to the light.

"It is dawn."

"You don't miss a thing, Fyx." Crisal dragged herself next to the old man. He turned and looked at the girl, soaked and mud-caked as himself.

"You must be tired, child."

"Ah, Fyx, there is fortune teller's blood in your veins."

The magician raised an eyebrow. "I see you've spent the night honing your tongue. Do you wish to rest or not?"

"Of course." Crisal cocked her head at the drenched landscape. "But where?"

Fyx reached into his robe and handed Crisal a black wad of raw cobit dough. The lump was crusted hard and weighed heavily in the child's hand. "Pick a spot with neither trees, weeds nor grass."

Crisal looked around, walked ahead to a sandy place on the east side of the road. "Here?"

Fyx nodded. "Listen carefully. When I tell you, crush the dough ball hard and throw it in the center of the clear spot." Crisal looked at the innocent lump in her hand. "You must be very quick, understand?"

"Yes."

"Then, now!"

Crisal crushed the ball and felt it warm her hand even

before she threw it. Before it landed on the sand, it exploded into a blinding column of flame. Crisal turned to Fyx. "Yudo's pyre."

"Yes. With your right hand, feel inside the right sleeve of your robe. Do you feel a pocket?"

Crisal felt about and found an opening. "Yes."

The magician handed her five more of the black dough balls. "Put these in that pocket. You know how they can be used." Fyx nodded at the fire, almost gone out for lack of fuel. "It burns hot, but very fast. The sand will be dry, but only warm."

Crisal put the balls into her sleeve pocket. "Is this to be my first trick, Fyx?"

The magician laughed. "No, child. Your first trick will be learning how to sleep without rolling over on your sleeve!"

Crisal dragged herself onto the warm sand, stretched out and fell asleep, her right arm straight out from her body.

If Crisal dreamed at all, it was of sleep. The clearing skies and rising sun warmed and dried her robe, and she wriggled happily as she fought back the wakefulness that gnawed at the edges of her sleep. She snuggled her face, cupped by her right hand against the sand, then remembered the dough balls. Sitting bolt upright, she saw that the loose sleeve of her robe had not been under her.

"Ah, child, you are awake."

Crisal turned to see a woman in singer's white and green sitting next to a tall blonde man wearing the black and scarlet. The man nodded to Crisal. "Dorna invited me to warm my backside on your sand, little magician."

Crisal nodded back. The man was young and very strong looking; the woman, as young, had black flowing hair and dark brown eyes. Crisal cursed her own freckles and muddy appearance next to the beautiful singer. "Have you seen my master?"

The young magician shrugged. The singer shook her head. "I suppose you should wait here for him." Dorna looked down at the magician's hand around her waist, then nodded her head toward Crisal. Shrugging, he removed his hand, and lay back on the sand, propping himself up with his elbows.

Crisal studied the young magician. "You are not from this planet, are you, magician?"

The man laughed. "No, child. My name is Ashly Allenby. I come from the parent planet."

"Yet, you wear the black and scarlet."

"Even I must eat. What are you called?"

"I am Crisal. I am apprenticed to a great magician."

"His name?" Allenby sat up.

Crisal looked at Dorna and read her eyes. "His name is of no consequence, Allenby." The girl waved her hand around indicating the sand she had dried.

Allenby raised his eyebrows and nodded. "The few movills I have already weep from loneliness. Would you observe a new trick of mine in exchange?"

Crisal shrugged. "If I can determine how you do it, I will still want payment."

Allenby chuckled and withdrew a deck of cards from his robe. As he handed the deck to Crisal, he smoothed the sand before him with his hand. "Pick seven cards you can remember."

"I can remember any seven—or the entire deck, for that matter." Crisal thumbed off the first seven cards and handed them to Allenby.

"No, don't give them to me. Put them in a row, faces up, on the sand." Crisal put out the cards. "Do you have them memorized?"

"Of course."

Allenby spread his fingers above the cards and turned all seven over without touching them. "You're sure you have them memorized?"

"Yes."

"Then, turn over the three of clubs."

Crisal sighted the third card from her left, imagined the tiny hands of her mind under the edge of the card, and heaved. The card turned over, exposing the eight of diamonds. Allenby laughed at the expression on her face. "But the eight is here." She pointed at the card on her far right.

"You are sure?"

Crisal reached for the card and turned it with her fingers. The six of spades. Dorna the singer nodded in admiration. "An excellent trick, Allenby." The young magician smiled his thanks and gathered up his cards. Crisal frowned.

"Can you tell me how I did that, Crisal?" Allenby tucked his cards away and stood.

Crisal broke her frown long enough to deliver a curt nod. "It is a good enough trick."

Allenby threw the hem of his robe over his shoulder and pointed south with mock drama. "Begads, with such lavish praise at my back, I must hasten to Tarzak and bedazzle the crowds."

Dorna stood. "Must you go, Ashly?"

Allenby bowed and took Dorna's hand, brushing it with his lips. "Aye, beautiful Dorna. I must make Tarzak. A cargo shuttle is said to be there. It is the first since I came to Momus, and I must catch it to send my news back to the Quadrant Secretary of State." He bowed toward Crisal, then hefted his sack and stepped onto the road heading south. Dorna and Crisal both watched until long after he was out of sight.

The girl turned toward the singer. "Dorna?"

"Yes, child?"

"I read something in your eyes, but I cannot fathom what I saw in them. Where is my master?"

The beautiful Dorna smiled, covered her face with her robe, then lowered it. Fyx's toothless smile grinned at the girl.

"Fyx, by Momus's boiled behind—it is you?"

The old man cackled. "Turn your back, child."

"What will you do then? Turn yourself into a lizard, or me into a boy?"

"Turn around. I must reverse my robe."

Crisal turned. "All this playacting, Fyx; what did it accomplish?"

"A young magician would guard his tongue more closely with the Great Fyx than with lovely Dorna. You may turn around now."

Crisal turned and saw Fyx before her in his black and scarlet. "Was that no magic, too, Fyx? Where did your wrinkles go?"

"Make a frown, Crisal, and feel your forehead."

Crisal did as she was told. "So?"

"You are young, yet you can make wrinkles. I am old, and can make my skin smooth, although it takes much effort."

"Very well, Fyx, but explain the beautiful Dorna's teeth.

You haven't one in your entire head."

"Neither did Dorna."

Crisal folded her arms. "She did too!"

"Think, Crisal. Those wide sensuous lips smiled, but never parted unless a hand or sleeve was before them."

The girl frowned. "I remember . . . no, I feel I remember. You are right; I saw no teeth." Crisal shook her head. "What had the magician to say that was of value?"

"Here, eat." Fyx reached into their sack and produced two soggy cobit cakes. "Allenby comes from as far north as Dirak on the other side of the Snake Mountains. He also passed through Miira on his way to Tarzak. Both towns are black with despair. Rogor is leaving his mark."

Crisal swallowed a piece of cobit, then dropped the remainder into the sack. "Fyx, can we go around Miira?"

"You are thinking of last night in Porse."

Crisal nodded. "These people do not know what faces them. We do not know. I want no more horrors."

Fyx finished his cake and studied the girl. "You think my actions harsh?"

Crisal shrugged. "I understand why they acted as they did."

Fyx nodded. "Imagine this, Crisal: you have a knife in your hand held at Salina, your mother's, throat; I am holding you with a knife at your throat. I tell you that if you do not kill Salina, I will kill you. What would you do?"

Crisal bowed her head, walked to the edge of the dry sand, then walked back. "I would like to think I would die. Is that what you want to hear?"

"That was Porse's choice, Crisal, and they failed."

The girl looked into the old man's eyes. "Will we pass through Miira?"

Fyx nodded. "We must. That is where we pick up our provisions and transportation across the mountains." The old man picked up the sack and handed it to the girl. "We must be off if we are to get there before nightfall."

As they climbed the steepening foothills into Miira, the setting sun picked out with red, orange and yellow the untended fields, half cut and dressed timber logs and deserted streets. The houses, now made of wood, stood empty. Fyx pounded on several doors, but all those he knew in the town were gone. Walking farther into the town, they entered the square. Crisal gripped Fyx's arm and pointed at the center of the square.

"Look, Fyx, another murder!"

The old magician followed the direction of Crisal's finger and studied what he saw. In the back of a two-wheeled pull cart, a huge man garbed in the freak's green-and-yellow was sprawled on a few sacks, his massive arms and legs hanging over the sides and end of the cart. "Come, Crisal. He only sleeps."

As they approached the cart, the huge man opened one eye, then nodded. "You are the Great Fyx."

Fyx nodded. "And you?"

Quick and graceful for his size, the man sat, then leaped from the cart to the ground. He bowed, aiming his bald pate in Fyx's direction. "Great Fyx, I am Zuma, strongman of the Dirak freaks."

"Dirak?"

"From the other side of the Snake Mountains, Great Fyx."

The old magician nodded, then passed his hand around the square. "Where are they?"

Zuma chuckled making a rumble that seemed, to Crisal, to vibrate the ground. "The news of your judgment in Porse arrived hours ago. The good citizens of Miira have taken to the hills."

"And you?"

"Me?"

"How do we find you snoozing in the square amidst this rush to return to nature?"

"Hah!" Zuma laughed and slapped Crisal's shoulder, sending her sprawling. "I am Zuma. No more needs to be said."

Crisal picked herself up and scowled at the strongman. "He is here for a reason, Fyx."

Zuma nodded. "That scrap of an apprentice speaks the truth. The town of Dirak has sent me to bring you across the mountains."

Fyx rubbed his chin. "Dirak knew, then, that Miira would take this vacation?"

Zuma spat on the ground. "Rogor's arm is felt even on this side of the mountains. Dirak takes no chances that you might be late for lack of transportation."

"You do not fear the Dark One, then?"

"Fear him? Hah!" Zuma flexed his mighty arms, stooped and wrapped them around the wooden cart. Standing, he lifted the cart over his head. "Zuma fears no one." The strongman lowered the cart to the ground as gently as a feather. Turning, he frowned at Fyx. "If I could find the sorcerer, there would be little need for you, magician. But . . ." The huge man shrugged.

Crisal's eyes narrowed as she tried to read the strong man's eyes. "Zuma, my master is hired by the town of Ikona to rid them of Rogor. You are from Dirak."

Zuma nodded. "All four towns in the Emerald Valley, Dirak, Ikona, Ris and even the fishing village of Anoki have contributed. Ikona has gotten the worst of it, and they made the contract." Fyx looked at the girl, his eyebrows raised. Crisal only shrugged. "Shall we go then?" He tossed Zuma a purse.

Fyx and Crisal climbed into the cart and settled themselves among the boxes and sacks. Zuma stooped under the pull handle at the front of the cart, stood and gripped it with his powerful hands. As they clattered through Miira, Crisal studied the back of Zuma's head. Turning to the old magician, she tugged his sleeve. "Fyx . . ."

Fyx touched a finger against her lips and shook his head. "Try and sleep."

"Sleep?" Crisal threw up her hands at the absurdity.

Fyx looked into her eyes. "Sleep." Crisal fought against it, but her mind clouded, then grew dark.

Crisal looked down from a great height and saw a wooden handcart being pulled by a powerful man. In the back of the cart were two figures dressed in black and scarlet. The cart left houses behind and made its way up a gentle incline. At times, a turn in the road or an overhanging tree would obscure the travelers, but as the cart pulled onto a high mesa and worked its way around the shore of a small lake, she felt herself drawn to the vehicle. She swooped down, coming up behind and just above the cart. In the cart she saw herself, asleep, her head cradled on Fyx's lap.

Fyx! She called out, but had no voice. *Fyx, what is this?*

See ahead, child, the man pulling the cart?

Fyx, I am frightened.

Do you see him?

Yes, yes, but Fyx . . . Crisal saw the cart turn from the lakeshore to follow a steep road into the mountains.

Crisal, you will enter Zuma's mind and tell me what you see.

Crisal looked at her own sleeping face, then up into Fyx's. *I can't, Fyx. What if he is Rogor?*

You suspected something, then?

I could not read his eyes.

Perhaps what you read was out of your experience. Have you ever read murder?

No.

Then, you would not recognize it.

Fyx, if it is Rogor, will he know I am there?

Crisal saw the old magician look down and stroke the face of the sleeping child, pushing a tangled lock of red hair away from her eyes. *If it is Rogor, he will know, but I will protect you. Do you believe this?*

Yes, Fyx. What must I do?

Look at Zuma's head. Do you see the aura?

Crisal turned and saw a pale glow rippling above the strongman's skin all over his body. *Yes, I see it.*

When I tell you, go to it and blend with it. But, remember, child, whatever happens to you, do not try to speak to me. Do not cry out, and neither fight what you find there nor try to change it. Do you understand?

Yes, Fyx.

Then, go.

Crisal saw the road's incline steepen, and as she touched, then wrapped herself around Zuma's aura, the cart turned, exposing a cliff falling away to the left. The aura was foreign, but she felt herself change a particle at a time until a harmony between herself and the aura was achieved.

Zuma looked over the edge of the cliff and chuckled. No one would ever find the old man and the child down there, he thought. Rogor will line my purse with coppers instead of plague for my crops. The strongman shook off a twinge of guilt. No one can fight Rogor's magic. I must do as I am told.

Seeing the sharp turn in the road ahead with a flat place carved into the wall opposite the cliff, Zuma turned back toward the old magician. "We will stop here and rest." He pulled the cart onto the flat and lowered the handle. Stepping out from under the handle, Zuma began picking up dead twigs and sticks along the road. "I will have hot food for us in a moment."

Fyx nodded and shook the sleeping child's shoulder. Crisal started awake, her eyes wild with fear. Fyx touched her lips and stroked her face. "Come child. While Zuma prepares our food, there is something I would show you. This part of the Snake Mountain cliff is the highest. It is very beautiful, even in starlight."

Trembling, Crisal stepped down from the cart, followed by Fyx. The old magician took her hand and walked to the very edge of the cliff. "Fyx . . ."

"Hush, child. Just look down and listen."

Crisal looked down, but could not see the bottom of the cliff in the dark. Wind whistled and echoed from the walls, and very far away, she could hear water flowing. Fyx stooped over, picked up a rock and moved so close to the cliff's edge that their toes hung over. Holding Crisal tightly about her shoulders with his right arm, he tossed the rock into the chasm with his left. Crisal listened, but heard nothing but the wind and the water far away. "Fyx, should we stand so close . . ."

"Observe nature's beauty, child, and listen."

Crisal listened and heard the crackle of the fire Zuma had started. She also heard soft footsteps padding up behind them. She tried to pull back from the edge of the cliff, but the old man's grip held her tight. The footsteps came closer, then began running. Crisal turned her head, and three full strides to her right, Zuma ran to the edge of the cliff, arms outstretched, and sailed over, plummeting into the darkness below, followed by a trail of screamed question marks.

Crisal looked up at Fyx. "Why . . . ?"

"That's where he saw us, child. Poor fellow must have an eye problem." Fyx cackled and turned back to the fire. "Come, Crisal. Zuma was kind enough to build our fire, but I'm afraid we'll have to prepare our own food. Pity."

Crisal looked into the darkness hiding the scattered remains of the strongman, then turned to watch the old magician, a smile on his face, setting up rocks around the fire upon which he would cook their cakes. As she walked slowly to the fire, she thought again about Bianice's comment about a vapor being caught between a sledge and an anvil.

The next morning, having determined that neither Fyx's magic nor their combined strength could move the heavy cart, while Fyx prepared their morning meal, Crisal searched among the sacks and boxes hoping to find enough provisions to support them to Dirak. "There is more than enough, Fyx, if we can carry it all; even blankets for the mountain nights." Crisal continued moving the contents of the cart around, examining the contents of each sack and box.

"Child, if you've found enough food, leave the cart alone so we can eat and be off." Fyx saw that he was being ignored, shrugged and sat by the dying fire. As he bit into a cobit cake spread with sapjam, Crisal stood in the cart holding a small package in her hands. She climbed down from the cart and walked to the fire.

"See this, Fyx?" She held the package out.

The magician put down his cake, took the package and turned it over. It was white with rounded corners forming two halves held together with a clear, seamless cover. It had no markings. "Do your fortune teller's eyes tell you what it is?"

Crisal shook her head. "I saw in Zuma's thoughts he was bringing something for Rogor. Dare we open it?"

Fyx held the package to his ear, shook it and shrugged. With his fingernail, he pried up an end of the clear cover, stuck his finger beneath it and made it stretch until the opening was large enough to remove the cover. With the cover removed, Fyx placed the package on his lap and lifted off the top half. Firmly held in place by the molded bottom half was a mechanism, blue-black with a handle extending from a curved plate. At the top of the plate were numerous black, red and orange cubes from which hair-thin wires came. Toward the front of the plate, the wires gathered into a cable and terminated at a threaded cylinder that hung loose at the end of the cable. The front of the handle was shaped into five rings, the one closest to the plate larger than the others and containing a metal lever that extended back into the handle. The back edge of the handle had two rings together of the same size. Fyx looked up at Crisal.

"Well?"

"What is it, Fyx?"

The magician lifted the object from the molded half and turned it over in his hands. Holding the curved plate upright, he clasped his hand around the handle, putting his thumb through the top rear hole and his fingers through the top front four. He cocked his head at Crisal. "Stand out of the way."

Crisal moved aside while Fyx aimed the object at the chasm wall opposite their perch. He pulled the metal lever back with his forefinger; nothing happened. Fyx lowered the thing to his lap and shrugged. "I thought it might be a gun of some design, but it does nothing."

Crisal pointed. "Look, Fyx." The girl's finger tapped the extra ring beneath Fyx's little finger, and again the extra ring beneath his thumb. "If it's a handle, it wasn't meant for hands like ours."

The magician nodded, then handed the object to Crisal. "What do your fortune teller's eyes make of our future now?"

Crisal took the object and sat on the sand next to the fire. She looked at the handle, turned it over and shook her head. "Fyx, I haven't assembled enough information to make any sense of the present, much less talk about the future." She took the moldings and cover and reassembled the package, placing it in her sack.

"It doesn't do anything, child. Why drag the extra weight?"

Crisal stuffed some cake in her mouth and talked around it. "Allenby, that young magician from Earth, he said he was trying to meet a cargo shuttle. I think Zuma picked this package up there for Rogor. It is something Rogor wants, and now we've got it."

"But, we don't know what it does, nor where it comes from."

Crisal squinted her eyes, looked at her lap, then at Fyx. "Allenby said he had news to send to Earth—no, to the Quadrant Secretary of State. What news?"

Fyx shrugged and reached for another cake. "Some prattle about sending a diplomatic mission to Momus. Also, that his news had attracted the newstellers and that the law they require should be made by the time whoever it is shows up."

Crisal took the remainder of her cobit cake and threw it at the old magician's head. "Old fake!"

Fyx stood, his eyes narrowing in anger. "Brat. Have you lost your mind? I could turn you into ashes in the blink of an eye."

The girl stuck out her tongue and made a rude noise. "I see where you cannot Fyx. Now, tell me the whole truth. I cannot see the things I have to see without it."

The old magician pursed his lips, nodded and resumed his seat by the fire. "Allenby is an official of the Ninth Quadrant. He has come to Momus to arrange for military protection for our planet."

"Protection? From whom?"

Fyx shrugged. "The Ninth Quadrant suspects an invasion of Momus by the Tenth Quadrant Federation."

Crisal nodded. "And this law, what is that?"

"Momus must ask for the protection, otherwise it would violate laws that govern all the quadrants."

Crisal felt the outline of the package in her sack, then picked up another cobit cake, eating it slowly. "Fyx, what do you know of the Tenth Quadrant worlds?"

"As much as I know about the worlds of the Ninth, child—next to nothing." Fyx stood and hefted his sack. "Can you continue your cogitations while we walk? The morning is aging rapidly."

Crisal nodded, picked up her sack and walked to the cart. "Will your magic keep you warm, or do you want a blanket?"

Fyx snorted, turned his back and began climbing the steep road. Crisal picked up two blankets, tucked them under her arm, threw her sack over her shoulder and followed.

Three mornings later, Fyx and Crisal stood on the north foothills of the Snake Mountains looking out over the Emerald Valley. Toward the sun, green fields dotted with brown extended to the horizon, leaving space for only a lake, and above the lake, a small village. Fyx pointed his stick at the village. "That is Ikona."

"The two towns before us?"

"The first is Dirak, and the second at the base of the mountain is called Ris."

Crisal looked to her left to see more green fields, dotted with brown, extending until they met a wide expanse of water. She pointed to a small settlement at the edge of the water. "Anoki?"

Fyx nodded. "The brown you see in the fields must be the dying crops."

Crisal studied them, but there seemed to be no pattern, save the fields closest to the mountain on the other side of the valley had no brown. "What is the mountain opposite us called?"

"Split Mountain. You will see why when we get to Ikona. A great movement in the crust of Momus caused a crooked rent in the mountain that extends deep into its center."

Crisal pointed at the town straddling the road before them. "Dirak, at least, has a welcome planned for us."

Fyx rubbed his chin. "Keep alert; Rogor can plan welcomes, too." He nodded his head toward the three men who stood at the entrance to the town gate.

The old magician hefted his sack and stepped off, working his way down the road to Dirak. Crisal followed a few paces behind, studying the men at the gate. All three wore the black and tan short robes of roustabouts and stood motionless, waiting. When she could see their eyes, Crisal moved up beside Fyx. "I read mayhem in their eyes, Fyx."

The magician nodded. As they approached the three, Crisal saw Fyx's left hand disappear into its sleeve and return again as a fist. The old man put a smile on his face and nodded at the three toughs. "A pleasant morning, friends."

The roustabout in the middle glanced at his companions, then walked toward the two travelers. "You are the Great Fyx?" The man offered nothing for the information.

"Yes. And your name, friend?"

The man looked up the road into the Snake Mountains, then back at the magician. "I am Jagar. Where is Zuma?"

Fyx shrugged. "The strongman took leave of his senses and leaped from a cliff to his death. We could not stop him."

Jagar studied Fyx, then looked at Crisal. "Is this true?"

Crisal looked at Jagar and turned up her nose. "You doubt the word of my master?"

Striking swiftly, Jagar grabbed the front of Fyx's robe.

"The cart, old man, what have you . . ." Fyx passed his left hand before Jagar's face and the roustabout dropped to the ground, twitching.

Fyx arranged his robe and stepped over the body toward the two remaining roustabouts. "Rude fellow." Seeing their companion twitching in the dust, the two turned and fled through the town gate and disappeared down an alley. The magician turned around and knelt next to Jagar. "Crisal, come here." The girl stood across the body and looked into Jagar's face. The man's eyes rolled with terror and spittle dribbled from the corners of his mouth. "I will ask him some questions, child. Tell me what you see."

"Yes, Fyx."

The magician reached into his robe and withdrew a tiny vial filled with a colorless fluid. Opening it, he forced Jagar's teeth open and let three drops of the fluid fall into the man's mouth. In a few seconds, Jagar lay quiet. "Jagar. You hear me?" Fyx waited a moment, then slapped the man's face hard enough to make Crisal wince. "Jagar!"

"Spare me, Great Fyx." The man barely spoke above a whisper.

"Spare you? Jagar, I will ask you questions and you will answer me truthfully. Then perhaps we may talk of sparing your miserable life."

"I can't . . . talk to you of Rogor, Great Fyx. This is what you would ask?"

"It is. What will Rogor do if you talk?"

"Oh, Great Fyx, he will kill me!"

Fyx cackled. "Hear me, Jagar: you will tell me all I wish to know, or else I shall visit such horrors upon you that you will beg me for that same death."

"Ask, then, Great Fyx."

"The gadget in the cart Zuma was to bring, what is it?"

"I do not know." Fyx looked at Crisal and the girl nodded back.

"Was it for Rogor?"

"Yes. We were told to wait here for it."

"What were you to do with it?"

"It was to be taken to the fountain in Ikona."

"And?"

"That's all, Great Fyx. I swear it."

Crisal knelt next to Jagar. "He does not lie. Ask him if he's ever seen Rogor."

Fyx poked Jagar in the arm. "Well?"

"No. No one has ever seen the Dark One."

Crisal turned Jagar's face toward her with her hand and looked deep into his eyes. "Jagar, where are the people of Dirak?"

"Child, they are in Ris. All of the towns of the Emerald Valley are in Ris."

"Why?"

"The people assemble to form an army and declare Rogor king of Momus."

Fyx looked into the child's face. "Do you see something?"

Crisal nodded. "Yes. I feel I have the parts to an answer. I must still fit them together. We must leave the road and find a quiet place."

As Fyx led the way through the fields toward Ikona, Crisal stopped to examine both green and brown stalks of grain, healthy and rotting melon patches. Reaching some trees near the lake below Ikona, Crisal withdrew her clear glass marble and fell to her knees. Hearing her, Fyx turned and sat next to her. She held the ball in the sun, catching its rays, and used it to focus her mind. Pieces of the puzzle fit together, but something still lay out of her grasp. She dropped the marble to her lap and shook her head. "It is not enough."

"Can you at least see a question?"

Crisal smoothed the sand in front of her knees and drew Rogor's cross with her finger.

```
  R
  O
ROGOR
  O
  R
```

"Fyx, I must know the meaning of this."

The old magician shook his head. "It is as I told you, Crisal. It means nothing."

"Tell me what you can, Fyx. It is the part I need."

Fyx rubbed his chin. "It could be the hidden cross of a magic square."

"Magic square?"

Fyx shook his head. "There is no magic to them. They were believed to cure illnesses and drive away evil spirits long ago. On Momus, some magicians take names that can form such a cross."

"Show me a magic square."

Fyx smoothed the sand next to Rogor's cross. "This is a very old one. It is formed by two words, sator and opera. The words must fit frontwards, backwards and up and down. Like this." The old magician quickly drew the words and word arrangements with his finger.

S A T O R
A R E P O
T E   E T
O P E R A
R O T A S

"Now, all we do is add an 'N' in the middle, and the word TENET becomes the hidden cross in this magic square." Fyx added the "N" and smoothed out the rest of the letters.

T
E
TENET
E
T

"No magic in it; just a word game."

Crisal studied the word, drew in again the letters Fyx had erased, studied it some more, then erased the entire square. Erasing Rogor's cross, Crisal looked again at her marble.

Fyx raised his eyebrows as Crisal began making marks in the smooth sand. "Let us use the name of Dirak town the same as 'sator' in the tenet square."

D I R A K
I   A
R   R
A   I
K A R I D

"See?"

Fyx shrugged. "What of the rest?"

Crisal's finger flew at the sand. "The towns of Ikona and Anoki we use the same as 'arepo' and 'opera' in the tenet square . . . add a 'G' and there you are."

D I R A K
I K O N A
R O G O R
A N O K I
K A R I D

Fyx nodded. "And there is Rogor's hidden cross. But, what use is this to us?"

"Fyx, if this were a map and Dirak sat on the bottom 'D' of the square," Crisal poked it with her finger, "and if Ikona were here," she stabbed the "I" above the bottom "D", "and if the fishing village of Anoki were here," she poked the "A" in the bottom rank of letters, "where would the extra letter, the center of the cross fall?"

Fyx stood and looked at the square, then squatted next to it and drew in a few landmarks. "The 'G' falls at the end of the cleft in the center of Split Mountain." Fyx stood and pointed across Ikona toward the peak. "Now that we are here, you can see where the cleft begins."

Crisal stood and observed the crooked pass that led deep into the mountain, its walls hanging with bushy vines. The mountain itself was hidden beneath a heavy growth of trees except for its highest point which grew only scrub trees and brush. "This is your invitation from Rogor." Crisal pointed at the "G" in Rogor's cross. "We will find his lair at the end of the cleft. It is a trap."

Fyx nodded. "Rogor has gone to great pains to kill me, and yet he points the way for me to destroy him."

"There is more, Fyx. This thing in my sack that I got from Zuma's cart, it is a weapon, or a part of a weapon. It is what killed the farmers' crops. Look." Crisal pulled some half-brown, half-green stalks from her robe. "The part below is healthy, but look at the brown part. It looks as though it had been dipped in boiling water. Can your powders and other tricks protect you against such a thing?"

Fyx looked at the girl's eyes. "There is more, much more. Tell me."

"Fyx, what would happen if Rogor became king of Momus and then asked the Tenth Quadrant Federation for military protection against the Ninth Quadrant?"

Fyx shrugged, then looked down at the square. "As I understand it, the Ninth would have no choice but to let Momus be occupied, such as their laws are." He cackled. "But, child, Momus with a king? Perhaps Rogor can bully this small valley, but how could he become king of Momus? The ruler of Emerald Valley can't speak for the planet."

"Fyx, you saw the fear on the other side of the Snake Mountains, in Miira and Porse."

"And, child, I set them straight in Porse. Have no doubt about it. We can do the same everywhere south of the Snake Mountains. Neither of us will ever live long enough to see a king in Tarzak."

"But, when you are dead, Fyx, what will there be to stop King Rogor, his terrible weapons and his army of terror-driven thugs?"

"Dead?" The old magician pounded his chest. "I am far from dead, child."

"That is an obstacle Rogor and the Tenth Quadrant would like to remove. That's why Rogor offered the twenty thousand movills."

"Rogor? My contract is with him?" Fyx shook his head and frowned. "My brother was not a clever person, Crisal. Where does this devilish thinking come from? What powers has he discovered?"

Crisal spread out their blankets and stretched out on one of them. "His thinking comes from the same place that gives him his weapons, Fyx—another world." She patted the blanket next to hers. "Rest. We will need our wits about us tonight.

"We?" Fyx lowered himself to his blanket and put his stick aside. "Child, I promised Salina to turn you back once you had seen the answers to my questions. There is nothing left now but to pit my tricks against Rogor's."

"I told you, Rogor has powerful weapons, not tricks."

"Promise me you will not enter the mountain's cleft."

"But, you will . . ."

"It is my promise to Salina, child! Give me your promise."

"Very well." Crisal rolled over and turned her back to

the magician. "I promise to stay clear of the mountain's cleft."

Crisal awakened to a black, starless night. Rolling over, she felt for the magician, but found only his long cold blanket. Even straining her eyes, she could see little more than a dim outline of Split Mountain against the night sky. Fyx was somewhere within that great shadow preparing to do battle with the Dark One—or dead.

Crisal stood and mulled over the stupid promise Fyx had made her give. "What chance have you, old man, against weapons that can roast entire fields?" She stepped off to begin pacing, but stumbled over her sack. Regaining her balance, she pulled back a foot intending to deliver the sack a swift one. Hesitating, she squatted down, opened the sack and took out the white package. The roustabout at the gate to Dirak said he was to deliver it to the fountain in Ikona.

"Yes!" Crisal remembered Yudo, the barker, saying that his letter for Fyx had appeared at the fountain in Ikona. The girl held the package under her arm and stood, her back to the lake, facing the tiny farming village. From there she looked to the peak of Split Mountain. Reaching into her robe, she wrapped her hand around her glass marble. "The brown spots—there are none at the base of the mountain. Up there, on the peak, must be the weapon." Her feet carried her toward the town with its fountain. "And, if Rogor's friends have machines that can kill entire fields, moving a letter, a package," she smiled, "or a small child should be no great task."

Crisal stood before the unremarkable fountain in Ikona's tiny square. The streets and houses were deserted, and she examined the structure unafraid of discovery. The fountain itself was a simple column of mortar and stone with a weak spout of water rising from its center. The water dribbled down into a trough that surrounded the column, then drained off into a hole in the flatstone and mortar walkway that covered the center of the square. Looking behind her, Crisal could see that hers were the only footprints in the square, at least since the last rain. The path she had taken from the lake to the village was well traveled.

"Why do they go to the lake for water, unless there is

danger here in the square?" Crisal looked over the top of the fountain to see the peak of Split Mountain. Without stepping on the flatstones, she walked part way around the fountain, examining the walkway. Because of the dark, she could tell no difference, but on the side facing the mountain, she could make out a flatstone larger than the others. It seemed to shine, as if it had been scrubbed with sand many times. Picking up a handful of dust from the square, she threw it up, making a cloud between the stone and the mountain. Caught in the air, the cloud passed and settled to the ground undisturbed.

Crisal looked around the square until she found a rock the size of her fist. Taking it, she walked to the fountain and stepped gingerly on the flatstone walkway. When nothing happened, she let out her breath and slowly approached the large flatstone facing Split Mountain. Squatting next to it, she rolled the fist-sized stone into the center of its shiney surface. The stone sat motionless for a moment, then disappeared, leaving a sharp smell in the air.

Clenching her teeth, Crisal gripped the white package in both hands and jumped into the center of the stone. As she looked at the peak of Split Mountain, she felt tears running down her cheeks. She closed her eyes. "I am *not* afraid!"

"I'm pleased to hear that." Opening her eyes, before her stood a grinning figure in black and scarlet. He was old, stooped and had a blue "M" marked on his wrinkled forehead.

"Rogor!" Crisal dropped the package and reached into her sleeve for Fyx's fireballs. Her movements slowed to less than a crawl as the magician walked up to her and calmly removed the balls from her sleeve.

"You startled me, child. I thought Fyx had shrunk." Rogor took the fireballs and tucked them away in his own sleeve pocket. "Nasty little things."

The magician lifted Crisal and moved her from the platform where she had been standing. Carefully, Rogor examined every pocket in the girl's robe, then tied her hands at her back with a wire pulled from his waist. Having bound her securely, he pushed her to the ground and snapped his fingers. Crisal felt her muscles regain their normal speed, then she sobbed as Rogor went to the platform and picked up the package. He opened it and grinned as he pulled out the blue-black handle. "Ah, child, I should pay you. I have waited a long time for this."

Rogor walked across the platform and stepped down to the smooth hard surface beneath. Crisal noticed for the first time that the entire surface around her was smooth and hard, save for holes from which small trees grew. The magician stopped at a long, slender cylinder mounted on a metal-wheeled cart. He took a small threaded cylinder dangling from an opening on the bottom of the object and connected it to the handle. This completed, Rogor pushed the handle up into the larger cylinder and snapped it into place. "You have brought me the kingdom of Momus." He turned his head in Crisal's direction. "Know what this is?"

"No." She tried to move, but she felt the wire cut her wrists.

Rogor laughed. "Watch!" The magician worked controls at the base of the machine that Crisal couldn't see. The light from the controls cast a greenish glow on Rogor's face. He stepped back from the machine. With a low hum, the wheels turned slightly and the long cylinder tipped down. The hum grew louder for a moment, then ceased.

"That is how you kill the crops, Rogor."

He nodded. "Another unbeliever's crops have died. But, with this new trigger," he walked to the machine and aimed it into the air, "I have the very strength of Momus in my hands." A blinding white beam split the air and parted the clouds above them. Rogor stopped the beam and pushed the machine to the opposite side of the smooth area. "I can even melt mountains if I choose." Crisal pushed herself to her knees and got to her feet. Looking in the direction where Rogor aimed, she saw the great cleft in the mountain.

"No!"

Rogor looked at her. "Eh? Are you so fond of my mountain you could not bear to see me put a hole in it?" He cackled. "Or is there a little old man down in the cleft who might get hurt?" Rogor walked over to Crisal, held her chin with an iron grip and forced her to look into his face. "Is Fyx down there?"

Crisal tried to spit at Rogor, but her mouth was too dry. Laughing, the magician pushed her to the ground again. "No, child, this cannon would do the trick, but then Fyx would never know." Leaving the cannon, Rogor walked over to some bushes and pushed them aside exposing another wheeled contraption, this one a black cube. From its top, several large prisms were supported by metal arms. He pushed the machine to the edge of the cleft and began working the controls. "This is what took you from the fountain in Ikona, child. With it I can see anything within a two day's walk, and can bring it to my mountaintop if I choose."

Rogor turned the controls, all the time watching a screen. He frowned as he searched, then smiled. "Much of the path at the bottom of the cleft cannot be seen because of the turns and twists of the walls, but from here I can see the power station at the end of the cleft. Sooner or later . . . yes, that's him. Fyx."

Rogor pushed more controls, then turned to the platform, drawing a pistol from beneath his robe. In the blink of an eye, the back of a black and scarlet robed figure holding a stick appeared on the platform. "Fyx. It is you, isn't it?"

"Rogor?"

"Just so you know, Fyx." Rogor fired the pistol sending a pencil-thin streak of light through the figure on the platform. The stick fell and the robe collapsed. Rogor took a step toward it, then cursed, seeing the robe flat and empty. Quickly he leveled the pistol on Crisal. "Fyx, I have the little brat in my sights. Come out where I can see you, or I will cut her in two. Come out, and if I even sense your thoughts reaching toward mine, I will kill her!" Rogor looked around to his right, then his left. "Hear me, Fyx!"

"I hear you, Rogor." To Rogor's left, Fyx moved from behind some bushes, naked and looking small and helpless.

Rogor smiled, then laughed, turning the pistol on his brother. "I feel you trying to work my thoughts, Fyx, but I am stronger."

Crisal watched as Rogor straightened his right arm, aiming the pistol dead center. She closed her eyes and tiny hands searched Rogor's sleeve. Finding what they searched for, they wrapped themselves around a blackened dough ball and squeezed. Before she floated into black nothingness, she felt hot flame wash her face.

Crisal opened her eyes and looked up into a face lit with a red light. The face looked over her at the source of the light. "Fyx, it is you." The magician looked down and smiled a toothless grin. Crisal realized the old man was holding her in his arms. She threw her arms around Fyx's neck and held him tightly. "Fyx, it is you."

"Child," Fyx gasped, "you may succeed where Rogor failed. Let me breathe!"

Crisal relaxed her hold, but kept her head against Fyx's chest. "I killed him, didn't I?"

"You had no choice, Crisal."

"He was your brother."

"I tell you, you had no choice." Crisal looked into the old magician's eyes and read nothing but love. She turned toward the light and saw the sides of the cleft burning. Below, molten rock filled the cleft from side to side. "Let me down, Fyx." Once on her feet, and steady, Crisal looked away from the cleft. The smooth, hard surface was empty. "Where are the machines and the platform?"

She looked at the magician, and he nodded toward the river of molten rock. "Down there."

"Fyx, they could have made you the greatest magician on Momus!"

The old man raised his eyebrows and turned toward the girl. "Child, I *am* the greatest magician on Momus."

Crisal nodded. "But, what of the quadrant laws? Rogor didn't build these machines." She pointed at the red, flowing rock. "How did that happen?"

"I turned Rogor's cannon on the power station below. You are right; these are not Rogor's works."

"But, without the machines, how can we prove that Rogor had help from off-planet?"

"We can't. Hence, no act of war can be proven. No one from the Tenth Quadrant will tell of what was attempted here, and neither will we."

"But, if the law . . ."

"Child, what do your fortune teller's eyes show you if the Ninth Quadrant knew about this?"

Crisal frowned. "They would send their own force to counter the forces of the Tenth . . . and they would settle their differences here, on Momus."

The magician nodded. "Great powers usually find someone else's backyard in which to wage their wars. We have spared Momus that."

"What of Rogor's army forming in Ris?"

Fyx turned from the cleft and walked to the mountainside. Crisal followed behind as they began the long climb. Fyx talked over his shoulder as he felt his way down. "They will get tired of waiting for King Rogor. In a day or two they will drift back to their towns. Some will still talk in fear of Rogor, but next spring the crops will come up green. In a few years, nothing will remain of Rogor except children who will try to scare each other with tales of the ghost of Split Mountain."

Crisal followed until she stumbled, barking her shins on a sharp rock. "Fyx, wait. Let me rest."

The old man turned and stood next to her. "Here is a grassy spot, Crisal. We can rest here until morning."

The girl moved to the place and sat down, rubbing her legs. The magician lowered himself next to her and put his stick on the ground. Lifting up a hip, he plucked a rock from beneath it and tossed it down the mountain. Crisal bit her lip and turned to the old man. "Fyx, I know Salina agreed to let me apprentice to you at your request, but what happens now? Rogor is defeated. Am I needed anymore?"

Fyx let his head fall slowly to the ground and looked up at the cloudy sky. "Momus has drawn the interest of powerful forces. I shall return to Tarzak and do what I can. Our troubles do not end here."

"But, what of me?"

"You shall rest. Go to sleep."

Crisal felt her mind cloud. "Fyx, I don't like it when you make me sleep . . ." She saw herself in a black mist, floating free. All around her was black save a wisp of white floating to her left. *Fyx?*

Yes, child.

The black mist parted and Crisal saw stars above and a fluffy blanket of clouds beneath. The wisp of white turned and streaked toward the east. Crisal turned and followed. *Fyx! Fyx, what is this?*

We have done little but work magic, child. Now, I would show you some play!

Where do we fly?

We meet the sun. Hurry, we can go fast—as fast as we wish.

Crisal darted away from the clouds toward the stars, laughed, then dipped into the black mist and up again at Fyx. The magician dodged and cackled. *Fyx, my question.*

Will I still be your apprentice? Her companion mist flew a circle around her, then darted toward the yellowing sky ahead. *Well, Fyx?*

Yes, you shall remain my apprentice. She hesitated, then streaked far ahead of the magician. *Someday, Crisal, you shall be the greatest magician of us all.*

The sun burst upon Crisal's sight, and she outshone it.

The Second Law

As he stepped up the tiers in the spectator's section of the Great Ring, Lord Ashly Allenby paused to listen as a minor poet from Porse rehearsed his argument. The chubby fellow in blue and grey stripes cleared his throat, stood, bowed and recited:

"We're here to form the Second Law,
I'm not sure why we do,
The horrors of debate, it seems,
Not worth the revenue.
Lord Allenby has called us here,
To beg the Ninth to still his fear,
The evil Tenth will soon be here,
A frightful thing, if true."

As Allenby frowned and took a step toward the poet, he felt Disus, his chief-of-staff, pulling at his arm. He turned and saw the clown shaking his head.

"But, descendants of the circus ship,
CITY OF BARABOO,
I feel I have a question
I must ask of you:
We've lived here free with but one law
A hundred years without a flaw,
We need another? I say 'Pshaw!'
And now, I bid adieu."

As a few listeners applauded, Disus hustled Allenby to their seats. Allenby sat with a thump and shook his head. "Moon, spoon, June, I hope the armies of the Tenth Quadrant will be amused by the fool." He pushed back the black and scarlet striped hood of his magician's robe and leaned back on the cut stone step of the amphitheater, his elbows resting on the step behind. Disus arranged his own orange robe and adopted a similar posture. When the ambassador from the Ninth Quadrant cooled to a low boil, Disus reached into his purse.

"A movill for your thoughts."

Allenby held out his hand and the clown dropped a copper into it. "They find too much humor in my mission and, perhaps—" He smiled. "A little too much seriousness in me."

"You have much to be proud of, Allenby. Look at them." Disus nodded at the tiers filling with magicians, riders, trainers, clowns, newstellers, mimes, jugglers, freaks, acrobats, merchants and artisans. "Masters every one—look! There is Great Vyson of the Dofstaffl newstellers, and look! Great Kamera!"

Allenby smiled, knowing that Disus, a master clown himself, would be staring in adoration at the Great Kamera, master clown and delegation leader to the Ring from Tarzak. He felt his own heart skip a beat as he recognized Great Fyx, the ancient master magician, in the delegation. Leaning forward, then standing, both Allenby and Disus bowed as the delegation came abreast of the spectators' seats. Kamera nodded at Disus, but Fyx separated from the delegation and motioned for Allenby to come down to him. His heart racing, Allenby stepped over and around the other spectators until he reached the bottom tier where he stood before the Great Fyx.

"Allenby, I would have come up, but the years are gaining on my magic. What do you charge for the trip?"

"Nothing, Great Fyx. It is my honor."

Fyx nodded, then smiled a toothless grin. "Come down to the Ring. I wish to talk in private."

Allenby stepped over the low stone wall and stood on the sawdust next to the great magician. "How may I serve you?"

Fyx stood close, cupped a gnarled hand around his mouth and whispered. "Your trick of the seven cards, I wish to buy it."

"I am truly honored."

"How much?"

Allenby shook his head. "Forgive me, Great Fyx, but I seem to have lost my wits. That *you* should buy a trick from *me*... I am stunned."

"A good trick is a good trick no matter where its source, Allenby. I saw you perform it on the road to Miira."

Allenby frowned. "Impossible. Forgive me, Great Fyx, but I would have known you. You couldn't have seen it on the road to Miira."

Fyx cackled and stamped one of his spindly legs against the sawdust. "You are a master magician, Allenby, but a new one, nonetheless. Listen." Fyx composed his features, closed his eyes for a second and covered his face with his robe. When he removed the robe, the face of a young woman smiled sensually at Allenby. "I would go with you behind the dunes, Lord Allenby, Ashly—but I must save myself for my betrothed . . ."

"Dorna!" Allenby flushed, then bellowed in glee as Great Fyx recovered his face, returning with his original mass of wrinkles twisted in mirth. "Excellent, Fyx! Ever since, I have dreamed of that maiden."

"You were persuasive, Allenby, but it is well that I didn't give in to your charm; even I am not that good an illusionist!" The two magicians laughed until tears came to their eyes.

"Yes, Great Fyx, that is my price for the trick of the seven cards: the truth about Dorna. Perhaps now I can dream about other things." Allenby reached within his robe and took out a wallet. Leafing through the papers in it, he pulled one out and handed it to the old magician. Fyx stuffed the slip in his own wallet, removed another and handed it to Allenby.

"Your magic is coming along, Allenby, but as a bargainer you are pitiful. Take it. It is only a minor illusion in exchange for the trick."

Allenby took the slip with trembling hands. "I am very honored. Thank you."

Fyx looked toward the center of the Ring where a man in bright red robes busily instructed a hundred others dressed in white. "The Master of the Ring is instructing the cashiers, and I must join my delegation." Allenby bowed, the old man nodded and hobbled off toward the portion of the steps belonging to the town of Tarzak.

Allenby looked at the slip Fyx had given him. It was Fyx's illusion of the displaced person, a minor illusion to Fyx, but the centerpiece for any lesser magician's repertory.He tucked the slip in his wallet as he climbed the tiers to rejoin Disus. As he took his seat, a flash of the freak's yellow and green caught his eyes. "Disus, is that Yehudin?"

Disus turned, shielding his eyes from the sun. "Yes, it is. He hurries. Do you suppose the mission has already landed?"

Allenby frowned and they both rose to meet the freak. Yehudin, out of breath, came to a stop before them and held out his hand. Allenby dropped a copper into it. The skin of Yehudin's palm, as with the rest of his body, was thick, segmented and nut brown. "What is it?"

"Allenby, Humphries is here. He wants to see you at once."

"What is he doing here?" Allenby turned to Disus and dropped some coppers into the clown's hand. "Watch things and come for me if I'm needed." Allenby and Yehudin climbed down the tiers and walked around the Ring until they came to the spectator's entrance. Turning into the carved rock tunnel, Allenby pressed Yehudin's thorny shoulder. "Did Humphries say what he wanted?"

"I couldn't understand him, Allenby. He seemed very upset." They left the cool tunnel and turned down a dusty street flanked with white-painted single-story shops and homes. "He only appeared disdainful until I showed him his office at the embassy—then, he began calling me names!"

"I apologize for him, Yehudin."

"The apology is not yours to give."

Allenby nodded and they walked until they reached a two-story, white adobe building. Above the entrance appeared the words: Embassy, Ninth Quadrant Federation of Habitable Planets. Standing in the entrance, pink, chubby and glowering in the full regalia of a Quadrant vice-ambassador, Allenby saw who he assumed to be Bertrum Humphries, his second in command.

"I'm Allenby."

Humphries eyed Allenby from the top of his black and scarlet striped hood to his sandals and dirty feet. Waving his arm back toward the building, Humphries shouted, "Allenby, what is the meaning of this? Do you expect me to conduct myself as a proper representative of the quadrant in a . . . a hovel? And why are you dressed in that preposterous costume?"

"First, Humphries, you shall address me either as Lord Allenby, or Mister Ambassador." Humphries froze, then lowered his arm, his eyes narrowing. "Next, I believe you owe my secretary an apology."

Humphries pointed a finger at Yehudin. "That . . . that is your secretary?"

"That has a name, Humphries! This is Yehudin the alligator man of the Tarzak Freaks. His family is one of the most distinguished on Momus, *and* he is my secretary, Mister Vice-ambassador!"

The muscles beneath Humphries' right cheek twitched. Turning toward Yehudin, he cocked his head forward slightly. "I apologize for my remarks, Mister . . ."

"Yehudin." The alligator man smiled, exposing twin rows of teeth filed to sharp points, and held out his hand, palm up. Humphries looked at the outstretched hand, then looked at Allenby.

"Humphries, you *owe* him an apology. Twenty movills should be sufficient." Yehudin nodded.

"Do you seriously expect me to *pay* this . . . this . . ."

"Secretary, and yes I do."

Humphries reached into his breast pocket and withdrew his wallet. Opening it, he pulled out several credit notes. "What's the exchange rate?"

Yehudin folded his arms. "All the cashiers in Tarzak are at the Ring."

Allenby took several credit notes from Humphries' wallet and returned him twenty copper beads. "Here, I'll exchange it for you, Humphries."

Humphries took the beads, a puzzled expression on his face, and handed them to Yehudin. Yehudin pocketed the movills, smiled again, and then walked behind Humphries and opened the curtain covering the embassy door. "Gentlemen?"

In the ambassador's quarters, seated on one of several tan cushions placed around a low table, Allenby watched Humphries grow more uncomfortable by the minute. The man's high-collared blue uniform blouse was obviously choking him. Allenby hadn't the heart to tell Humphries that when he had leaned back against the whitewashed adobe wall, he had covered the back of his midnight-colored uniform with chalk.

"Look, Humphries, I'm terribly sorry we've gotten off on the wrong foot. It's important that our relationship be one of mutual respect and cooperation."

"I suppose I overreacted at the news, Lord Allenby."

"What news is that?"

"What news . . . why, that Momus hasn't yet authorized relations with the Quadrant federation!"

"These things take time, Bertrum—may I call you Bertrum?"

"Bert."

"Very well, Bert."

"You've been on the planet for two years, Lord Allenby. I'd think that to be time enough."

Allenby shrugged and held up his hands. "The news first had to spread, then there are town petitions, meetings, the formation of delegations, then there's traveling to Tarzak. The town delegations are gathering now in the Great Ring to form the Second Law . . ."

"Second Law?" Humphries frowned. "Did you say 'Second Law'?"

Allenby dropped his hands to his lap and nodded. "You see, Bert, Momus only has one law. The First Law was passed over a century ago, and no one really remembers why it was ever formed."

"What is this First Law?"

"It's their law for making laws. It's such a bother they haven't passed another law since. First, the people of each town must petition in their towns for a meeting to select a delegation . . ."

Humphries held up his hand. "Please." He lowered his hand and shook his head. "Do you mean that there is no established political body with which to deal?"

Allenby smiled. "Now, you've got it."

"Impossible. It goes against every tenet of accepted political theory for a population of this size to live . . . I mean, what do they do about taxes, crime, or little things such as representing the planet to the Ninth Quadrant Federation?"

Allenby drummed his fingers on the table and studied the ambassador. Sighing, he shook his head. "As to taxes, Bert, everyone pays for what he uses to the degree he uses it."

Humphries snorted. "And there's no crime, I suppose?"

"It's rare, but it happens. If you cheat or steal, you either pay back the victim or are exiled. If you murder, you are exiled."

"Exiled from what?"

"Exiled from the company of good people. Exiles are marked and sent into the desert. No one will give them or sell them talk, rest, food or comfort."

"Who does all this judging?"

"The people . . . Bert, have you ever seen a circus?"

Humphries raised his brows as his jaw fell open. "A circus?"

"Yes."

Humphries shrugged. "I suppose, as a child, on television . . ."

"It's a very closed society, Bert, steeped in custom and tradition. The very nature of these customs and traditions is why Momus has only one law, and probably could get along without that."

"Except for one thing, Lord Allenby: The Tenth Quadrant."

Allenby nodded. "True."

"Which brings us back to the question of what you have been doing for the past two years."

"Bert, I had to steal a lifeboat to get here, and when I landed, I had only the clothes on my back. First, I had to get their attention; then, I had to get their respect."

"Respect? You are an ambassador of the first rank!"

Allenby shrugged. "Politicians and diplomatic types aren't recognized as having legitimate occupations . . ."

"Legitimate!? And I suppose you get respect by wearing that ridiculous getup?"

"I earned my magician's colors, Bert, and to tell you the truth, they're a lot more comfortable than that straitjacket you're wearing."

"My God, man, your trousers! Isn't anything worn under those robes?"

"No, Bert, everything works just fine." Allenby snickered while Humphries shook his head.

"Lord Allenby, do you have any conception of how old that joke is?"

"Disus said it was a classic. Cost me ten coppers."

"Disus?"

"My chief-of-staff."

"I suppose he's a comedian."

"No. He's a clown."

"And you have the respect of these people?"

"I can prove it." Allenby reached into his robe and took

out his wallet. Removing a slip from it, he put the paper on the table in front of Humphries. "Great Fyx, the most honored magician on Momus, gave me this in exchange for my trick of the seven cards. It's his illusion of the displaced person."

Humphries shook his head. "May I be perfectly frank, Lord Allenby?"

"Go ahead." Allenby replaced the slip and returned the wallet to his robe.

"Before I left the Sol System, Bensonhurst, the Quadrant Secretary of State . . ."

"I know him."

"And, Lord Allenby, it appears that he knows you."

"Clarify."

"The secretary informed me that you were selected as ambassador to Momus because of your rather unorthodox approach to diplomatic tasks." Humphries' arms lifted at his sides, indicating the entire planet. "I have some inkling of why. But this . . ." He lowered his hands to his lap. "This is pitiful."

"That's the second time today that I've been called pitiful. As my superior, Great Fyx can get away with it. As *your* superior, you had best produce an explanation."

"An explanation? The diplomatic mission has been sitting in orbit around Momus for the past ten days, and the military mission will arrive in another three weeks. Here you sit in a bathrobe headquartered in a mud hut glorying in a new prank you've . . ."

"Illusion."

"Illusion, then. In any event, here you are playing magic act with a freak and a clown, while the legality of both diplomatic and military missions has yet to be satisfied!"

"I think that's enough frankness for one day, Humphries."

"There's one more thing you should know."

"What's that?"

"I am to report on you directly to the secretary."

Allenby nodded. He had expected nothing less. "What do you know about Momus?"

"I was briefed, of course."

"That's not what I asked."

"Very well. One hundred and seventy Earth Annual Units ago, the circus starship *City of Baraboo,* enroute to the first system of its intended circuit of Tenth Quadrant planets, established an orbit around Momus due to engine difficulties. Its orbit, due to the selfsame engine difficulties, was erratic, enabling only the performers and some of the livestock . . ."

"Animals."

"Forgive me—some of the animals to escape in the life-boats before the ship and crew burned in the atmosphere."

"And?"

"I'm afraid that's it, except for astrophysical data, Quadrant coordinates, things like that."

"In other words, you know next to nothing about Momus."

"From what I can see, Lord Allenby, it is one step removed from a primitive society. My . . . our primary interest here is to counter Tenth Quadrant territorial ambitions. I'm sure we and General Kahn can accomplish our mission without involving ourselves overly much with concerns about a bunch of fuzzy wuzzys in greasepaint."

"Fuzzy wuzzys . . ." Without changing expression, Allenby adjusted his robe and leaned toward the vice-ambassador. "Humphries, old man."

"Yes?"

"See this black mark between my eyes?"

The vice-ambassador leaned forward and squinted. "Hmmm, yes. What caused it?"

"Keep looking at it. Now, put your palms flat on the table." Humphries lifted his arms slowly and placed his palms on the cool surface of the table. Allenby smiled as Humphries' palms grew hotter and hotter.

"What's going on . . ."

"Now, Humphries, look down. Look down at the table." Humphries looked down, his eyes widening. In a second he was screaming, trying to pull his hands free. Allenby knew that Humphries saw himself whirling down into a bottomless pit of flames and brimstone, the skin searing, then roasting from his bones. He had been there himself, which is why he paid Noman two thousand movills for the illusion. He was almost happy Humphries had shown up; he had never found anyone else he disliked enough to send to Hell. Allenby clapped his hands, and Humphries collapsed on the table.

"My God . . . my . . ."

"Humphries, old man?"

"Allenby, what in God's name . . . ?"

"That is a minor illusion called Visions of Hell. Did you enjoy it?"

"Dear God, Allenby!" The vice-ambassador pushed himself up, unclasped his uniform collar and wiped the perspiration from his face.

"Momus is not a colony of fuzzy wuzzys, Bert, old man. Also, it would pay you to keep views like that to yourself. As I said, it's only a minor illusion." Allenby turned to the door. "Yehudin!"

The alligator man entered and stood next to the table. "So you finally tried the hotfoot?"

"Yes. Yehudin, please help Vice-ambassador Humphries to his shuttlecraft." Yehudin pulled Humphries to his feet and pocketed the coppers Allenby put on the table. "Humphries?"

"Yes?"

"You are not to come planetside again without my permission. That applies to all mission personnel. Is that clear?"

"Yes."

Allenby waved his hand and the alligator man took the shaking diplomat out the door. Long after they left, Allenby sat drumming his fingers on the table. He understood Humphries' attitude. Although considered a bit of a rough edge by the Quadrant diplomatic corps, Allenby had served it the better part of his adult life, and he knew and respected its customs and traditions founded upon centuries of diplomatic experience. He smiled as he recalled his own first encounter with an inhabitant of Momus, then frowned remembering Humphries' ominous statement about Bensonhurst. From their first meeting the Secretary made it clear that kicking Allenby out of the corps was one of his life's major aims. Reaching into his robe, Allenby withdrew the pocket communicator that had been left for him by the mission's initial landing party. That it was the only radio set on the planet seemed threatening, but how and to what he couldn't identify. He pressed the call button.

"Quadrant Starship *Elite*, communications," the palm sized box crackled with a magic from another time.

"This is Allenby."

"Yes, Mister Ambassador, how can I help you?"

"I want to speak with the commander of the military mission."

"General Kahn. One moment, please, Mister Ambassador." The box, silent for a few heartbeats, reurned to life with a deep, powerful voice. "Lord Allenby, this is General Kahn."

"General, I would like some information."

"Certainly, Lord Allenby."

"General, is the occupation and defense plan for Momus complete?"

"Yes it is."

"I want to see it—down here."

"You understand, Lord Allenby, that it's all on memory chips?"

"Is that a problem?"

"All our portable readers are with the military contingent. All we have on the *Elite* are the ship's computers and a field command unit. The *Elite's* shuttlecrafts aren't designed to take a command reader. It's not weight; size is the problem."

"General, I don't care if you have to take a shuttlecraft apart and reassemble it around that reader."

"Yes sir, and when do you want it?"

"How fast can you get it here?"

"That fast?"

"That fast. Allenby out." Allenby returned the set to his robe, stood and went to the open window looking out on the dusty street. Seeing the red-and-purple stripes of a barker, he called out, "Ho, barker!"

The barker ambled across the street and stood in the sun beneath the window, with his hand out. Allenby dropped a copper into it. "How may I serve you, magician?"

"Can you get me Great Tayla the fortune teller?"

"It will be a price to remember."

"I will pay whatever price she asks, and two hundred coppers for yourself if she is here within the hour." The barker disappeared down the street before the dust from his first step settled to the ground.

That evening on the desert west of Tarzak, Allenby eyed the interior of the cramped shuttlecraft and wondered what magic Kahn had used to fit the enormous holographic reader through the craft's tiny port. The sphere, which depicted

Momus under a hypothetical attack by Tenth Quadrant forces, barely cleared the ceiling. Tayla sat before the sphere, her black eyes darting from place to place, absorbing every detail of the imaginary battle. General Kahn, still irked at Tayla's lack of a security clearance, stood between Tayla and the reader's operator.

The fortune teller passed her wrinkled hands between her eyes and the sphere, then pushed back one side of her pale blue hood and looked at the general. "Kahn, make the planet large again."

Kahn nodded at the operator, who punched a button. The sphere filled with the planet, its forests, deserts, oceans and towns springing to life. "Show me the installations, Kahn, and this time explain them to me."

Kahn pointed to a screen on the console beneath the sphere. "Anything you want to know about a base will appear there."

Tayla looked at Allenby. "She is a fortune teller, General. She does not know how to read. Read it to her."

Kahn nodded at the operator, and the sphere went black, save for several tiny specks that remained the color of the terrain, reddish-yellow, green and brown. "Give me the Tarzak base." All but one of the reddish-yellow specks disappeared. The remaining one expanded until it filled Tayla's side of the sphere. The general cleared his throat. "This is the Tarzak base, which will be both the first and the largest. It will serve primarily as the military mission headquarters as well as housing for off-orbit personnel and their families."

Tayla held up her hand. "How many?"

"How many what?"

"Soldiers and others."

Kahn reached in front of Tayla and coded the request into the console. "Total personnel, military and civilian, will be two hundred and twenty thousand."

Tayla nodded. "The next installation, Kahn."

The general and the fortune teller went through the complete series of Quadrant military installations, from the combat training range located in the Great Desert to the wide and narrow defensive satellite systems. Orbital and planetside fighter bases, supply depots, commissary and post exchange facilities, raw materials acquisition operations, even educational, hospital, and recreational facilities for dependents were examined by the old woman. As the series ended, Tayla closed her eyes, her head bowed. "Turn it off, Kahn."

The general nodded at the operator, and the sphere became transparent and lifeless. Allenby went to the fortune teller and pressed her arm. "Great Tayla, are you well?"

She lifted her head, her eyes tired. "I see such things in your crystal ball, Allenby—such things." She shook her head. "It will take me time, and I must consult my own poor ball." She looked back at the reader. "I would give much for such as this, yet," she nodded, "even that is part of the problem." She withdrew a palm-sized glass sphere from her robe and held it, catching the beam of a service light on the reader's console. In seconds, her breathing slowed and she stared at the ball with unblinking eyes.

General Kahn poked the reader operator in the shoulder and motioned toward the cockpit of the shuttlecraft. Quietly, the soldier stood and left the compartment. Kahn left the reader, took Allenby by the elbow and steered him toward the back of the passenger area. "Lord Allenby, to follow your orders I've had to bend, shatter or throw out half a volume of Quadrant regulations, but this act with the crystal ball is a little much. What will she see in there she didn't see in the reader?"

Allenby shook his head. "She sees nothing in there, Kahn. She uses the ball's light to focus her thoughts. Right now her mind is working at top speed organizing, associating and abstracting all she knows, including the information she obtained from the reader. She'll take that information, weigh probabilities and draw conclusions from them."

Kahn frowned. "But, you call it fortune telling."

"Statistical forecasting by any other name . . ."

"But we have the equipment aboard ship to do sociological projections, and highly trained scientists to interpret and verify the information. All you'll have here is the word of an old woman."

"No, Kahn. I'll have the word of Great Tayla, the greatest fortune teller on Momus. What's more, she has capabilities your equipment doesn't."

"Such as?"

"Common sense, feelings, and a heart tuned to the interests of Momus and its people."

Tayla's head snapped up and she stood, letting her ball shatter on the deck. "Allenby!"

Rushing to her side, Allenby caught her as she began to swoon. "Tayla, what is it?"

"They will destroy us. Keep them away. The soldiers must not come on the planet."

Later that night, the street outside Allenby's window cool and quiet, Allenby and Kahn sat in the dark, sipping wine. Yehudin had escorted Tayla to her home, returned, and bid them a night's sleep. Allenby, his purse lighter for the day's events, put down his cup and looked across the table at Kahn. In the dark, the general resembled a great bear, hunched over the table sipping at his own cup.

"Well, General?"

The dark shape nodded slowly. "What the old woman says is true, Allenby. I've seen it before on Markab VIII."

"What's troubling you, then?"

"I've seen it before, but I never thought about it. It was always just a necessary evil of military occupation." Kahn drained his cup and refilled it. "The troops move in, those paper credits start flying around, the economy gets a sharp increase in wages and sales, and the next thing you know the bases are ringed with whorehouses, drug parlors, and clip joints. After that, it's only a question of time before crime gets to the point where a man on a horse is the only answer." Kahn emptied his cup. "Then the military steps in and sets up a government. Just having the size military mission that is scheduled to occupy Momus will attract trade from the rest of the Quadrant."

"Which means, more people, more scum, more crime . . ."

"And more government." Kahn shook his head. "You know, it shouldn't be hitting me this way. Like I said, I've seen it before. But that old woman—she was describing the death of an entire people; she was describing her own death."

"What would be worse, Kahn: that, or occupation by the Tenth Quadrant?"

"That is no choice. Depends on whether you like your death slow or fast." Kahn refilled his cup, slopping some wine on the table. "Sorry."

"No matter."

Kahn drank deeply and placed his cup on the table.

"Well, it's not our fish to fry, is it?"

"How so?"

"As I'm sure Vice-ambassador Humphries has already pointed out, we all work for the Quadrant. It's not just keeping the Tenth Quadrant off Momus; there's more at stake. The Tenth has put together an armada equal to anything in the galaxy, and they're prepared to use it. If they can move in without a fight, all well and good. But, they're not afraid of a fight. We've already had a few brushes with them."

"I heard nothing of this."

"Neither our Quadrant nor the Tenth admits to anything. Any official mention means certain war. They'd just as soon get as far as they can without spending ships and lives. This Quadrant is what they want to get, and if we stack the interests of Momus against the interests of the entire Quadrant . . ."

"Then we sacrifice the pawn."

"Spoken like a true diplomat." Kahn knocked his cup on the floor with a wave of his hand. "Damn, I'm drunk!"

"What about Tayla's solution?"

"The fortune teller?" Kahn shook his head. "Impossible. The only way we could keep them separate is to put the whole bloody military mission, dependents and all, in orbit. Even then, we'd still have to have the power and materials."

"Power and materials could be provided with a minimum of contact, couldn't they?"

"I suppose. But, here's the thing. The expense to put up and maintain the mission in orbit—the secretary wouldn't stand for it. Prohibitive."

"That's all there is to it? The expense?"

"Technically we can do it."

Allenby laughed. "Well, Kahn, that's it! Momus will pay for its own defense."

"What?"

"If they didn't pay for it, the people here would think the defenses worthless. It will be one grand haggle, but Momus will pay for your orbiting mission."

"That'll be some kind of first."

"How soon can you cook up an amended plan?"

"Cost is no object?" Allenby laughed, then nodded. Kahn thought a moment. "After I sober up, perhaps three, four hours. Everything is in the computer. All we'll be doing is altering a few factors."

"Noon tomorrow?"

"No. It'll take an hour to get to the ship, more to haul the reader in. What about doing it here, planetside? I can use the shuttlecraft and patch the reader into the ship's computers. I could have it out by noon."

"Good. I'll expect it then."

"Where do I sleep?"

"Just push a few of those floor cushions together and stretch out."

Kahn stumbled around for a few moments, then dropped onto the cushions. In moments he was breathing deeply, and promising to snore. Disus rose from a dark corner and placed some coppers on Allenby's table.

"A trip through another's mind—excellent, Allenby. The illusion of the displaced person is worth ten times the price."

"I'm surprised I got the moves right on my first try. Fyx will never make a living as a scribe."

"As I felt myself approach the aura, it seemed as though he would have noticed had he not consumed so much of your sapwine."

Allenby nodded. "I'll get the proper combination with practice. About what I asked you?"

"Kahn is an honest man, Allenby. He will try his best."

Allenby pushed his cushions together and stretched out. "I must rest, Disus. I want to be at the Ring early tomorrow."

Disus nodded and turned to leave. "Tomorrow you will be needed. Great Kamera will speak, and he opposes the Second Law."

Early the next morning, the sun warming only the upper edge of the amphitheater's west wall, Allenby watched as Boosthit of the Farransetti newstellers and his apprentice told once again the news Allenby had brought to Momus. The apprentice played the part of Allenby, and all having seen the news before, the element of surprise was lost. But, the performance was polished and drew many coppers. As the two newstellers bowed toward Allenby, seated in the spectator's section, the white-robed cashiers adjusted their money trays and took their stations among the delegates.

The Master of the Ring blew his whistle and the chatter of the delegates dropped to a lower volume. A cashier moved from the Tarzak delegation, walked to the center of the ring and handed the Master of the Ring a slip of paper. After blowing his whistle again, the Master of the Ring addressed the tiers.

"Laydeeeez and gentlemen! Great Fyx of the Tarzak Delegation would speak to the Great Ring!"

The cashiers moved among the delegates collecting from those who would hear Fyx and paying off those who would charge to hear the master magician. As they finished, the cashiers gathered at the edge of the Ring and presented their balances to the Master Cashier, who, in turn, presented his balance to Fyx. The old magician accepted his movills, stood and stepped into the Ring. Flinging up his hands, a ball of orange flame appeared high above his head, then turned to black smoke which drifted slowly in the quiet air.

Fyx pointed at the smoke. "A grain of sand is to a mountain as this little puff of smoke is to war." The delegates applauded the magician's opening, and Allenby clapped the loudest. It was an old trick, but it captured the attention. The crowd quiet again, Fyx lowered his hands and looked around at the delegates seated in the tiers.

"We have heard Boosthit of the Farransetti newstellers relate the news Allenby brought to Momus. We have heard of the evil designs of the Tenth Quadrant Federation. They would control this planet with or without our consent. With our consent, we would be slaves; without our consent," Fyx pointed at the drifting cloud of smoke, "they would bring terrible weapons against us and take what they want." He lowered his hand. "By protecting us, the Ninth Quadrant would save us from making either choice, but we cannot have this protection unless we give our consent."

The ancient magician motioned toward the Tarzak delegation and an apprentice scurried from the tiers carrying a gnarled staff. Handing the staff to Fyx, the apprentice returned to the tiers. The magician supported himself by holding onto the staff with both hands. He bowed his head for a moment, then continued. "The Second Law must, first, ask the Ninth Quadrant Federation to act in our defense. Second, it must create a means to represent Momus as an entire planet to plan and form the nature of that defense with the officials of the Ninth Quadrant." Lifting his head, he raised his staff above it. "We must do this. Remember what awaits us if we do not!" At that, Fyx's edge of the ring was filled with dense, white smoke. When it cleared, the old magician was again seated with the Tarzak delegation.

As the crowd applauded, Allenby turned to see Disus climbing the tiers to where he sat. "Have I missed Kamera's performance, Allenby?"

"No. Fyx did well enough, but I don't even see Kamera with his delegation."

Disus sat down and rubbed his hands. "He is the greatest clown on Momus, Allenby. He must have an entrance."

"What about Kahn?"

Disus looked confused for a moment, then nodded. "He says he will have the new plan by the time the sun warms the Ring." He held out his hand and accepted the coppers Allenby dropped into it. Pocketing the movills, Disus turned his attention toward the north entrance to the Ring. A cashier ran from the entrance and handed a slip of paper to the Master of the Ring.

"Laydeeeez and gentlemen! Great Kamera would speak to the Great Ring of Tarzak!"

The cashiers scurried about their business, and the Master Cashier had to take an apprentice to carry Kamera his balance, for many valued his performances. The two were swallowed by the darkness of the north entrance, then returned to the Ring, trying to stifle their snickers as they resumed their places.

Allenby looked around the tiers, stopping on Disus. Every member of the crowd, save himself, was watching the north entrance and preparing to laugh themselves silly. As he turned his own eyes toward the entrance, Allenby shrugged off his feelings of apprehension. They quickly returned as a pitiful "Squeegee! Squeegee!" sound came from the entrance and triggered a wave of laughter. As the laughing began to slack, a flat paper mask emerged into the light, looked left, then right, then straight ahead that all but the few behind the entrance could see. Allenby shuddered at both the thunder of laughter caused by the mask, and by the mask itself. With wide, abnormally large blue eyes, pink cheeks and a mouth formed into an "o," it was the face of a small boy in wonder, as well as a grotesque representation of Allenby's own face.

To the sound of "Squeegee! Squeegee!", the figure entered the Ring. The sound, caused by enormous fake feet worn backwards, was soon drowned by the laughs and applause from the crowd. The master clown, holding the mask before his face, wore a magician's robe on his right side and a newsteller's robe on his left. The loose ends were wrapped and tangled around his body and held in place by a belt from which dangled and clattered a variety of objects. As he reached a spot well into the Ring, Kamera stopped and held up his free arm for quiet, the sleeve flapping loose over his hand. The end of the sleeve immediately began smoking, and Kamera's attempts at trying to stamp out the fire with his outsized backwards feet soon had even Allenby shaking his head and laughing.

The fire apparently out, Kamera again held up his free arm, the sleeve still loose over the end of his hand. He turned his face and mask toward his upraised arm, and the crowd quieted as the sleeve-covered arm began to shake. After a moment, the sleeve slid down Kamera's arm exposing his fist. The arm stopped shaking and the clown seemed to cower as he watched his own fist slowly open. The fingers fully open, Kamera turned and showed the open hand to everyone in the tiers. "Laydeeeez and gentlemen! I give you the Illusion of the Reborn Hand. Ta-daaa!"

Allenby frowned and turned to Disus. "He goes too far! I'd like to show him the illusion of the fried clown!" Already laughing, upon hearing Allenby, Disus doubled over and fell off the tier. Shaking his head, Allenby turned to look at Kamera who was again holding up his hand for quiet.

"I speak to you, ladies and gentlemen, as Allenby, magician . . ." Kamera looked at the black left sleeve of his costume. "No, this is a newsteller's sleeve. Then, I speak to you as Allenby the newsteller . . ." Switching mask hands, the clown looked at the black-and-scarlet-striped sleeve on his right arm. "Ahhh! I am a magician! How else could I dazzle you with my fine magic?" He paused. "But, if I am not a newsteller, how did I bring you the news of the Ninth Quadrant's offer?" Switching hands again, he looked at his left sleeve. He started at the sight, then reached to his belt and took from it a band. Using the band, he secured the mask to his face, then held both arms in front. He looked first at one sleeve, then at the other. Dropping his arms to his sides, he shook his head.

"Let it pass for the moment; I will remember by and by." He held out his arms. "In any event, I speak to you as Allenby of the town of... the town of... Why, I don't seem to remember that either." Kamera turned toward the Tarzak delegation. "I live in Tarzak, but have I ever been accepted by the town?"

A priest decked in black and white diamonded robe stood above the delegates. "No."

Kamera turned his back on the Tarzak delegation and shook his head. He began pacing in a small circle, his feet going "Squeegee! Squeegee!" He spread his hands, palms outward before his chest and walked around the Ring. "Am I from Kuumic?"

A priest in the Kuumic delegation stood and answered, "No."

(Squeegee! Squeegee! Squeegee!) "Am I from the Town of Miira?"

"No."

The clown went from delegation to delegation, shaking his head, scratching it, rubbing his chin, pulling on his nose between delegations. At last, he stopped near the center of the Ring and shrugged. "No matter, it will come to me, by and by." He held up his right hand and pointed it at the crowd. "At least, I speak to you as Allenby! I'm sure of that!" He dropped his hand, then lifted it to scratch his head. "Pretty sure..."

Allenby pointed at Kamera and turned to Disus. "Will this never end? He's killing me down there!" Disus, tears streaming down his face, could only nod and gasp for air. Allenby looked at the Tarzak delegation, and sitting in the front tier of laughing delegates, he saw Fyx sitting quietly studying Kamera.

The great clown held up his arms again. "I remember now. I *am* Allenby." As the cheers from the crowd died down, Kamera lowered his hands, clasping them in front. "I am an ambassador, I remember that too. I am from the Ninth Quadrant Federation of Habitable Planets, and I have a plan. My plan is to have you represent Momus to the Ninth Quadrant by electing a clown to do this service..."

"NO!" shouted the delegates, most of whom were not clowns.

Kamera scratched his head. "At least, I thought that was the plan... perhaps a magician?"

"NO!"

"A freak?"

"NO!"

The clown shook his head. "I see now that wasn't the plan. Perhaps it was a town, instead. A town has all trades, and Tarzak is the largest town. Shall Tarzak represent all the towns? Was that my plan?"

"NO!" shouted the delegates, most of whom were not from Tarzak.

Kamera nodded. "I see now that it wasn't. I'm sure I had one . . ." The clown stood straight and assumed a Eureka pose, finger held in the air. "I remember, now! This Great Ring represents all the towns and all the trades of Momus. My plan is to keep all of you here for the rest of your lives, here in the Great Ring, to represent Momus to the Ninth Quadrant! That was my plan, wasn't it?"

"NO!"

Kamera's shoulders slumped and he shook his head. "I see now that it wasn't." Straightening slightly, he shrugged and began walking toward the north entrance. (Squeegee! Squeegee!) "It seemed so clear to me for a moment . . . Perhaps I had another planet in mind." (Squeegee! Squeegee!) He stopped at the entrance, removed his mask and bowed. Allenby swore he could feel the stones of the Great Ring shake with the applause.

As the applause died down, Allenby turned to Disus. The clown was drying his tears with the sleeve of his orange robe. "Well, Disus?"

Disus looked at Allenby, then burst out in laughter. Others looked in their direction, and soon the entire spectator's section was rocking with everything from titters to guffaws. "Forgive me, Allenby . . ." The clown placed several coppers in the ambassador's hand. "What was your question?"

"The applause—was it for the performance, or for the position?"

Disus nodded, snickered, then nodded again. "For both. He does not oppose the Ninth Quadrant defending Momus, and for that we are fortunate indeed. But, as the ambassador from the Ninth, Allenby, who will you deal with? This is the question you must answer."

Allenby turned his head to the front, glowered a freak in the spectator's section into silence, then shook his head.

"This is not my question to answer, Disus."

"True. Momus must choose its own way." Disus nodded toward the Ring. "But, I think your question is coming up."

A cashier ran from the Tarzak delegation and handed the Master of the Ring another slip. Allenby looked at the delegation and saw a figure dressed in the fortune teller's blue preparing to stand. "Tayla!"

Disus squinted. "Yes, it is. I didn't know she was a delegate."

Allenby smacked his left hand with his right fist. "She wasn't. She must have joined it this morning."

"Laydeeeez and gentlemen!" The crowd quieted. "Great Tayla of the Tarzak delegation would speak to the Great Ring." The cashiers scurried among the delegates and the Master Cashier went to Tayla. Allenby could see her reach into her robe and hand a purse to the Master Cashier.

"Tayla is respected. Why must she pay a balance?"

Disus smiled knowingly. "Kamera is a tough act to follow." Allenby nodded as Tayla stood and spread her arms.

"I, Tayla, speak as one who has seen what can be." The old woman's voice was faint, and the crowd became as silent as stone to hear her. "I have seen much in the great crystal ball from the Ninth Federation starship—much. I have seen a great army descend on Momus to destroy us. It turns our movills to paper and our acts to shame. It tempts our children with glitter, turning them from the ways of their fathers and mothers and sending them away from Momus . . . to fester in the sinkholes of a thousand worlds. This army approaches us now from the Ninth Quadrant Federation . . ."

The crowd exploded in chatter while the Master of the Ring blew his whistle for quiet. The noise tapered to a buzz, then ceased. Allenby motioned for a cashier. A spectator at the edge of the Ring hissed at a cashier and pointed at Allenby. As Tayla continued, the cashier climbed the tiers and bent down next to him. "The speaker's balance is twelve hundred movills," the cashier whispered.

Allenby pulled two heavy purses from his robe and dropped them into the cashier's tray. "I have no question; I would speak. I am Allenby, the magician."

"Your town?" The cashier looked up from his notepad.

"I have no town."

The cashier frowned, then raised his eyebrows in recognition. Stumbling down the tiers, he ran across the sawdust and gave his paper to the Master of the Ring. The Master read it and waited for Tayla to conclude her remarks. Allenby noticed a barker pointing his way from the spectator's entrance, then saw Humphries next to the barker.

Tayla concluded her remarks and resumed her seat, as Humphries began climbing the tiers.

"Laydeez and gentlemen, Allenby the magician would speak to the Great Ring." As the cashiers sped about their business, Humphries arrived, puffing from the climb.

"Allenby, what are you doing?"

"I'm trying to save the Second Law, but I thought I gave orders that you were to stay on the ship."

Humphries sat down next to Disus. "I am here under the direct orders of the secretary . . ."

Allenby motioned for Humphries to be quiet as the Master Cashier climbed the tiers and presented Allenby with four bags of movills. Allenby handed the bags to Disus, stood and spread his arms. "I, Allenby, speak as the Ambassador to Momus from the Ninth Quadrant Federation of Habitable Planets." The crowd buzzed, then fell silent.

"Great Tayla speaks the truth." The silence became heavier. "The truth she speaks is if the Quadrant military mission is based planetside, which was our plan. But, the plan has changed." Allenby noticed the sunlight edging into the Ring. "At this moment General Kahn of the Quadrant military mission is completing a new plan that will keep the mission in orbit and off-planet—away from the people of Momus . . ."

Allenby felt his sleeve being tugged and turned to see Humphries pulling at it. "Stop, Allenby! You can't say that. I have orders from the secretary . . ."

"Have I been removed as ambassador?"

"No, but . . ."

"Then, be quiet. My orders still bear the authority here."

"But, the secretary . . ."

"Silence!" Allenby turned to the assembly, took a deep breath, and continued. "For five hundred movills, I would have Tayla tell you what she saw if the forces were thus separated from the people, and what she saw if Momus had no defense against the Tenth Federation." Allenby sat down and Disus paid off the cashier, while Tayla rose and accepted and the remaining cashiers paid and collected for Tayla's response. While they worked at their tasks, Allenby turned to Humphries. "Now, explain yourself."

"Under orders of the secretary, I have sent Kahn back to the ship. I am down here to get things moving . . ."

"Let me see those orders." Humphries reached into his blouse and handed Allenby a folded sheet of paper. Opening it, Allenby read, his eyes widening in horror. "You did all this?"

"Yes . . ."

"You seized the embassy and posted armed guards?"

"My orders . . ." Before Humphries could finish, Allenby raced up the remaining tiers to the top of the wall. Looking south toward the embassy, he could see a thin wisp of smoke and the beam of an energy pistol cutting through the noon haze. In seconds, Humphries stood next to him. "What is it?"

"You fool!" Allenby felt tears burning his eyes. "You damned bloody fool!"

At the embassy, seated at his table, Allenby stared at Humphries, hoping that anger could drive the scene of carnage he had witnessed from his mind. Two shops across the street were still in flames while four Quadrant soldiers and seventeen citizens of Tarzak lay dead in the dust, among them Yehudin the Alligator man. Humphries sat, elbows on the low table, clenching his fists and staring at the young newsteller seated across from him. The newsteller had his head bowed in meditation while Disus worked to bind the young man's wounded arm.

"I've had enough of this!" Humphries pointed at the newsteller. "Speak up! What happened?"

Allenby grabbed Humphries' collar and held him. "Shut up, you ass! Haven't you done enough?"

Humphries pulled away, rubbing his throat. "That is unpardonable, Allenby. The secretary shall hear . . ."

"I said shut up, Humphries." Allenby nodded toward the newsteller. "Be quiet. He must prepare his material."

Disus completed his dressing. "That's all I can do, Allenby. It should hold."

"Thank you." Allenby put some coppers in Disus's hand. "See about Yehudin." Disus nodded and left the room. The room was quiet for a moment, then the newsteller lifted his head and pushed back his black hood. His face was bruised, dusty and sweat streaked.

"Allenby," he said, "you earned your black robe with Boosthit on the road to Tarzak from Kuumic. You know why I should take my news on the road."

Allenby nodded. "I understand, Zath, and I swear it shall not be repeated. Tell us what you saw, and you have our silence and a thousand movills."

"It will play the Great Square."

"I know."

The newsteller shrugged. "Very well." He closed his eyes for a moment, then opened them, his palms facing the two diplomats. "This news is of the glorious battle of Embassy Street between soldiers of the Ninth Quadrant Federation and the travelers and residents of the street."

Allenby nodded. "A good opening, Zath. Continue."

"Gorgo the strongman of the Tarzak Freaks stood across the street from the embassy passing the time with Yehudin the alligator man, when Ellena the magician's assistant passed by and bid them good day."

Allenby held up his hand. "I would use more dialog, Zath . . ." Humphries slapped his hand on the table.

"Will you quit interrupting?"

"How else will he know where to improve his act?"

Humphries frowned and shook his head. Zath continued, "A soldier standing in front of the embassy door whistled at Ellena and made a rude remark. Gorgo went to the soldier and asked him to apologize. The soldier laughed. Then Gorgo lifted the soldier off the ground by his neck with one hand and asked him again.

"Another soldier coming through the embassy entrance saw this, drew his weapon and fired at Gorgo, killing him. And then . . ." A fire lit behind Zath's eyes. ". . . and then, Yehudin issued the ancient battle cry. He called 'Hey Rube!' The call to war.

"Yehudin sank his teeth in the neck of the second soldier, killing him, while two more soldiers ran from the embassy entrance, their weapons blazing. Yehudin dropped, cut in two by their terrible guns.

"By then the people of the street, freaks, roustabouts, barkers, even merchants, were running and charged the soldiers with sticks, rocks, teeth and nails. The terrible guns killed seventeen and wounded many more before all the soldiers lay dead."

"Excellent, Zath. It needs work, but well done." Allenby pushed two purses across the table to the newsteller. Zath tucked the purses in his robe, stood and left the room. Humphries fumed.

"By the living God, I'll have every person responsible for this before a firing squad!"

"Planning on committing suicide?"

"What do you mean?"

"The man responsible is sitting on your cushion right now, Humphries."

"Nonsense!"

"Is it?"

"I committed no crime, Allenby. I followed the orders of the secretary . . ."

"And disregarded mine."

"I followed the orders of the Quadrant Secretary of State, and four of my men were brutally murdered. We have enough officers on the *Elite* for a tribunal. You will form one and punish those responsible!"

Allenby drummed his fingers on the table, then poured himself a cup of wine. "There will be no tribunal, Humphries." He drank deeply from the cup, then lowered it to the table. "Until the second law is passed, the Quadrant has no jurisdiction or right of extradition on Momus. But, you are right about one thing."

"Yes?"

"A crime was committed. You made it possible, but you did not commit it."

"And the guilty parties?"

"They have all been tried, sentenced and executed."

Humphries struggled to his feet. "You plan doing nothing?"

"As I indicated, the courts of Momus have ruled; it is out of Quadrant jurisdiction."

"My great God, Allenby! Are you forgetting your oath? Are you a member of the diplomatic corps, or are you one of those freaks? Whose bloody side are you on?"

Allenby looked at the table top, without an answer. "Get out, Humphries. Go back to the ship."

"You think the Secretary will ignore this?"

"I said *get out*!"

Humphries stormed from the room. Refilling his cup, Allenby sat alone drinking. As the light from the window grew dim and then ceased, Allenby still had no answer to Humphries' question. He wept, thinking of his friend Yehudin. The young newsteller had done a poor job; he should have learned the names of the dead and the wounded. Allenby was grateful. He could only imagine the additional friends he had lost or were maimed in the battle. He heard Disus enter, but it was too dark to see through tear-filled eyes.

"Have you taken care of Yehudin?"

"Yes, Allenby, it is done."

"Who . . . who else was killed?"

"Tomorrow." Disus lit an oil lamp and held it under his chin. His face, white-painted with broad red lips, appeared under a huge purple fright wig. Prancing across the floor, his orange robe replaced by great plaid bags of trousers which bounced up and down on thick yellow suspenders, he lit another lamp and did a cartwheel, landing flat on his face.

"Stop, Disus. You make me laugh!"

"That is what clowns are for, Allenby. Laugh, for tomorrow comes all too soon."

While Disus entertained Allenby, Fyx and Kamera sat together looking out upon the Great Ring. Empty and dark, the amphitheater seemed to swallow their voices. Dressed in his orange clown's robe, Kamera shook his head. "A terrible business."

Fyx leaned back and propped his elbows on the tier behind. "Gossip so far, Kamera. We haven't heard from a newsteller yet."

"Do you believe the gossip?"

Fyx nodded. "Tayla seems to be right. Even if the Ninth defends us, we must keep them away."

Kamera leaned back and waved a hand at the black sky. "How can we keep them away, Fyx, without something to look out for our interests?"

"You made your point well this morning." Fyx leaned forward and turned toward the clown. "But aren't these weighty and morbid things ill fare for a clown's ears?"

Kamera shrugged. "I find little to laugh at, that is true."

"Would the greatest clown on Momus care to purchase

a joke from a poor magician?"

Kamera raised an eyebrow and smiled. "Comedy from a magician?"

Fyx shrugged one shoulder and nodded. "Today I saw magic from a clown."

Kamera sat up. "What do you have up your sleeve, old trickster?"

"I'll tell you this much: it's something more substantial than the famed Illusion of the Reborn Hand."

"How much would you charge for this amateur effort?"

Fyx smiled. "How much would you pay for the greatest joke you ever played?"

Kamera laughed. "My, but age has made you modest."

"Kamera, it is a joke that will pale all your previous performances, for it will be heard throughout the quadrant—perhaps even the galaxy."

"Fyx, there is barker in your blood." The great clown rubbed his chin, then nodded. "Very well, I'm listening."

The next morning at the Great Ring, the amphitheater's tiers packed and silent, the Master of the Ring opened the slip of paper handed him by the spectator's cashier. He read the paper, looked at the quiet delegates and cleared his throat. "Laydeeeez and gentlemen! Allenby the magician would speak to the Great Ring!"

The cashiers moved silently among the delegates. The Master Cashier climbed to Allenby's tier and bent down. "Allenby, if you would speak, you owe eight hundred and thirty movills."

Allenby turned to Disus and nodded. "Pay him." The clown counted out the coppers and handed them to the Master Cashier. Allenby stood and looked around the Ring.

"I, Allenby, speak to you . . . only as Allenby. This morning, only minutes ago, the Secretary of State of the Ninth Quadrant Federation of Habitable Planets ordered me removed as ambassador to Momus." The crowd whispered, and a few booed. The crowd silent, Allenby dropped his glance to the backs of those sitting before him.

"From the Tenth Quadrant, you face quick and thorough annihilation unless you are defended. But, from the Ninth Quadrant, if not so quick, your annihilation will be no less thorough. You heard Great Tayla speak." Allenby looked around the tiers, stopping on Kamera. "You also heard Great

Kamera and know why Momus cannot decide on a representative to treat with the Ninth Quadrant. But, I tell you this: if the Second Law appoints no one to look out for Momus's interests, then no one will.

"This afternoon, Ambassador Humphries would speak before the Great Ring and have you vote to leave the form and method of Momus's defense to his office. The Secretary of State has ruled that this will satisfy the laws of the quadrants. If this is what you do, then Great Tayla's tale will come true..." He faltered, and looked down again. Disus rose and stood by him. "I... I feel that I have brought you to this. The mines of Momus do not contain enough copper for my apology." Bowing his head, Allenby sat down. Disus looked around the Ring, then took his seat next to Allenby.

From the north entrance, a cashier ran across the sawdust and handed the Master of the Ring a slip of paper. "Lay-deeeez and gentlemen! Great Kamera would speak to the Great Ring!"

As the cashiers moved among the delegates, Disus turned to Allenby. "Do you wish to leave?"

Allenby shook his head. "Even as children playing pranks while their house burns, they are entitled to their fun. I will stay."

As the Master Cashier and his apprentice returned from the darkness of the north entrance, Allenby noticed Humphries and two aides enter from the spectator's side and take seats on the bottom tier. The silence of the Ring was broken by a familiar "Squeegee! Squeegee!" then laughter. The laughter sounded different—almost bitter.

The mask that emerged into the light was still one of boyishness, but one of sadness, too. The large blue eyes brimmed with jelly tears and the corners of the mouth were turned down. To applause, Kamera squeegeed into the Ring wearing his half-newsteller's, half-magician's costume and backwards fake feet. He held up his arms for quiet.

"I speak to you as Allenby the lost soul. But, I would not be lost, if a town would accept me." He held his arms out and turned around (Squeegee! Squeegee!). "Will no town accept me?"

Amidst the laughter, a number of "No's" could be distinctly heard. Kamera lowered his arms, slumped his shoulders and hung his head. "Then, no town owes me loyalty, and I may not give my loyalty to any town." Twin streams of tears literally sprang from the mask's eyes, then stopped. Kamera held up his hand and stood straight. "Wait! I am at least a magician . . ."

"No!" All turned to see Fyx standing amidst the Tarzak Delegation. "You are no magician, Allenby. You never apprenticed, and you wear the newsteller's black. The magicians owe you nothing!" Fyx sat down to applause.

Kamera turned and ran to the Sina delegation (Squeegee! Squeegee! Squeegee!). "Boosthit, I apprenticed under your wing. Am I of the newstellers?"

Boosthit stood and shook his head. "No, Allenby. You gave up your newsteller's robe to masquerade as a magician. The newstellers owe you nothing."

In mock panic, Kamera ran (Squeegee! Squeegee!) and stopped before Humphries. "Am I at least an ambassador?"

Humphries stood and looked nervously at the garish representation of Allenby pleading before him. "I thought . . ." He pointed up the tiers at Allenby, then turned back toward Kamera. "Ashly Allenby has been removed as ambassador to Momus. In addition, you . . . uh, he has been cashiered from the Ninth Quadrant diplomatic corps. He no longer has any claim to authority."

Tears again sprang from Kamera's mask, soaking Humphries' uniform. He turned to face the delegates (Squeegee! Squeegee!). "Then, there is nothing left for me! Nothing!" The volume of tears increased, then stopped. "Nothing, except to be the representative of Momus to the Ninth Quadrant." The tiers fell silent. "I put it to the vote. Shall I become Great Allenby, Statesman of Momus, to treat with the Ninth Quadrant on Momus's behalf?"

Allenby began snickering, then saw Humphries' confused face staring back at him. Allenby pointed at Humphries and laughed. The laughter spread from the spectator's section throughout the Ring, and soon the delegates took up the chant "YES! *YES!*" Kamera removed his mask and bowed toward Allenby, but the gesture was lost. Allenby, Great Statesman of Momus, had fallen off his tier.

Round-hoof'd, short-jointed, fetlocks shag and long,
Broad breast, full eye, small head and nostril wide,
High crest, short ears, straight legs and passing strong,
Thin mane, thick tail, broad buttock, tender hide:
Look, what a horse should have he did not lack,
Save a proud rider on so proud a back.

—Shakespeare, VENUS AND ADONIS

Proud Rider

From the hills surrounding Miira, on the rutted road to Porse, four white stallions tossed their heads in unison and pranced in perfect step. Bareback on the left lead horse, hands on hips, a glower on his face, a young boy in a brown jerkin turned his head toward the old man mounted on the left rear horse. The old man held one hand on hip; the other held a pair of rude crutches.

"Father, we won't sell them, then. But if we could rent them to Davvik the logger . . ."

"Silence! No more of that!"

The boy looked forward, his glower deepening. Noticing the hoof prints leading off the left side of the road into the sandy wastes of the desert, he pressed his left knee lightly against the horse's shoulder. The horse and its companion wheeled left, followed by the old man's horse and its companion. The boy turned and looked back at the mountains, crowded with great trees. Davvik would pay four hundred movills a day for the horses.

"I know what you think, Jeda," the old man called. "You would take them and make dray animals out of them. Not while I live, Jeda. Not while I live."

"Father . . ."

"Hold your tongue!"

The boy shrugged and let his horse find the path to the flats. As they reached the hard sand, he squeezed his knees together and his pair of mounts stopped. The old man nodded at his empty horse, and it stopped while he pulled along side his son and called his horse to halt.

"I saw them move. Both times I saw your knees move."

"What of it, father?" The boy spread his arms to encompass the desert and empty hills. "Where is my audience?"

"No audience would sit still to watch such clumsiness." The old man lifted his right leg up and over his mount's back. "Help me down."

"Yes, father." Swinging his own leg over, the boy slid to the sand and walked to the left side of his father's horse. He gripped his father around the waist, and the old man leaned his crutches against his horse, put both hands on his son's shoulders, and slid down. With his crutches, the old man moved out onto the hard sand.

"The cord, Jeda."

The boy unwound a string from around his waist and handed one end to the old man. Pulling the six-and-a-half meter cord tight, Jeda walked a circle around the old man, dragging his foot every few steps. As the circle closed, he walked back toward the center, gathering up the string. "What shall it be first, Father?"

"Dressage. You need work on it." The old man hobbled outside the ring, turned, and faced Jeda. He watched as the four stallions pulled abreast of the ring and stood motionless. Jeda, just as motionless, began putting the four animals through their drills. He watched the boy closely but could detect none of the signals the boy made to the horses as they reared, wheeled, paraded, and pranced as a perfect team. The boy needs no work on that, thought the old man; all he needs is an audience. He's good, better than I was. "Voltage, now Jeda!"

Jeda ran to the lead horse, leaped up and over it, falling in perfect position to jump the next stallion in line. As the boy jumped the next horse, and the next, his taut muscles standing out against his tanned skin, his father imagined the boy decked in the rider's silver spangled tights, silver bows in the braided manes of the gleaming white stallions. The old man had seen that once before, when he was only a boy himself, and his own father, mother, and uncle dazzled the crowd at the Great Ring in Tarzak. Now, the sun dipped into the horizon, Jeda began his tricks, balancing on one horse, tumbling off, then leaping to the next to balance on his hands. He flipped from the horse's back only to land and pirouette on the next. The old man watched Jeda's face and could tell the boy was no longer thinking of their argument. Glowing in rapture, the boy and the stallions were one.

This is how it should always be, thought the old man. But after a moment, he shook his head, knowing that it might never be. Tonight the house would be quiet and sullen, until either Jeda or Zani, Jeda's mother, would begin the argument again. The spell broken, the old man turned from the ring.

"Come, Jeda. We go home."

Davvik turned to Zani, shrugged, and looked back at the old man, silently concentrating on his meal. Jeda, seated on a cushion across the low table from Davvik, between Zani and the old man, shook his head and pushed the tung berries on his plate around with his finger. Davvik leaned on the table. "Hamid, you are unreasonable. Look at Zani, your wife. When will she get a new robe?"

The old man broke some cobit and dropped the two pieces of bread on his plate. "You sit at my table to insult my wife, Davvik?"

"It is not an insult, Hamid, but the truth. Don't trust my words; look for yourself."

The old man lifted his eyes and turned to Zani. Her robe, like Jeda's and his own, was many times patched and mended. Her hair, still streaked with black, framed a tired face bowed in shame. Hamid looked back at the logger. "Miira is not a wealthy town, Davvik. We are not the only family in patches."

"I have no patches, Hamid." Davvik waved his hands about the room. "No one in Miira, or anywhere on Momus for all that, need wear patches. Not if they have any sense. The new market centers are prospering, and my wood is bringing good prices. Think what you could do with four hundred movills . . ."

Hamid slapped his hand on the table. "They are liberty horses, Davvik! They will not pull your sleds. Never have their mouths felt a bit nor their backs a harness." Hamid shook his head and turned back to his meal. "What can a roustabout understand about liberty horses?"

Davvik clenched his fists and flushed red. "And you, Great Hamid of the Miira riders, you understand, do you?"

"Yes."

"Then, understand this, as well. I am no roustabout; I am a logger—a businessman. There are no more roustabouts, Hamid, because the circus is dead, gone, naught but a dream in an old man's brain!"

The old man pushed his plate from him, and peered through shaggy white brows at his wife and son. Both seemed very concerned with their plates and eating utensils. "Zani."

She looked up, not meeting his glance. "Yes, Hamid?"

"Why have you invited this bastard son of a carnival geek to eat our bread?"

Davvik stood, his lips twitching with unspoken oaths. Turning, he bowed toward Zani. "I am sorry for you. I tried, but it is no use." He turned toward Jeda. "Boy, my offer of thirty-five coppers a day still holds. I can use a good rider—" He looked at Hamid. "To drive horses at useful work." Bowing again, he turned from the room into the street.

Hamid turned back to his meal, but Zani clasped his arm with a fierce strength. He saw tears in her eyes. "Old man, you asked me a question; now, you hear my answer! I want my sons back. That's why Davvik sat here tonight, and you shamed me. Your son and I—we are ashamed!"

"Wife . . ."

"But whose wife will it be, Hamid? Not yours, unless Jeda stays in this house and my three other sons come home!" Hamid winced. The old woman's threat was empty, but it hurt all the same. He watched as she stood and walked into her room, pulling the curtain closed behind her. The old man sighed and turned to look at his son. His eyes cast down, Jeda sat holding his hands in his lap.

"And you, my son?"

Jeda shrugged one shoulder. "Am I a barker, father, to find words when there is nothing to say?"

"You think I am wrong, then."

The boy looked up at nothing. "I don't know." He looked at Hamid, his hand on his breast. "Everything I feel agrees with you, father." He dropped his hand, shaking his head. "But everything I see agrees with Davvik. We aren't like the magicians or clowns; our act can't play the roadside fires. We need a ring."

"There are rings, Jeda. Here in Miira, the . . ."

"Father, to use the ring our act must draw coppers. When did the ring in Miira, or the Great Ring in Tarzak, last see riding?"

The old man shrugged. They both knew the answer. "There may be fairs, again. When I was a boy, the fairs had grand circuses."

"It has been a long time since you were a boy." Jeda placed his hand gently on the old man's arm. "Father, there will be no more fairs. The people of Momus trade differently now; there are stores, shops, markets."

"Then, why not a circus in itself? Ancient Earth had circuses that were on their own. Even the ship that put our ancestors on this planet made its way through the hundred quadrants bringing the circus to countless planets. They were wealthy."

"They had audiences, father. Momus has been a show without an audience for almost two centuries. The people have turned to other things. We must eat."

The old man studied the boy. "You want to be a rider, don't you? You must; it is in our blood."

"Yes." Jeda withdrew his hand. "As did Micah, Taramun, and Desa, my brothers before me. But they wanted to marry, eat, provide for children. Is that wrong?"

"Bah!" The old man shook his head. "They are not riders. They are . . . *teamsters*! They left this house—" The old man made a fist, then dropped it in his lap. "They . . . left this house. What about you, Jeda? Will you drive nags for Davvik?"

"Father, we cannot survive without an audience. The jungle acts, trapeze artists, dancing bears—where are they all now? An act like ours is not a circus. We must have many acts and an audience willing to pay to see them."

"Momus has people . . ."

"Father, they think they are circus people. They have already seen the show. Perhaps a circus every five or ten years to honor the old traditions, but they would not pay to keep a circus together between times. What do we do then?"

Hamid remembered the streak he had seen in the sky. "The soldiers, Jeda. There are many soldiers out there on the satellites."

Jeda shook his head. "They may not see us, father. Great Allenby has decreed it. You know that."

"Allenby—a newsteller turned tricksters!"

"The Great Ring made him our Statesman, father. It is the law." Jeda stood and brushed the crumbs from his robe. "I must look to the horses."

Hamid nodded. "Jeda."

"Yes, father?"

"Jeda, will you ride for Davvik?"

"I haven't decided."

The old man pulled himself to his feet with one of his crutches. "If you do, Jeda, you are welcome to remain here in my house."

Jeda nodded. "Thank you. I know it was difficult to say."

Hamid nodded and the boy went through the curtain into the street. Hobbling to the door, the old man looked after his son until he was swallowed by the dark. Listening, Hamid could make out Pinot on the other side of the fountain, singing to herself. No longer a singer, thought Hamid, but a cobit gatherer, selling roots instead of songs. His sons, no longer riders, but teamsters. And where, he thought, where are the lions, elephants, and bears? Where are those golden boys and girls who walked the highwire and flew above the sawdust from bar to bar? Where are the bands? The music and laughter gone, replaced by cheese making and pillow stuffing.

Hamid stepped through the door and looked up at the night sky. Even straining his eyes, he could not see them. "But *you* are there, and if I must move Heaven and Momus, I will have you as an audience for my son, the rider!"

In the swamps north of Arcadia, a great lizard exposed its belly to the sun and settled back in the ooze. After scraping a handful of bottom slime from below, the lizard smeared its warming belly, sighed, and dreamed of Mamoot's breadcakes. Mamoot's mother stuffed them with tung berries and coated them with thick crusts of salt. Opening one slitted eye, the lizard noted the position of the sun. Mamoot would not show at the edge of the swamp for two more hours. Seeing movement, the eye locked on a fat waterwasp and tracked it as it buzzed around closer and closer to the seemingly innocent lump of mud. Curling its tongue, the lizard tensed for the strike, then relaxed, letting its pink snake of a tongue flop from its mouth into the water. Fly away little morsel, thought the lizard. Mamoot would be angry if I spoiled my appetite.

"Stoop! Stoop!"

The lizard lifted its great head and turned in the direction of the call. It's Mamoot, thought the lizard. He is early, and I haven't finished my bath.

"Stoop! Come here right now, you ugly moron!"

Rolling over, the lizard stood on its hind legs and began wading toward the noise.

"Stoop! Are you coming?"

"Oz, ahoot, oming!" answered the lizard.

"Coming now?"

"Oming ow!" The lizard shook its head and rolled up its tongue. Mamoot was angry already. There's no help for it but to hurry. Reaching the swampbush, the lizard pulled itself up on the spongy soil and shouldered through the underbrush.

"You better hurry, you smelly fat toad!"

The lizard pushed its way into the clearing and looked down to see Mamoot, hands on his hips, stamping his foot in anger. Next to Mamoot was a larger version of the boy, holding some papers in one hand and his nose in the other. "Hake?"

The boy ran to the lizard and delivered a swift kick in a shin armored with thick, almost nerveless skin. "Look at you, you stinking lump! I'll give you cake, all right! Go wash! I've brought my father to see you."

The lizard looked at the larger human with curiosity. The man pointed toward the clear-watered lake, and made a show of holding his nose. "Old."

The boy kicked the lizard again in the tail. "I don't care if it's cold, you foul-smelling slime snake! Get in there and wash!"

Imagining the icy lake water closing over its head, the lizard bent down at the shore and tested the water with its toe. A shiver ran from its toe throughout its mud-caked body. It turned back toward the boy and smiled. "Hake?"

The boy folded his arms. "You wash, Stoop! Right now!"

Stoop faced the boy, rose to its full height, and folded its arms. "Hake!"

The boy narrowed his eyes, trying to stare down the lidless lizard's gaze. After a few determined minutes of futility, the boy stamped his foot and turned to his father. "Show him, father."

The man picked up a sack from the floor of the clearing and held it up for Stoop to see.

"Hake?"

"Yes," answered the man. "All the cake you can eat."

Stoop grinned and leaped into the water, hardly feeling the cold as it thought about the cake, a whole sack of cake. Its body clean, Stoop's head broke water as the lizard walked toward the shore. Mamoot stood on the shore soaking wet. "You, you, *Stoop*, you! Look at me!"

The lizard walked out of the water and grinned at the boy "Hake?"

"Here, Stoop." The man held up a breadcake. "Come over here and get it."

Stoop lumbered over, took the cake from the man's hand, and sat on its hind legs to eat. Mamoot stormed over and stood next to his father. "Well, father?"

The man looked at the papers, and then at Stoop. "It's big enough, all right. What can it do?"

"Stoop can do anything an elephant could do, and then some. I've trained him the same way you said great great grandfather trained the elephants."

The man shook his head. "If we only could, Mamoot. Momus hasn't seen a great-beast act in over a century! And now, a circus." He handed one of the papers to the boy. "But, look, Mamoot, we will need more than one."

Mamoot took the paper headlined **"HAMID'S GREATER SHOWS Now Organizing At The Great Ring In Tarzak. Auditions Daily."** Below the type, a parade of great Earth beasts was depicted, dressed in tassels with knobs of brass on the tips of their long white tusks. Each beast's nose curled around the tail of the beast in front of it. Mamoot held the paper out to Stoop, who took it with one hand while the other, claws extended, picked the tung berry pits from between its teeth. The lizard shivered at the sight of the frightening Earth animals, but something stirred inside his green-armored hide at the sight of the colors, clowns, horses, and . . . all the humans, all different sizes and shapes, stacked in tiers to be looked at while the fearsome beasts passed by.

"See the elephants, Stoop?" Mamoot jabbed the paper.

"Ssseee."

"That's our act, but we need more lizards. Smart ones, eleven more."

Stoop held the paper down so the boy could see, and poked the picture with a distended claw. "Phats ow?"

Mamoot shook his head. "No, they're all gone. The last elephant on Momus died before you were hatched."

Stoop nodded. "Or zards. Ow uch?"

"Four breadcakes a day for each lizard, but no deal unless we get eleven more."

Stoop rubbed its chin. "Ive."

"Four, and that's it!"

Stoop folded its arms and looked down its long snout at the boy. Friendship was one thing, but business was business. "Ive."

Mamoot fumed, stamped around, waved his arms, and ground his teeth. "All right! Five, you thief, but you better be back here in one hour with eleven more lizards, or no cakes for anybody!"

Stoop fell to his front legs and ran for the swamp, cutting a wide swath through the underbrush. As he hit the water, he heard Mamoot call. "Stoop!"

"Oz?" The lizard stopped in the water to listen.

"You tell 'em that everybody washes every day. You hear me?"

Stoop scratched his head and cursed himself for not holding out for six cakes. He shrugged, thinking of the spectacle of humans to be seen at the circus. In a moment, Stoop decided that the spectacle was compensation enough for the missing cake.

"You hear me, Stoop?"

"Oz," answered Stoop, "alla tie assshh." The lizard swam off in the muck, hoping to find eleven other lizards smart enough to learn to talk and perform, but not smart enough to figure out that they didn't really have to give Scoop one of their cakes every day in return for the job.

Tessia held the bar, waiting for her father, who was hanging from his knees with outstretched hands, to reach the top of his swing. As he came up, his body almost parallel with the grassy ground beneath, she pushed the bar from her. It swung down, drawing an arc through the empty air that reached its zenith at the moment her father reached the bottom of his swing, his body perpendicular to the ground. She saw herself releasing the bar, balled and somersaulting, and reaching her father, his back and arms arched to receive her, as he reached a point halfway through his outside swing. She would fall a long way, but the space was needed for the quintuple somersault. A slight breeze brushed her face, and she watched the leafy whips of the trees move. Catching the bar, she timed it and sent it back, empty.

"Good," called her father. "Wait for the perfect moment. Dead wind."

Tessia looked down, and the net as always seemed too small. But it had caught her every time she had tried the quintuple before. It was big enough. Kanta, her mother, stood beside the net, smiling. Tessia waved and looked back at the trees, which were still moving. This time I will make it, she thought, catching the bar and sending it back. In her heart, her pride at this knowledge met her pain. After she made the quintuple, the equipment would come down—the ropes, bars, stands, posts, and net sold for nothing; the family on the road as tumblers. But if I miss this time, she thought, the trapeze will stay up. We will be flyers for another day.

The wind died as the bar returned. "Wait for the next one," called her father. Tessia caught the bar and sent it back. As she pulled herself up to the high perch, she knew she could not fail on purpose. This was the moment. Kanta and Vedis both knew it; Tessia knew it. As the bar swung up, Tessia dove from the perch to meet it. Its cool weight in her hands, she used her own weight to increase the swing, heels over her head as she reached the top. As she descended, she swung her legs and body down, the gravity tugging at her cheeks.

"Ready!" Her father's voice came as if from a long distance away. As she reached the outside of her swing, using her arms to draw her shoulders well above the bar, a strange hush fell over the deserted glade. Her audience of insects, avions, and ground animals stopped to watch the golden girl in sequined blue drop down, down, swinging her legs forward. At the top of her swing, she left the bar, spinning—two, three, four, and—five! She didn't find her father's strong hands wrapped around her wrists anything remarkable. It was over. She had made the quintuple. Tears sprang to her eyes as she looked up into her father's beaming face.

"You did it, Tessia! You did it!" Vedis pulled her up and kissed her forehead.

"But it is the end, Father. Let me drop to the net."

Vedis released her at the bottom of his swing and she fell, landing in a sitting position. One bounce, then two, then she grasped the edge of the net and somersaulted over it. As she dropped to the ground, Kanta rushed to her, kissing and embracing her. Tessie hugged her mother, wishing the moment would never end. Opening her eyes, she saw an old cripple in rider's brown at the edge of the glade. Realizing that he had been seen, the old man raised a crutch in the air and waved it. "Hallo! I am Hamid of the Miira riders."

Kanta turned and looked. In seconds Vedis was down from the net standing next to his wife and daughter. "What is your business here, rider? We come here to be alone."

The old man hobbled closer and stopped next to the net. Looking at Tessia, he smiled. "I saw you, child; it was beautiful."

"Thank you, but you interrupt a moment dear to my family."

The old man looked at the three in turn, stopping on Tessia. "Child, I am here that the moment will never end."

Great Kamera leaned back from his table and clasped his hands over his large belly. The barker, in dusty red-and-purple robe, stood before him. "This thing you said in the street, barker. Repeat it."

The barker bowed deeply. "Of course, Great Kamera, but there is a small matter . . ."

"You will be paid."

"Of course. I never doubted . . ."

"Get on with it!"

"Yes, of course." The barker grinned, exposing yellowing teeth. "Great Kamera, I advertise auditions for the greatest show on Momus, a grand circus operated by the Great Hamid of the Miira riders . . ."

"A rider?"

"Yes, Great Kamera. Owner of the finest . . ."

"You will tell me a rider will operate the shows?"

"Yes. But as Great Kamera has undoubtedly learned through his many years, the first circus was started by a rider, Philip Astley . . ."

"Barker, you presume to instruct me on the history of the circus?"

The barker bowed deeply. "No, no, Great Kamera. If I may repeat . . ."

"No!" Kamera held up his hand. "Not that. What shows has he?"

"There will be Jeda, Hero and Great Emperor of all the horsemen, riding Hamid's own quartet of white stallions. There will be the Flying Javettes, featuring Tessia and the quintuple somersault. Then, the Rhume Family and its Great Phant Lizards, featuring Mamoot and . . ."

"Barker. Phant lizards?"

"A great-beast act, Great Kamera, with fierce monsters whipped and driven from the swamps of Arcadia, tamed and trained by a small boy, who . . ."

"Go on. What else?"

"The Great Riettas of the high wire will dazzle the crowds with its four-tiered pyramid. Yarouze, the brave lion tamer, will put on a spectacle of daring . . ."

"Barker, I've never heard of any of these names. Who are these people who pretend to bring a circus into being?" Kamera rubbed his bald head and thought for a moment. "In fact, I do not remember ever seeing a high-wire act before in my life. Nor flyers, not even those lizards. Is this some kind of joke?"

"Upon my life, Great Kamera. The acts assemble now in the Great Ring."

"Koolis undoubtedly knows of this."

"Yes, of course. The Master of the Great Ring has paid ten thousand movills for the privilege of exhibiting Hamid's Greater Shows."

"Koolis *paid* for the privilege, you say?"

"I arranged the contract myself."

Kamera rubbed his chin. "Koolis parting with coppers can only mean he sees a greater amount returning."

"It is the truth, Great Kamera. For his payment, Koolis will get a quarter of the gate."

"And, barker, I suppose Hamid, whoever he is, is looking for clowns, is he?"

"A circus is the proper setting for a clown, Great Kamera. Do I not speak truly?"

Kamera nodded. Years ago he had played a circus, a poor thing at one of the last fairs ever held. It had been better, almost a spiritual experience. "I make a good—no, an excellent living playing by myself here at the square in Tarzak. What would this Hamid pay if I condescended to lend my name and talents to his bill?"

The barker grinned and shook his head. "The Great Kamera does not understand. Because you are master clown of Momus, Great Hamid will allow you billing for only one thousand movills."

"I must *pay* to perform?"

"Yes."

"That is nonsense! You said yourself, I am master clown of Momus!"

"True, true, Great Kamera." The barker rubbed his hands together. "But, the star clown of Hamid's Greater Shows *will be* master clown of Momus."

Kamera nodded. "I see. Was Koolis swayed with similar logic?"

"Great Koolis also gets a quarter of the gate. You, Great Kamera, will get half of one percent for your coppers."

"And Koolis gets twenty-five by paying ten?"

"Koolis also has the Ring."

"Hmmm." Kamera reached under his table and pulled a purse from beneath it, dropping the pouch in front of the barker. "Before you lift those coppers, satisfy me on a point."

"If I can, Great Kamera."

"The circuses died on Momus for lack of an audience. Has this Hamid found an answer?"

The barker shrugged. "Great Hamid, when I asked this same question of the Great Hamid, his answer was cryptic."

"He does not depend on the soldiers, does he? Allenby will not allow them on the planet."

"He only looked up, Great Kamera, and said, 'An audience shall be provided.'"

Koolis looked down at the old man sitting on the low stone wall surrounding the Great Ring. Hamid stared at the sawdust. The Master of the Ring looked at Jeda and Davvik, shrugged, and tried again. "Hamid, I not only talked to Disus, but to Great Allenby himself. He will not be moved; the soldiers stay in the satellites."

Hamid moved only his lips. "Did Allenby see the parade?"

Koolis let out a sigh. "It makes no difference."

"If Allenby saw the parade, he could not deny the circus life."

"Hamid, Allenby's concerns encompass the entire planet of Momus. The circus is not his entire world, as it is with us."

"Us?"

Koolis looked offended. "Yes, us."

"If the circus dies, Koolis, you will still have the Great Ring. We will have nothing."

Koolis spat in the sawdust. "Hamid, you know nothing. I've beggered my family to give your circus a place to exist."

"For a quarter of the gate."

"Without an audience coming through that gate, it is twenty-five percent of nothing." Koolis slapped his hands against his legs. "Without the soldiers, your circus—my Ring—will be lost. It is my world too, Hamid!"

The old man looked up and nodded. "I owe you an apology, Koolis." He reached for his purse, then shrugged. "But I owe many people for many things."

Koolis smiled and sat next to the old rider, patting him on the knee. "I'll put it on your account."

Hamid looked from Koolis to his son. "Well, Jeda, say it."

Jeda lifted an arm, then lowered it. "There are no coppers, Father. I see no other way."

The old man turned to the logger. "Well, Davvik, you get your way. The horses . . . are yours."

Davvik looked at his own feet, then shook his head. "This is not what I want, Hamid. Believe me, I would rather you could keep them." He nodded his head at the great lizards being trained on the far side of the Ring, then up where roustabouts strung supports for the high wire and trapeze. "But neither my wishes nor yours will feed your flyers or beasts."

Hamid nodded. "Take care of them, Davvik."

Jeda walked to Hamid and placed a gentle hand on the old man's shoulder. "I will be there, father. I'll watch them."

The old man looked up into his son's face. "You go with Davvik?"

Jeda nodded. "I'm a rider, and . . . your circus has no horses."

"I will pay him well, Hamid." Davvik put his arm around Jeda's shoulders. "And if you can get your show going, I'll sell you back the horses."

"Thank you, Davvik."

The logger nodded, then turned to Jeda. "We must go, then."

"Good-bye, father."

Hamid put his hand over his son's, pressed it and nodded, his eyes closed. He felt the hand leave his shoulder and listened as the two left the Ring.

Koolis shook his head. "After we sprinkle a few movills on our creditors, Davvik's coppers might keep us going another month—perhaps less. What then?"

"My mind is as empty as my purse, Koolis . . ." The old man looked up and saw a roustabout on the high-wire platform playing at stepping out on the wire. The man stumbled, but quickly caught the post behind the platform. Koolis stood and cupped his hands around his mouth.

"Break your neck, fool, and you pay your own funeral."

Koolis turned to see Hamid hobbling off on his crutches. "Hurry, Koolis; assemble the company. Hurry!"

Master Sergeant Levec scanned the indicators and adjusted a control with a feather touch. As the huge machine chewed through the blue-green sulphide vein, an extra drop of oil fell into the crushers dispersing a slight foam accumulation. "You got to keep your eye on that, Balis. Too much foam can really gum up the works."

"I apologize, Sergeant." Balis's hand left the control and reached for the purse beneath his lavender-and-white juggler's robe.

"Get back on that control!" Levec shook his head as the juggler's hand sped back to the steering buttons. "Look, Balis, I thought we had a deal; you don't pay me every time you make a mistake. Just don't make it again."

"Yes, Sergeant. I got confused."

Levec caressed the cab frame he was using for support and patted it. "You'll get the hang of it. In another two weeks, the Montagnes will be back up in the statellites and you boys will be operating the pit."

Balis scanned the controls, indicators and progress track.

"We are on the straight, Sergeant."

"Good. You can put it on automatic."

Balis flipped a switch, leaned back in his seat and sighed. "It seems so much to learn in two weeks."

"A little more involved than tossing around a few balls, eh Balis?" The juggler smiled, reached into his robe and produced four red spheres. Levec took them, sighed, and moved to the back of the cab for the additional headroom. A look of determination on his face, the sergeant made sure of his footing, fixed his eyes on the imaginary high point of the trajectory and began pitching the balls. His hands moved with a steady rhythm keeping no less than two balls in the air at once.

"Now, Sergeant, one hand!" Levec threw three complete cycles one-handed before he broke rhythm, dropping the balls. Balis laughed. "You'll get the hang of it."

Levec gathered up the balls and handed them to Balis. "Here."

"Keep them, Sergeant. I brought them for you."

Levec nodded. "Only to pay for your apologies, of course."

"Of course." Balis smiled. "I will miss you when the Montagnes return to the satellites."

Levec opened his utility bag and put the balls in it. Standing again, he nodded at the juggler. "Well, the Montagne must follow its orders." Levec slapped Balis on the shoulder. "But this does not mean we shall never see each other again. A detail will be down every few weeks to do maintenance."

"Still . . ."

"It's been a while. You better check the indicators." Levec turned and looked through the dusty sideport at the pit. A kilometer across and eight hundred meters deep at its lowest point, the pit resembled a great, stepped bowl. On each step, a line of huge processors connected by water, slurry and power ducts, chewed their way around the bowl, widening it and producing copper, silver, iron, and arsenic for the satellite defense rings and orbiting bases of the military mission.

A movement in the pit caught his eye, and Levec reached to the console in front of Balis and slammed an orange panel. Power to the processors stopped. "Sergeant, what is it?"

"Something in the pit. Call it in." As Balis radioed pit control, Levec undogged the side door and stepped out on the catwalk. Far to his right, an enormous green animal was leaping down the steps of the pit. In a matter of seconds, it reached the bottom and began swimming the evil-smelling slurry pond. "Balis! Come out here and bring the monocular." As Balis came through the door, Levec took the monocular and focused on the animal in the pond. "Lookit that! Balis, I swear you can have my stripes if I've ever seen anything like that!"

Balis squinted against the sun. "It is one of the great lizards of Arcadia, Sergeant. I've never seen one out here on the desert so close to Kuumic."

"It's pulling something." Levec played the monocular back along the path the lizard had taken. "It looks like a cable or a rope. Look at the top of the rim."

Balis took the monocular and focused on the rim. A crowd was gathered, watching the lizard. The other end of the rope appeared to be anchored to a high pole on the edge of the rim. Balis turned. On the opposite edge of the pit, another crowd was gathered. The lizard, having traversed the slurry pond, leaped up the steps to the left, still dragging the rope. As the animal disappeared over the opposite rim, the slack in the rope was taken up. Levec took the monocular and saw the rope being anchored to another high post. A figure climbed the post and stood on top, waving to the crowd. From where he stood, Levec could hear the cheers. The figure was handed a long, white pole. Balancing the pole across the rope, the figure began walking out over the pit. In moments the figure had only air between a swaying, narrow path and certain death. Levec switched to a higher powered lens and saw that the figure was a man, an old man. "Balis, who is that?"

"Sergeant, that is Great Tara of the high wire Riettas. He is enough to make one's heart stop."

"He's so old." Balis watched Levec move and shift as the Montagne Sergeant walked the rope vicariously with the Great Tara. As he reached the center of the rope, the wind across the pit picked up and snatched at the old man's yellow robe. Levec held his breath as the old man sat down on the rope and leaned his pole into the wind. The wind gone, the old man did a backwards somersault on the rope, coming up to his feet again. He teetered for an instant, then resumed his walk above the pit. Lifetimes later, the Great Tara stood atop the anchor pole on the other side of the pit. At both ends of the rope a cheer went up accompanied by signs, each one a letter, spelling **HAMID'S GREATER SHOWS—TARZAK.** Then, the crowd was gone. Levec looked at Balis, confused. "They were all with that circus."

"Yes."

"But, between Montagnes and trainees, there can't be more than twenty people here in the pit."

"True, Sergeant, but I heard that Tara put on a spectacle yesterday at the microwave relay station by climbing one of the guy wires supporting the broadcast antenna. There were only eight soldiers at the station."

Levec shook his head. "I don't know much about advertising, Balis, but it seems they're going about it the wrong way. Soldiers aren't even allowed planetside." Levec played the monocular along the rope, watching it sway in the wind. "But I sure wish I could see that show."

Balis smiled, entered the cab and pulled some flyers from his robe. In seconds he had them stuffed into Levec's utility bag.

Captain Bostany knew the perspiration running down her back was imaginary, but as she stood at strict attention before General Kahn while he traced little circles on his command desk with a wicked-looking swagger stick, she swore her boots were filled to overflowing.

Kahn dropped the stick on his desk with a clatter, folded his hands and pursed his lips. "Let's try it one more time, Captain, shall we?"

"I . . . I await the general's pleasure."

Kahn pressed a panel on his desk causing the bulkhead behind him to part, disclosing an activated, holographic command reader. "You know what this is I suppose?"

"Yessir."

Kahn smiled. "That will save some time. Captain, as you can see, the Ninth Quadrant Federation has enough hardware in orbit around Momus to destroy utterly any kind of force the Tenth Federation cares to send against us—" The general held up a finger. "If, I repeat, if everything is functioning smoothly. With me?"

"Yessir."

Kahn picked up a sheaf of papers from his desk. "These

are summary courts' records, Captain. As mission sociological officer, you will be interested to know that the Momus military mission has the worst petty disciplinary rate in the Quadrant."

"Yessir."

"Captain, that includes the Quadrant bases around all three penal colonies!"

"Yessir."

"Captain, the men and women manning this mission are Montagnes, the most professionally disciplined soldiers in the Quadrant forces. This cannot go on. First, I want you to tell me why, then I want to know what you are going to do about it."

"Yessir. The positive so—"

"So help me, Captain, if you start talking sociological parameters, biofeed responses, or negative poop loops again, I will eat your head off!"

"Well, General, it's a combination of things—that caused the disciplinary problems, that is. The analysis just completed . . ."

"Skip that and get to what it is."

"Ah, yessir. Well, sir, to be overly simplistic about it . . ."

"Impossible."

"Yessir. Well, sir, it's what we call acute environmental awareness."

"That's what you call it; what would I call it?"

"Cabin fever?"

"Go on."

"Well, sir, it's just that the isolation from the planet's surface is beginning to have neg—ah, well, sir, it's beginning to get to the troops."

"Now, Captain, we are at a point we could have reached an hour ago. Cabin fever, huh?"

"Yessir."

"I can think of maybe twenty military missions offhand that are similarly isolated for political reasons, environmental conditions, any number of reasons." The general waved the stacks of papers. "None of them has this problem."

"Yessir, I mean, nosir. Everyone brought up on charges so far has undergone analysis to determine the soc—uh, to see if there is a common cause. Using that information, my department conducted additional surveys and found that the pattern extends to dependent families and civilian employees."

"And?"

"Well, sir, it's probably a lot more complicated than it sounds. Doctor Graver, the chief of psych, says that it's probably symbolic for..."

"What is it, Captain?"

"Sir, uh... the personnel, they... want to go and see the circus."

"Circus."

"Yes... sir."

Kahn studied an empty spot in the air until Captain Bostany had to break the silence or run screaming from the compartment. "Sir, we traced the information about the circus to the crews operating the relay station, the open-pit mine operations..."

"Momus doesn't even have a circus."

Bostany reached into a folder and placed some papers in front of the general. "We obtained these from the crews rotating from planetside."

Kahn studied the flyers and shook his head. "Captain, would you tell me why men, women, and children who have at their disposal a variety of the most sophisticated recreational facilities known to modern science want to go see a circus?"

"Yessir," Bostany smiled and pulled a bound set of papers from her folder. "I'm writing a paper on it..."

"Just *why*, Captain."

"Yessir. Outside of actual sports activities, virtually all of our recreations are remote sensory. There is an unreality about them that leaves unfulfilled certain needs."

"Unreality? Captain, have you ever used a fantasizer? You can climb the Matterhorn if you want, and even be frostbitten."

"Yessir. But, before and after the experience, you know that the experience never was and that no challenge existed. Doctor Graver agrees with me that this phenomenon is actually a reach for reality."

Kahn held up a flyer depicting a huge lizard in pink tights and tassels, holding a small, turban-wrapped boy high over its head with one hand. "You call this reality?"

"That's what it seems to represent to the personnel."

Kahn looked at the flyer and nodded. "I guess it is, for Momus." He looked up. "Your recommendation?"

"General, we have to let mission personnel get in some time planetside on a regular basis to see the circus, go backpacking, or just walk around and breathe fresh air."

"You have another plan? Allenby would kill that one in a second, and you know why."

"No other plan that is practical. Either get them planetside or replace the entire complement. We ran the sociological progressions, and visiting planetside on a rotating basis would have no adverse impact. The impact Lord Allenby fears happens only if the mission uses planetside bases."

"Your department checked out the fortune teller's story, then?"

"Yessir, and her accuracy is uncanny, except for this. Her recommendation was complete separation. It's strange that she could be so accurate with the one and miss so badly on the other. But, she's hardly a computer."

Kahn snorted out a short laugh. "Tayla the fortune teller has Allenby's ear; your computer doesn't." Kahn reached for the communicator built into his desk. "Get me Ambassador Humphries." He turned back to Bostany. "Put together the best case you can, Captain. You are about to meet the cashiered former Ambassador and present Statesman of Momus, Great Allenby, magician and newsteller." Kahn shrugged. "Part of that reality we're reaching for, I imagine."

While Captain Bostany explained her sociological progression tables, charts and diagrams, Allenby looked at the people seated on cushions around his table. Ambassador Humphries, as usual, scowled impatiently. Seated next to the ambassador, General Kahn remained properly impassive. Across from Allenby, Hamid of the Miira riders looked at the center of the table, seeing nothing. Next to Hamid, Tayla the fortune teller watched Bostany's performance through hooded eyes. Bostany collected her papers and concluded: "Therefore, Lord Allenby, while the complete separation protects Momus from undesirable socio-impact, it is having an undesirable impact on the military mission. As

I have repeated, my department has determined that there will be no adverse impacts as a result of limited interaction between . . ."

"No!" Tayla held up her hands, palms toward Allenby. "I have seen what will be and what can be, Great Allenby. I say that the soldiers must stay in the sky."

Allenby shrugged. "Then, Ambassador Humphries, that is my answer. The mission personnel remains off-planet."

"Lord Allenby, be reasonable, man. Captain Bostany is more than qualified to determine whether or not there will be problems from limited contact. She has the command of the latest computerized investigation tools. Against this, you would take the word of a spiritualist?"

"Humphries, from birth Tayla has been trained to absorb information, associate it, weigh probabilities, and project outcomes given a certain set of circumstances. There is nothing spiritual about it. She couldn't tell you how she arrives at a particular conclusion, but I can tell you the conclusions are accurate. I think the general can support what I say."

Kahn nodded. "I saw Tayla observe our original occupation and defense plan of Momus, then point by point list the sociological results. This has since been verified by captain Bostany—that is, except the need for complete separation, as I think she has shown."

Allenby nodded at Bostany. "Captain, I do not doubt your qualifications. However, a skilled fortune teller can do anything your computers can do, and a lot faster. In addition, Tayla knows Momus. There must be a factor, some seemingly unimportant fact, you failed to include. Mission personnel will not come planetside."

"Great Allenby." He turned to see Hamid looking at him through hazy blue eyes. The old rider's face was tired as death. "Great Allenby, I beg you. If the soldiers do not come down, the circus will die. We have been open now for only three nights, and already the tiers at the Great Ring are half-filled. The main attractions cannot continue without the soldiers."

"You have heard Tayla speak. Can I sacrifice the way of an entire planet's life for the sake of a few attractions?"

"I would ask Great Tayla a question." Hamid turned to the fortune teller. "Great Tayla, how is it that a few soldiers visiting my circus will destroy us when the ancestors of

Momus, the old circus, traveled among worlds of strangers for many centuries?"

Tayla closed her eyes. "I see what I see."

Allenby stood. "Then, if there is nothing else?"

Hamid pulled himself along on his crutches until he stood in the light coming from the Great Ring. Still outside the spectators' entrance, he could not bring himself to enter. Moving to the side to stand alone in the dark, the old man listened to the music coming from within. He watched the pitifully few customers walking up and down the midway, peeking into stalls and tents, reading the signs and listening to the barkers. The side attractions were falling off as well. But, thought Hamid, it is nothing to them. When the circus dies, they will play the squares and fires as before. But for us... He stood back in the entrance and for a moment watched Tessia and her parents high above the sawdust. He turned away. For us there will be no tomorrow. As a cheer erupted from the Ring, Hamid lifted his eyes to see a fortune teller's stall. Inside, a lone woman in the blue robe sat playing solitaire, unmindful of the noise and music. Hamid thought, shook his head, and thought again. It was so simple. Smacking his head, he hobbled off in the darkness.

"Great Tayla." Hamid nodded his head.

The old fortune teller squinted at him from her place at her table, then nodded. "Enter, Hamid. Be seated." The old man hobbled into the dark room, propped his crutches against the wall and lowered himself to the single cushion before Tayla's table. On the table, a single oil lamp illuminated the room. "What brings you?"

"It is your greatness that brings me."

She read the old man's eyes, disliking what she saw there. "Be clear, old rider."

Hamid nodded. "The captain fortune teller of the soldiers does not understand. I did not either."

"Understand?"

"Great Allenby spoke truly when he said you could do anything the captain's machines could do, and at greater speed." Hamid grinned. "But, our Statesman did not honor you enough."

"Get on with what you have come to say, Hamid."

"Great Tayla, you can do something the captain's machines cannot."

"Which is?"

"You can lie."

Tayla's face froze. "I told what I saw. All those soldiers and others here on Momus—they would absorb us. We, our way of life, would cease to be. It is the truth!"

Hamid nodded. "As much of it as is told. But the bases, all those soldiers, live up in the orbiting bases and stations. Our way of life is safe from them."

"No!" Tayla shook her head. "They must stay there. We can be safe only if they stay off Momus—all of them."

Hamid rubbed his chin. "Tayla, what did you see of the circus, if the soldiers only visited? You saw the circus born again, didn't you?"

Tayla closed her eyes. "I am tired, Hamid. Leave me."

"You saw it born again."

"Yes!" Tayla flinched at the loudness of her own voice. "Yes, but that only among other things..."

"You saw riders, high-wire walkers, flyers, great beast and jungle acts standing where they have not been for many years, center ring, main attractions..."

"Hamid, there is more."

"Yes, you saw more, Tayla. You saw fortune tellers tucked away in a little stall off the midway—sideshows, reading palms and leaves, telling the rubes what they would like to hear."

The old woman's eyes brimmed with tears. "Old man, Allenby will listen only to what I say."

"What if I took this to your daughter Salina? She is respected. What would her visions be? What if I took this to all the great fortune tellers on Momus? Allenby will not believe the captain, but would he believe ten, fifty, or a hundred fortune tellers?"

"They will see the same things I saw."

The old man shrugged. "Perhaps not. They are younger. Perhaps they will be able to see beyond a vision of a sideshow."

Tayla laughed. "What can you tell me about what they would see, old rider?"

"I think they would see that fortune telling has changed since the days Momus was first settled. Riders, flyers, trainers—we are the same as we were. But fortune telling has changed. It has grown. Great men and women of business come and sit before your table to hear the future and make their plans. You have outgrown the circus. I think they will see that."

The old woman frowned, then reached beneath her table and withdrew a clear glass sphere. She placed it on the table and adjusted the oil lamp. She sat for only a moment, staring deep within the glass, then closed her eyes and nodded. "I did not look beyond that vision. Understand my loyalty to the fortune tellers, Hamid. I saw this, and . . ."

"And lied!" Hamid gripped the edge of the table and pushed himself to his feet. He took his crutches, placed them under his arms and turned toward Tayla. "You will tell Allenby?"

Tayla looked into the old man's angry face. "Yes, I will tell him." Hamid hobbled toward the door. "Hamid?"

He turned to face her. "Yes?"

"I am ashamed. But tonight in Great Allenby's quarters, I saw an old cripple prepared to destroy an entire people, just to put his son on a horse. Is my shame any greater than his?"

Hamid looked at the old woman, then bowed his head. "No, Great Tayla. You see better into my own heart than I do."

"It is my trade."

Hamid looked at her and smiled. "Do I owe you for this visit?"

The old woman smiled and shook her head. "No, Hamid, I think we are even. Must you go?"

Hamid laughed. "Yes. I must see a man about a horse."

Allenby bid Koolis, Master of the Ring, good-bye and turned his attention to the tiers packed with Montagne soldiers, civilians, and, best of all, hordes of excited, wide-eyed children. The Ring stood brightly in the glow of eight searchlights General Kahn supplied to replace the rows of oil lamps, while from the bandstand, the musicians delivered a lusty march in preparation for the Great Parade. Disus, Allenby's chief-of-staff, walked up and stood beside him next to the Ring. "A marvelous spectacle, is it not?"

Allenby nodded. "The man behind this, however, is the real marvel. Koolis told me that Hamid began this without a movill in his purse; yet look at the acts he has assembled and the audience he has attracted."

Disus shrugged and waved an idle hand at the soldiers. "If Hamid cannot go to Montagne..."

"Don't finish that if you value your life. See to our seats." Grinning, Disus bowed and went off to negotiate for seating space.

Opposite the entrance, high on the last tier, an old man leaned on a crutch and surveyed the amphitheater. Before the night's show, Koolis had stood before him shaking his head. "Every last percentage of the gate has been exchanged for acts, food, materials, and supplies. I keep the accounts, Hamid. No matter the success, you will not find yourself a movill richer."

"I have my reward, Koolis," he had said.

The Master of the Ring shrugged and shook his head. "A high price to pay for sentiment, my friend."

"It is not sentiment."

"What then is your reward? I do not understand." Koolis left, shaking his head and fondling his fat purse.

As the Great Parade began, the old man leaned forward to see four brothers in silver-spangled tights mounted on four gleaming white stallions enter the Ring at the head of the parade. Four brothers whose sons and daughters will ride, and all their sons and daughters after them.

"Yes, Koolis," the old man whispered, "my fortune *is* made."

Dueling Clowns

Lord Allenby raised his eyebrows at the newsteller's apprentice, but the apprentice only shrugged. Allenby looked back at the master newsteller. His eyes fixed on the fire, Boosthit sat cross-legged, elbows on his knees, chin on his hands and a black scowl on his face. "Come, come, Boosthit. I've known you too long for this." The newsteller sat unmoving.

The apprentice scratched his head. "It's no use, Lord Allenby. He's been that way for a week."

Allenby shrugged. "I came by this fire and saw my old friend and expected to have grand times getting reacquainted. When I first came to Momus as the ambassador of the Ninth Quadrant, it was Boosthit who took news of my mission and played it in Tarzak."

The apprentice nodded. "He won't even talk to me."

Allenby looked closely at the apprentice. "You're one of the Montagne soldiers, aren't you?"

"Yes. In a year I'll be taking my retirement here on Momus. I'm on leave now looking into newstelling as an occupation for when I get out."

"Your name?"

"Forgive me. Sergeant Major Gaddis. I'm top soldier at orbital fighter base twenty-six."

Allenby nodded. "I'm pleased to meet you, Sergeant. Has newstelling been to your liking?"

The apprentice turned toward Boosthit, shook his head and turned back to Allenby. "I have no idea, Lord Allenby. I've been with him for a week, but I haven't heard any news yet."

Allenby looked at Boosthit. "Come, old friend, you haven't hit a dry spell, have you?" Boosthit's scowl deepened. "Why, there's news of galactic significance transpiring this very moment, with the commission from the United Quadrants coming to Momus. Then, there's the military buildup of the Tenth Quadrant forces to counter the Ninth's defense of this planet, and the ambassador from the Tenth

Quadrant will be here in a few days to present his credentials. Even my own office as statesman of Momus is in doubt. The UQ Commission will rule . . ."

Boosthit held up his hands. "Still yourself, Allenby; I have news!"

The sergeant major applauded. "Congratulations. That's more than I've heard him say for the entire week."

Boosthit glowered at the apprentice, then aimed his expression at Allenby. "As I said, I have news. I do not choose to recite it."

Allenby smiled and nodded his head. "That bad, is it? I understand . . ."

"It is the best news I have ever had. It is great news! And, you would *not* understand!"

"Dear friend." Allenby held up his hands in a gesture of peace. "We have been through and seen much together over the past six years. You think I would lack understanding, or not appreciate great news?"

"It is what I think."

"What caused this? A newsteller with great news refusing to recite it? Do you think I wouldn't pay?"

Boosthit stood, walked to the boulders outside the light of the fire, then returned and sat down. He lifted an eyebrow in Allenby's direction. "You really want to hear my news?"

"Of course. I also want you to explain your strange behavior."

Boosthit pursed his lips, then nodded. "Very well. First, I shall tell you why I am reluctant." He turned to the sergeant major. "I recited my news to others such as this one, and I was treated very badly."

Allenby frowned. "You mean, to soldiers?"

"They were apprenticed, as this one is, but they were soldiers, yes."

Allenby turned to Gaddis. "The rules for visiting planetside are being observed, aren't they?"

"Yes, Lord Allenby. We are all familiarized with customs, traditions and occupations. When I am on duty, that training is part of my responsibility."

Allenby rubbed his chin and turned back to the newsteller. "Tell me what happened, Boosthit."

Boosthit gave the apprentice a suspicious glance, then held up his hands. "Very well. It happened at the first fire from Tarzak several days ago. I had rehearsed my news, and was anxious to take it on the road. As I said, it is great news."

"As you said."

Boosthit shrugged. "I approached the fire in the evening, and heard laughter coming from behind the rocks. I thought to myself that this was a lucky stroke, having a good audience my first night. But, when I stepped through the boulders, I saw that they were soldiers."

"You said they were apprenticed. How did you know they were soldiers?"

"They wear their robes badly, and sit funny." Boosthit cocked his head toward his apprentice. Gaddis had his knees together and sat back on his legs.

Gaddis shrugged. "It takes time to get used to going without trousers."

Allenby nodded. "I remember. Go on, Boosthit."

"Well, I turned to go, but they made such a fuss about me staying, that I changed my mind. That meant, of course, sitting through all of their amateur acts, but, I thought, business is business. I stayed. There was a priest's apprentice, and apprentices representing storytellers, tumblers, knife-throwers, and even one representing your own magicians, Allenby.

"After we bargained and ate, the first to rise was the apprentice priest. He did an almost acceptable job of reciting the epic of the circus ship *Baraboo* that brought our ancestors to Momus. Reluctantly, I parted with two movills for the fellow's performance, thinking to collect twenty times that amount after I dazzled those apprentices with my news.

"Then, the knife-thrower did a few turns on a piece of board he carried with him, but the act was of no consequence since he had no one standing in front of the board. Nevertheless, I parted with another two movills. Let it suffice to say that the tumblers and the magician were of similar quality. I could hardly keep my eyes open.

"Then, may his master's throat turn to stone, the apprentice storyteller began. He went on and on about a boy in a strange land named Pittsburg, and I could find no start nor middle to the tale. I recognized the ending because he stopped talking and another movill left my purse. But, then—" A strange fire lit behind the newsteller's eyes as he stared off in a trance. "Then, my turn came. I looked among their eager faces, and began:

"I, Boosthit of the Farransetti newstellers, sit before the fire this evening to tell you of the great duel between Kamera, Master of the Tarzak clowns, and Spaht, new Master of Clowns from Kuumic. It is news of heroics, a defense of the mighty being attacked by a hungry jackal. I, Boosthit, was witness to this event.

"Four days ago, I sat at the table of the Great Kamera, exchanging my news for entertainment, when the curtain to the street opened. Standing in the doorway was Spaht, garbed in yellow trousers with black polkadots, a vest of green and white stripes over a naked torso. On his bare neck, he wore a collar and bowtie. He wore white greasepaint with red nose and upturned lips, the entire effect being capped with an orange fright wig and derby. He bowed to Kamera, and said, 'Now is the time, Kamera; be on the street in five minutes.'"

"Kamera laughed. 'Fool, I cannot be bothered with challenges from every apprentice that passes my door.'

"'Apprentice? I am Spaht, Master of the Kuumic clowns!'

"Kamera waved an idle hand in the direction of the door. 'In that case, out damned Spaht! Out, I say!'

"Spaht bowed. 'I see I have entered the wrong house and found only great chimera.'

"Kamera squinted his eyes. 'Leave me. I shall be out as you requested.' Spaht bowed again, then left. In the quiet room, I saw the great clown sigh and reach under his table for his paints. His face was very sad.

"'Surely, Great Kamera,' I said, 'this upstart does not worry you?'

"Kamera adjusted a looking glass and began putting on his makeup. 'Boosthit, it is ever thus for the greatest clown on Momus. Always there is another young punslinger lurking in the corners, waiting to build a reputation. It is not an easy life.'

"Kamera finished his makeup and put on a pure white suit, with large pompoms down the front. On his hairless head, he placed a white peaked cone. as he put on white slippers, I could see the frown under the painted smile.

"'Spaht is different than the usual run of challenger Great Kamera, isn't he?'

"He nodded. 'You saw what he was wearing. That garish costume, and the bowtie—he winds it up and it spins! Spaht has no sense of tradition, no honor. On the street this day, anything can be expected.'

"The two clowns squared off in the center of the dusty street. Warily, they circled each other, then Spaht opened, 'My uncle, a tailor, once made a magician very angry by making him a shirt that didn't fit.'

"'Put him in a bad choler, did he?'

"'Aye, and he turned my uncle into a tree.'

"All could see Kamera struggling, but he had no choice but to feed Spaht the straight line. 'Did it bother your uncle?'

"'He didn't say; he was board.'

"'Knot he?'

"'But, I avenged my uncle by thrashing the magician and throwing the rude fellow at my uncle's wooden feet.'

"'That was casting churl before pine.'

"As the dust cleared from the opening exchange, the two each had the other's measure. Kamera circled to get the sun out of his eyes. Spaht had a look of confidence on his face.

"'Did you know,' said Spaht, 'that my nephew is related to the tiny flying cave creatures?'

"'Yes, Spaht, I know. I stepped on one once and heard your nephew say, 'Oh, my akin bat!'

"The crowd moaned. Cued by this, Spaht returned, 'Why should the clowns pay homage to you, Kamera? It seems that you are in your anecdotage.'

"Kamera smiled. 'Obeisance makes the heart grow fonder.'

"Staggered, Spaht circled and began spinning his bowtie. 'My uncle, the tree,' he began.

"'I saw him the other day, Spaht. I said, "That's yew all over."'

"'We were so poor that at his funeral we could afford no music. All you could hear was the coughing . . .'

"'There was catarrh playing, then?'

"'Well, there was a coffin.' Spaht tried to rally, but Kamera scented blood. 'My . . . nephew lost consciousness and fell into a vat of stain . . .'

"'The good dye stunned.' Spaht fell to all fours and began crawling out of town. A cheer erupted from the crowd, and Kamera followed the beaten clown down the street. 'Crawl in a straight line, Spaht, or you will get contusions of meander . . .'"

Boosthit looked down to deliver the punchline at Allenby, but the Great Statesman of Momus was gone. "He . . ." He turned and found Gaddis missing as well. Rushing between the boulders, he could see two dark shapes running together toward Tarzak.

"Strange," said the newsteller, rubbing his chin, "if Allenby knew what the soldiers did, why did he ask?"

The Quest

On the planet Momus, south of the Town of Tarzak, lies the village of Sina nestled between the Fake Foot river delta and the glittering expanses of the Sea of Baraboo, named in honor of the ship that stranded the original circus on Momus two centuries before. The sun, just peeking over the edge of the sea, bathed the rooftops of Sina in red, while tufts of idle clouds warmed themselves in the glow above the water. Far below them, two figures dressed in hooded robes of purple stood upon a rotting wharf. The taller of the two scratched, then pulled, at a long white beard as he stared out across the Sea of Baraboo. He turned and looked at the scowling face of his corpulent companion. "Please, Durki. Try to understand."

Durki raised one thick black eyebrow and settled the scowl on his face more deeply. "You will kill yourself, you old fool!" His voice, high and nasal, grated on the ear. "You will drop dead from age, if you escape the storms, the exiles, and monsters. I say it again, Pulsit, you are an old fool!" Durki folded his arms.

Pulsit raised his brows. "Now, Durki, that is no manner in which to address your master. You are a terrible apprentice."

Durki snorted. "I might say a thing or two about your qualities as a master, Pulsit. I am over forty years old, yet I am *still* an apprentice!"

Pulsit winced. "Ah, Durki, please keep your screeching voice to a bearable volume." He shook his head. "How can I turn you loose on an audience with that voice? That's why no other master storyteller would take you on. But, I took you on, Durki. You owe me something for that."

Durki turned down the corners of his mouth, raised his eyebrows and nodded. "True." He reached within his robe and extracted a small copper bead. He held it between thumb and forefinger and dropped it into Pulsit's hand. "I trust this squares our accounts?"

"One movill? That's what you figure your debt is after

eight years as my apprentice?"

Durki shrugged. "I may have been too generous, but keep the change. It helps ease my mind for allowing you to go off and kill yourself."

Pulsit turned his gaze back out over the sea. "Bah! What concern is it of yours, you disrespectful wretch?"

"I have plans on becoming a storyteller, Pulsit, not your partner in suicide. You've never been off the central continent; I doubt you've even been as far as Kuumic—"

"I have too!"

"—and now you want to travel the girth of the entire planet Momus! You know nothing of the dangers! Nothing!"

"Keep your screeching down!" Pulsit looked up the wharf toward the houses along the shore. "Everyone in Sina will be demanding coppers from us for driving them out of bed at this hour. Where is that fisher?"

Durki looked up the wharf, then back out over the ocean. "Perhaps Raster thought better about it. Perhaps he would feel responsible for your suicide."

Pulsit frowned and turned toward his apprentice. "You must stop saying that! I have no intention of killing myself. I am a storyteller, Durki, and I must have experiences to draw upon. All the priests have to do is record history; the newstellers relate events; a storyteller," Pulsit tapped the side of his head, "must have imagination."

Durki shook his head. "You have been a storyteller for many years without having to leave the continent to fuel your imagination."

"My fires—"

"Which were none too hot to begin with."

"My fires . . . are cold. It is only a great adventure such as I have planned that can replenish them." Pulsit looked back up the wharf. "Ah, at last. Here is Raster now."

Durki turned and watched as an enormous hulk, garbed in the yellow-and-green stripes of the freaks, reeled out from between two buildings and staggered onto the wharf. Under the fellow's left arm were two large jugs, while a third hung from a finger. He grasped a fourth jug with his massive right hand, taking gulps of the contents every few steps. between gulps, he would wipe dry his black beard with the sleeve of his none too clean robe. Durkie shook his head and looked at Pulsit. "To whom should I send your belongings?"

The freak pulled up next to the two storytellers and looked down upon them as he belched out a great cloud of sapwine fumes. Durki waved his arms and backed off. Raster smiled, exposing teeth that might more properly be called "slabs." "I apologize, Pulsit, for making you wait." He sloshed the jug in his right hand. "It took me considerable time to convince Fungarat the merchant to leave his bed and sell me this medicine." Raster raised an eyebrow and leaned toward Durki. "To keep off the sea's chill."

Pulsit held up a hand. "No apology is necessary, Raster. Which boat is yours?" Pulsit waved his hand in the direction of the many sleek sailing vessels belonging to the fishers of Sina. Raster squinted his bleary eyes in the indicated direction, then shook his head. He took a step toward the edge of the wharf, bent over and pointed, jug still in hand. "There." Pulsit and Durki looked down and observed the craft Raster indicated. The single-masted wooden craft wallowed next to the pilings amongst the garbage discarded by the other ships. If it had ever been painted, the paint was gone. Tatters of ropes hung from mast and railings, while coils and tangles of rope littered the few places on the deck not occupied with piles of empty brown jugs. On the boat's stern, lettered in fading yellow paint, was her name, *Queen of Sina*.

Durki took in the sight and nodded. "You spoke the truth, Pulsit. It will not be suicide; it will be murder!"

Raster jumped from the wharf onto the *Queen*'s deck, and the two storytellers, held their breaths while the small boat rocked under the force of the freak's landing. Raster kept his feet and walked forward to the tiny cabin to store his medicine. Pulsit stood and placed a hand on Durki's shoulder. "You will not join me in my adventure, then?"

"I am only an apprentice storyteller, Pulsit. It would take the great magician Fyx, himself, to survive a voyage in that leaking tub."

Pulsit dropped his hand. "Very well. Good-bye, Durki, and I hope you can find another master before too long." The master storyteller went to a ladder and began climbing down to the boat.

Durki leaned over the edge of the wharf. "Another master? Pulsit, where am I to find a master with this voice of mine? Come back, you old fool! The fish will eat you, you know that?"

Pulsit reached the level of the *Queen of Sina* and jumped over the side, stumbled and fell on the deck. He stood and arranged his robe. Raster stumbled out of the cabin and began pulling on a rope. A once-white sail, now decorated in black and grey-green mildew, commenced its halting journey to the top of the mast. Pulsit waved, then turned and went into the cabin. Still holding the rope, Raster looked up at Durki and threw a few coppers up on the wharf. "Release the lines, will you?"

"You would make me an accomplice to murder?" Durki snorted, stooped over and picked up the coppers. After he had stuffed them into his purse, he went to the pilings fore and aft, lifted the frayed rope ends and let them splash into the water. As the sail reached the top of the mast, its triangle filled with a gentle breeze and began drawing the boat away from the wharf. Durki looked up at the clear sky, muttered either an oath or a prayer, then scampered down the ladder and jumped onto the deck of the *Queen of Sina*.

Raster secured the mast line and weaved over to where Durki kept a wistful eye on the shrinking houses of Sina. "If you are coming, Durki, it will cost you fifty coppers, the same as your master."

Durki turned and glowered at the freak. "You get my coppers, Raster, when I reach my destination alive!"

Raster shrugged. "Fair enough." The freak went back to secure the tiller.

Durki looked back toward Sina, sickeningly confident that his fifty coppers were as safe as if they were on loan to a cashier from Tarzak.

That night, the Town of Sina long gone from view, the *Queen of Sina* pitched and plowed through the dark, shrieking outrages of a summer storm at sea. Durki, his face a delicate hue of yellow-green, turned from the tiny glassed-in porthole and watched Raster take a gulp from a jug. The three adventurers sat upon built-in benches surrounding a rough plank table that occupied most of the cabin. A fishoil lamp swung and sputtered above the table, emitting an evil smell. Raster belched, and Durki's shade changed to green-yellow. Durki pointed aft with a shaking finger. "Raster . . . who is steering this misbegotten thing?"

"Steering?" Raster scratched his head, then shrugged. "I know not, Durki." Raster pointed at Pulsit, Durki and himself, in turn. "One, two, three. We are all here; then no one should be steering."

The apprentice storyteller plunked his elbows on the table and gently lowered his face into his hands. "Tell me, oh great man of the sea, what is to keep us from swamping or piling up on some rocks?"

Raster shook his head. "It is a good question, Durki." The freak smiled and held out his hands. "But, I have never been one for intellectual talk—"

"By the crossed eyes of the Jumbo!" Durki lowered his hands. "Raster, why aren't *you* out there steering?"

Raster grinned and slapped the table top, causing everything upon it, including Durki's elbows, to leap in the air a hand's breadth. "Hah! By my coppers, that's one I can answer! I would get wet."

"Wet? *Wet!*"

Pulsit placed a gentle hand upon Durki's shoulder. "Calm yourself. I believe Raster has secured the tiller. This fine ship can steer itself, you see?"

"See?"

Pulsit nodded and held out his other hand toward Raster. "Our captain says we are days away from any land or rocks—"

"Days?" Durki grabbed his mouth with both hands, swung his feet over his bench plank and rushed through the cabin door, out onto the deck. Raster stood, reached out a long arm, and pulled the cabin door shut. He seated himself, hefted his jug and took a long pull.

Pulsit stretched his arms, clasped his hands behind his head, and leaned back against the cabin wall. "Ah, my captain, I can feel my storyteller's blood stirring already. This will be a fine adventure." He brought his hands down and cocked his head. "Listen!" A long, low moan could be heard. "Listen to it wail. Is it a sea dragon? The ghosts of a stricken ship?"

Raster lowered his jug and pointed an ear in the direction of the sound. "It's Durki. He's got the shipslops."

Pulsit sighed. "Of course, Raster, of course. But the mournfulness of it—doesn't it stoke up your imagination?"

Raster took another pull from his own brand of fuel, lowered the jug and listened to the apprentice wretching, cursing and wailing at the wind. The freak nodded. "Now that you point it out, Pulsit, it does sound . . . well, the way

I always thought of the slave souls sounding."

Pulsit raised his brows. "Slave souls?"

Raster shook his head. "Only a myth of the fishers in these parts. The slave souls were victims the sorcerer pirate Bloody Buckets enchanted, then strapped to his mainmast to keep watch."

Pulsit rubbed his hands as Durki gave out with another moan. "Bloody Buckets! Excellent!" A dreamy look came into the storyteller's eyes. He spread his arms. "The tormented souls of Bloody Bucket's victims howled a warning, that wind and storm driven night, as the . . ." Pulsit lowered his hands and looked at Raster. "What was the ship's name?"

"Ship?"

"Bloody Bucket's ship."

Raster wrinkled up his face in confusion. "I told you, Pulsit; it's only a myth."

"I know, but I am a storyteller. I must let my imagination run free. Here we can take myth, coat it with belief, and make a story—no, *live* a story!" Pulsit reached out and picked up Raster's jug and took a gulp. He replaced the jug, shook his head and held up a finger. "The ship."

Raster warmed to the task and rubbed his hands together. "The *Black Tide* is his ship; the foulest most evil barge upon the water."

"A great name." Durki issued another moan. "Captain! Captain Buckets! What does the watch say?" Pulsit nodded toward Raster. "You shall be Bloody Buckets."

Raster grinned. "Then, mate, call me 'Bloody.' I lay bare the guts of any swab what calls me 'Buckets.'" Raster took another pull from his jug as Durki howled again. The jug dropped to the table as Raster held his hand to his ear. "Avast! Mate, avast there!"

Pulsit finished another gulp at the jug. "Aye, Bloody, what be it?"

Raster waved his hand above his head. "The wretches up there signal us of an approaching prize. Call out the hands!"

"Aye, Bloody." Pulsit pushed open a porthole glass and shouted. "All hands on deck! Bloody has need of your evil hands and steel blades." Above the port, a scream, then a whimper evidenced that Durki had not yet been washed overboard. "The crew is assembled, Bloody."

Raster glared at the wall. "Aye, and a scurvy lot they are too." The freak looked around the cabin, and pulled loose two narrow planks that served as trim between the wall and overhead. He handed one to Pulsit. "Your blade, mate."

Pulsit stood and swung the plank around his head. "It shall be always in your evil service, Bloody."

Raster swung his own plank, tried to stand, but staggered back against the wall. "Avast, ye swabs! On the horizon sails a fat merchantman. Helmsman, aim the *Black Tide* down her gullet, and you line monkeys—up top! Stay the mainsheets, matten down the batch covers and mizzle the fizzenmast! Har! There shall be rapine, loot and killing for all before the sun sets—" Raster stabbed a thumb into his own chest. "Or my name ain't Bloody Buckets."

They both dropped down on the benches and refueled on sapwine. After an impressive pull, Raster placed the jug on the table. "What now?"

Pulsit nodded. "The other ship—what shall we call it?"

Raster rubbed his chin. "Should it be a special name?"

"Yes. The *Black Tide* is evil. To fight evil, we must have good. The name of the merchantman must reflect good."

Raster nodded. "The *Honor Bright*, carrying a cargo of . . ." His bleary eyes fell upon his jug. "Medicine to ease the sufferings of a stricken city."

Pulsit clapped his hands and missed. "Excellent, and I shall captain the *Honor Bright*. Captain John Fine is my name."

Raster weaved to his feet, shielded his eyes from an imaginary sun with one hand and pointed with another. "Captain Fine! Captain Fine! Abaft the bort peam, there!"

"Aye, Mister Trueheart? What is it?"

"Captain, bearing down on us is a pirate ship." Raster fell back against the wall and held his hand to his neck. "The *Black Tide!*"

Pulsit stood next to Raster and placed an arm around his huge shoulders. A hint of a smile played on the storyteller's lips. "Have courage, Mister Trueheart. Our ship is fast, and our crew is the finest to be found in any port."

"But, Captain, it is Bloody Buckets!" Durki issued a drawn-out howl. "Listen! Hear his ghost watch!" The sound diminished to a moan, then to a whimper.

Pulsit nodded gravely. "The poor souls. But stiffen your spine, Mister, else we shall fail and a city will die."

Raster pushed himself away from the wall, held his plank before him and nodded. "Aye, Captain. I am all right now."

Pulsit looked at his own plank and turned to Raster. "We must have blood. What do you have?"

Raster turned to a locker next to the cabin door, stooped and opened it. With both hands he emptied the locker of odd bits of line, empty brown jugs, a half-bolt of sailcloth, paint-caked brushes, and finally a large closed bucket of paint. "Here it is. I must use this to mark my trapbuoys."

"What color is it?"

Raster opened the wooden top, and stood out of the way. The paint was bright scarlet. "And, there is your blood."

Pulsit closed his eyes and held out his hands. "Although the *Honor Bright* was swift, the *Black Tide* quickly closed the distance, driven by Bloody Bucket's sorcery. Grappling hooks flew from the pirate ship, and in moments, the two ships were bound together. Bloody's crew swarmed over the side." Pulsit dipped his plank into the paint and jumped up on one of the benches. "Defend yourself, Bloody!"

Raster dipped his plank and mounted the bench on the opposite side of the table. "Hah, Captain Fine! I'll have yer soul strapped to my mizzenmast, or me name ain't Bloody Buckets!" The freak lunged at the storyteller, slapping his arm with the plank. "First blood!"

Pulsit diverted the next blow, but Raster's onslaught drove the storyteller to the door of the cabin. As he narrowly avoided a killing blow, Pulsit drove in and poked Raster in the stomach. "Hah, Bloody! Take that!"

Raster picked up the paint and sloshed it down his front. "Curses, Fine! Ye have marked me, that's true. But, I am Bloody Buckets, with the strength of ten!"

"Then, up with your blade, pirate, and have at it!"

Pulsit swung, knocking the bucket across the cabin, splattering them both, as well as the cabin, with paint. As Raster stepped into a large puddle of paint, he slipped and came crashing down on the deck. Pulsit leaped to the fallen freak's side, lifted his plank, and brought it down next to Raster's neck in a mock beheading. "And, die, Bloody Buckets! Die!" Pulsit stood and looked in the direction of the overhead. "And Captain Fine, wounded and bleeding, stood atop the deck of the *Honor Bright*, his victory sweet on his tongue, while the flesh of the evil pirate grew cold." Pulsit listened and could hear nothing but the creaks of the ship, the shrieks of the wind and the snores of Raster. "And, at last, poor souls, you are free!" The storyteller backed up against a wall, slid down, and passed out.

Durki opened the cabin door, stepped inside and saw both his master and the fisher on the deck, soaked in red. More red covered the walls, table and overhead. "Whoops!" Durki covered his mouth and staggered back on deck. In moments the moans of the slave souls once more stole across the waters.

The next morning, the waves of the night before calmed to gentle swells, Durki pushed himself up from the railing and placed his hands gently against his aching ribs. He thought upon it for a moment, then concluded that his stomach had finally given in to its fate. He looked around the deck, found a canvas bucket attached to a rope, then picked it up and drew some sea water. He splashed it over his head, rubbed his face and dried it in the gentle wind coming from the northwest. "Perhaps," he said to the fingernail of new sun coming over the horizon, "perhaps this will not be so bad after all." He turned and walked forward of the cabin, coming to a halt at the ship's prow. The *Queen of Sina* dipped into the gentle swells ever so slightly, and Durki was delighted at the lack of response from his bowels. "An adventure will do much to fuel my own storyteller's imagination. I now understand torment."

Durki clasped his hands behind his back, assumed a deep frown, and began pacing back and forth in front of the cabin. "This is a king's man of war, Ponsonberry, not a pleasure ship! I *said* fifty lashes, and I *meant* fifty lashes! Now, strip that wretch to the bones, and be quick about it—lest you find yourself touched by the cat!"

Durki stopped, turned and held out his hands. "Captain Cruel, I would rather stand the lashes myself, than subject an innocent man to them."

"You would, eh Ponsonberry! Then order back the master at arms. It would never do to have a common seaman lay bare the back of a king's officer. *I will swing the cat myself!*"

A thumping came from the deck. "Have mercy, Durki, and still your mouth!"

Durki squatted next to one of the cabin ports. "Ah, Raster, you besotted freak. You are up then?"

"Of course I'm up, and with a head the size of the universe!"

Durki snorted. "You must pay the price for your ways, Raster." He heard a scuffle from inside the cabin, then Raster speaking Pulsit's name. "Raster, what is it?"

The freak's face, eyes as red as the paint splashed on his skin, appeared in the porthole. "Come down quick, Durki. I think your master is dying."

Durki and Raster sat on opposite sides of the table, while on the third bench, his face drawn and grey, Pulsit lay prone, covered with sailcloth up to his neck. His grizzled head rocked from side to side with the motion of the ship. Durki turned away and closed his eyes. *Amar looked down at the broken body of the great flyer Danto, then up at the trapeze, still swaying against the canvas of the big top. He looked one more time at Danto, then began climbing the ladder, ignoring the pain from his crippled left leg. "The crowd was told they'd see the backwards quadruple tonight, and if it takes my last breath, they will!"*

"Durki, what are you mumbling about?" Raster gulped from his jug and slammed the container on the table.

Durki shrugged. "I was thinking. The deathwatch is an old story."

"Too depressing. I like stories with action, glitter, and pretty girls." Raster belched.

"Aren't you soaking up the sapwine a little early?"

Raster shrugged. "A scale from the dragon that bit me." The freak cocked his head at Pulsit's quiet form. "Your master, do you think he will be all right?"

Durki shook his head. "I don't know. He is an old man." *They gathered like vultures around the old man's deathbed, rubbing their hands, smiling to each other in secret, counting their inheritances before the body grew cold . . ."* Durki reached for the jug, took a gulp and replaced the container on the table. "You are right, Raster. This is too depressing. What would you like to talk about?"

Raster rubbed his chin and raised his eyebrows. "What do you think about the new ambassador to Momus—the one from the Tenth Quadrant?"

Durki shrugged. "I am a storyteller, Raster, not a newsteller. I do not follow politics."

Raster laughed. "Neither am I a newsteller, but I take an interest in whether or not I will become a slave."

"What are you talking about?"

"The ambassador—a Vorilian, Inak by name—is in Tarzak right now. He would get the Great Ring to vote away the defenders from the Ninth Quadrant and accept those from the Tenth."

Durki rubbed his chin. "What do the defenders from the Ninth Quadrant defend us from?"

"Why, from the Tenth Quadrant, of course."

Durki shrugged. "Then, if we were defended by the Tenth, we would be safe, wouldn't we?"

Raster frowned, held up a finger, then dropped it. He shook his head. "Our statesman, Allenby, doesn't see it that way. He thinks we must keep the Vorilians away from Momus. I agree."

Durki waved his hand impatiently. "Let's talk of other things, Raster. This holds no interest for me."

"No interest?" Raster held out his hands, his eyebrows arched in wonder. "Things are happening that will change the courses of planets—of quadrants, or perhaps the entire galaxy! Your storyteller's blood is thin indeed if it cannot draw inspiration from such events."

"As I said, I am no newsteller." Durki reached for the jug.

"You mean to say that the idea of a great war—perhaps one in space—is of no interest to a storyteller?"

Durki put down the jug, turned his face to the overhead and closed his eyes. *Tadja jetted to one side as the Vorilian glopfiend's bolt sped past. The vapor trail from a passing ship obscured his vision as he tried to sight his weapon on the Vorilian . . .* Durki looked back at the jug, then shrugged. "Stories like that might interest some, but I don't think you'll find them among the better sorts of people."

Raster frowned, then stabbed himself in his chest with his thumb. "*I* like stories like that!"

Durki nodded. "I rest my case. You see, Raster, most of the listeners we storytellers have at fires along the road, or in the squares of the large towns, don't happen to be wine soaked, overmuscled, frustrated freaks." Durki raised his eyebrows. "No offense."

Raster grabbed the jug, stood and stomped to the cabin

door. "I must go on deck."

The door slammed behind the freak, and Durki turned toward Pulsit as his master began mumbling and moaning. "Pulsit?"

"Durki . . . is that you?" The old man's voice was weak.

"Yes. Are you all right? How do you feel?"

Pulsit reached out a hand and grasped the front of Durki's robe. "Did you see him? Where's the body?"

"Him? See who?"

"Bloody Buckets. We fought all night." Pulsit relaxed his grip and fell back onto the bench. "Ah, it was glorious!"

Durki stared. *"Humor him, doctor, otherwise the maniac will kill us all!"* "Did, uh, Mister Buckets fight well, Pulsit?"

The old man cackled. "Did he fight well? Look at me you fool! Anyone who could put Captain John Fine on his back fights well!" Pulsit's eyes rolled up, then the old man relaxed and fell asleep.

Durki shook his head. *"You lock me behind these doors, thou cowering knave in white! But, who is to judge the sane? Are you locking me away from the sane? Or, are you keeping me safe from all those out there? That is it, isn't it? I am the last sane man in the world—ha, ha, ha, ha, ha . . ."*

For the next few days, Pulsit raved, Raster swilled, and Durki wretched their collective way across the Sea of Baraboo until they came in sight of the continent of Midway. Actually, it was the *Queen of Sina* that came in sight of Midway, rather than her passengers, since Raster's state of constant blindness relieved itself only for as long as it took to find more medicine. Pulsit, of course, lay on his bench in the cabin, traveling the bruised reaches of his mind, while Durki hung from the railing, praying for death. The continent of Midway was named in honor of the collection of sideshows that filled the hold of the lone shuttle stranded there in the disaster of the circus ship *Baraboo*. It was isolated from the rest of the planet Momus. Few ships came to its shores, which caused the inhabitants of the coastal village of Mbwebwe to gather on the beach as the *Queen* came into view. Since the original inhabitants of Midway were comprised of a troupe of Ubangi Savages who also did seconds as Wild Men Of Borneo, and another troupe of acrobatic midgets, it was a curious lot that stood upon the beach examining the *Queen*. After a time, Azongo, the village headman, came to the obvious conclusion. He looked down at Myte, the meter-tall village priest, and held out his arm toward the approaching ship. "It is obvious, Myte. That unfortunate vessel has been attacked by sea pirates. Look at its tatters of rope and sail, and the rotting bodies draped over railings and deck."

In the cabin, Pulsit sat on his bench, peered through one of the front portholes, and also came to the obvious conclusions. *Cannibals!* His eyes went from the dark savages with their great shaggy heads, to the lighter-skinned midgets that stood beside them. *Giant cannibals!*

Pulsit leaned against the cabin wall and held a hand against his forehead. *What am I doing here? My crew depends upon me—and that city! We haven't delivered the medicine for that city . . . city—why can't I remember its name?* The old man's hand dropped to his lap, he turned his head and looked out of the porthole. The inhabitants of Mbwebwe were moving closer to the water. *The cannibals are attacking, and my crew without a leader!* Pulsit weaved to his feet, pushed his way across the cabin, and picked up a paint-smeared plank leaning in the corner. He hefted it and swung it about his head. *As long as I have breath in my body and a blade in my hand, John Fine is not defeated. I'll not have my crew garnished for a savage's gullet!*

Pulsit opened the cabin door, pulled himself up the four steps to the deck, then swooned against the roof of the cabin. "Mister Trueheart! Where be you, man? Call the hands on deck! Stand by to repel boarders!"

Raster pushed from his face the pile of rags and ropes he had covered himself with the night before, opened his eyes and saw a gaunt visage standing over him shouting and swinging a bloody blade. His eyes opened wide, and he pushed himself back in fear. His mouth worked a silent scream as he saw the tangle of ropes on his legs and feet. "Snakes! Oh, merciful Momus, God of Ridicule, spare me!" Raster bounded off the deck, throwing the ropes aside, then ran to the railing and flung himself over the side.

"Mister Trueheart!" Pulsit staggered to the railing and watched Raster swim toward the shore. "Trueheart, you coward! Come back and stand your ground, man!" The bottom of the *Queen* grounded, knocking Pulsit off his feet.

As he pulled himself up, he looked over the railing to see the inhabitants of Mbwebwe wading toward the ship. He backed up against the cabin, then turned and ran to the other side of the ship. *More cannibals! Waves of them!* He saw Durki hung over the railing and swatted the apprentice across the buttocks with the plank. "Awake, there, crewman! Arm yourself!"

Durki moaned, opened his eyes and saw the golden beach and trees of the village. "Land! Dry, hard, solid land!" He smiled, pulled himself over the railing, and fell into the shallow water with a smack. Pulsit looked down to see Durki wading toward shore.

What is this? Do I command nothing but cowards? Do the gods test my courage with these things? First one brown hand, then another and another grasped the railing. Pulsit smacked one with his plank, heard a curse, followed immediately by a splash. "Hah! Defend your heathen selves!" Pulsit ran up and down the railing, smacking hands with the plank and glorying in the curses and sounds of bodies falling into the drink. "If he need must, John Fine shall take on your entire cannibal nation!" For a moment, no new hands appeared on the railing, and Pulsit leaned over the side to see the last of the dark natives wading away from the *Queen*. The old man raised a fist toward the shore and shook it. "I am Captain John Fine, commander of the *Honor Bright!* I cannot be defeated! I say this to you: Send me *more* cannibals!"

He tossed his head back to laugh, then felt strong arms grasp him from behind. He turned his head to see dark faces and shaggy heads swarming over the deck. *I am captured!* The plank was taken from his hand, and he felt himself being moved to the other side of the ship, lifted over the railing, and lowered into waiting brown arms. *Still, I am John Fine!* "Hear me, you heathen devils!"

"I beg your pardon!" answered one.

"Do not trust your mouths when they water for this body! You shall choke on John Fine!" Pulsit laughed, then became quiet as a great darkness came over him. Those who carried him exchanged puzzled looks, then shrugged and headed toward the beach.

Even though he eyed the food suspiciously and had developed the habit of jumping at the slightest sound, Pulsit appeared well enough by that evening to join his companions at Azongo's table. Coppers were exchanged for the repast, and Durki felt blessed as he enjoyed the packed feeling of the first solid food he had been able to hold down for days. But, recalling his own screech of a voice, he listened with envy as Azongo conversed in rich resonant tones. As a pause in the conversation came, Durki nodded toward the headman. "I would give much to have been born with a voice such as yours, Azongo."

The headman laughed, exposing a glare of teeth filed to needle points. "So would I, storyteller. But, I was not born with this sound. It came only after long practice for my wild man act."

Durki looked around the table, then turned back to Azongo. "Since we are finished eating, I would lay a few coppers in your palm to see your act."

Raster waved his hand and shook his head. "I've seen several wild man acts, and they are good sleeping aids, but nothing for an evening's entertainment. They couldn't scare a child."

Azongo raised his eyebrows. "And, freak, would you care to wager your coppers on that?"

"No, but I'll stake a jug of sapwine against a jug of this cobit brew of yours." Raster held up his cup.

Azongo rubbed his chin, then nodded. "Done." He reached forward and extinguished the oil lamp in the center of the table, leaving only a single lamp on the wall to illuminate the room. He stood, turned his back on his dinner guests, and removed his robe. "Hhuurrraaaaggh!" Azongo leaped about in a crouch, his body scarred and tattooed in bright, fantastic patterns, his face contorted such that his eyes and filed teeth seemed larger than life. In the flickering half-light of the lamp, there was little doubt that the creature before them was a primitive, unreasoning machine of blood lust, coiled and ready to strike. Azongo leaped over the low table and landed next to Raster with his hands held forward, claws extended. "Aaarrrgggh!"

Raster backed up against the adobe wall of the room. "Very well, Azongo! Enough!"

The headman relit the table lamp, collected his coppers and sapwine, then returned to his place. Pulsit watched all of this, but kept his silence. *The natives are restless. When the time is ripe, I must try to convince them that I am a god.*

Raster shook his head. "Even the wild man act of the Tarzak freaks does not compare to your performance, Azongo. If you came back with us to the Central Continent, you could gather coppers by the sackful."

"Indeed."

Raster nodded. "But the act is only better, not very different." He rubbed his chin. "What you need is a victim. Play out a drama of life-and-death." Raster nodded again. "Yes, that would put the act in the Great Square in Tarzak."

Azongo sipped at his cup, mulling over Raster's words. "It would do me good to make my living with an act again." He held out his hands. "Since we are mostly all wild men, there is little demand for such an act here. And, there are others better than I. Being headman of this village is the only way I can keep a roof over my head." Azongo lowered his hands and shrugged. "But, where would I find such a victim?"

Raster stuck his thumb in his chest. "Me." He leaned forward. "I am a strongman with the Sina freaks, but there are many who are stronger, and with better acts. My pitiful performance as a fisher is all that allows me to keep myself in sapwine. But, together we shall become rich!" Raster turned toward Durki. "Durki, do you think your master would devise a story for Azongo and I to act out?"

Durki turned his head and looked at Pulsit. The old storyteller stared with unseeing eyes at the lamp on the table. Durki looked back at Raster and shrugged. "Pulsit is still in the grip of his imagination. If he were well, he could devise a fine story."

Azongo scratched his head, then pointed a finger at Durki. "There is talk of a doctor two day's ride from here."

"Will he treat my master?"

Azongo nodded. "It is said that the doctor treats those who come to him in exchange for plants and animals. It is also said that he has seven fingers on each hand."

Raster shrugged. "That is nothing. Vorub of the Tarzak freaks has sixteen fingers, yet he cannot make a living at it."

"You do not understand, Raster." Azongo lowered his voice. "The talk is that the doctor does not come from the planet Momus."

"Is he a Vorilian?"

Azongo shrugged. "It is all talk. Still, he may be able to help your master. If Pulsit becomes well and writes Raster and I a story, we can put together a great act."

Durki nodded. "perhaps the doctor can do something for my voice as well."

Azongo laughed. "That I can do. You must exercise your voice by forcing the air out of your body sharply, and growling with your throat, like this. Azongo took a deep breath, then forced it out. "Hhhoooowaughhhh!" the headman nodded. "It will thicken up your voice if you practice it every chance you get. Try it."

Durki took a deep breath. "Hoowah."

Pulsit's eyes came to life, darting between Durki and Azongo. *What is this? What heathen ritual?*

Azongo shook his head. "You must force the air out faster. Hhhoooowaughhhh!"

"Hhoowahh!"

"Hhhoooowaughhhh!"

"Hhooowaugh!"

"Much better." He nodded toward Raster. "If you are to be my victim, you will need a good scream. Try this." Azongo took another breath. "Aaaaaah!"

Raster nodded. "Aye, it chills the bones." He took a deep breath. "Aaaaaaah!"

As the three screamed and growled, a tear trickled down Pulsit's cheek. *The peasants of the field—listen to them suffer the tortures of the damned! Look, beyond! A dragon! What horror!*

"Hhhoooowaughhhh!"

"Aaaaaaaaah!"

Pulsit weaved to his feet and placed a hand on Raster's shoulder. His other hand held an imaginary lance in Azongo's direction. "Fear not, sweet maiden, for I, the Golden Knight, shall slay yon dragon and lay its carcass at your feet!"

Azongo leaned forward and spoke to Durki. "Is your master well enough to tell us a story?"

Durki sighed. "This is no story to Pulsit's troubled mind, but reality. He sees the dragon—" He nodded toward Raster. "And the maiden."

Azongo shook his head. "With the morning's light, then, we shall set off to find this strange doctor."

* * *

Two days ride from Mbwebwe, deep in the Donn:ker Basin, stood a compound surrounded by tall, vine-hung, saptrees. Surrounding the compound were tall metal fences, the enclosed area being divided again and again into smaller areas containing representatives of Momus's peculiar life forms. In its center stood a blue metal building from which curious apparatus bristled, giving the structure the appearance of a bowl-cut porcupine. Inside, Doctor Shart clasped his seven-fingered hands together and groveled before an image on his laboratory's telescreen.

"All I need is a little more time, Ambassador Inak. If I can have just a little more time—"

"Enough!" The image scowled, then pointed a couple of fingers at Shart. "I don't know what halfwit approved the funding for your project, Shart, but when the Council of Warlords receives my report, someone is in for a roasting!"

Shart wrung his hands together. "Inak, the experiments are very complicated, and I am the only one at the station. If you could see your way clear to approving my request for an assistant—"

The image raised its thin yellow brows. "You astound me! You expect the Tenth Quadrant to expend *more* monies in support of your demented theories? Fantasy. Utter and complete fantasy!"

"Inak, just think of the benefits to the government if I am successful. Think of being able to control the entire animal population of a planet. Think of it—being able to spread diseases at will using specially adapted carriers—"

"Think of it?" Inak's brows dropped into a frown. "That's all we can do, Shart, is think about it. We certainly haven't seen any results."

Shart smiled and held his hands out at his sides. "If the Ambassador will remember, the Warlords looked favorably upon my project. It would place a great weapon in their hands, and—"

"Only if you begin getting results, Shart. No more of this—when will you have something positive that I can report?"

Shart shrugged. "Perhaps . . . thirty days. My experiment on the virus is almost completed. After that, its just a matter of tuning and adjusting the control banks."

Ambassador Inak rubbed his pointed chin, then nodded toward Shart. "Perhaps, then, we will be able to send a very glowing report to the Warlords. Yes, that will be just about right."

"If I might inquire, Inak, right for what?"

"The commission from the United Quadrants will be here soon, and then there will be a long period of investigation and negotiation. Allenby, the puppet of the Ninth Quadrant, refuses to consider our proposal . . ." Inak leaned forward. "But, if I can show the Great Statesman of Momus that not accepting our proposal would bring disaster to his people . . . Do you get my meaning?"

"I will do my best, Inak—"

"No, Shart! You will succeed!" The image faded and the screen went blank.

Shart placed the thumb of his right hand against the tip of his nose and wiggled the remaining six fingers in the direction of the screen. "Yaaaaaaaah!" He dropped his hand and half turned away when the automatic sensor alarm began to buzz. "What now?" He sighed, then switched the function selector on the screen control. Four figures, riding in one of the clumsy Moman lizard carts, were approaching the station. "Not another patient." Shart shook his head, then remembered toying with the idea of training a Moman to handle the multitude of simple tasks around the laboratory that ate up his time. Now that Inak had turned down his latest request for an assistant, and had stepped up the timetable, what choice had he?

Shart deenergized his screen, then turned and entered a corridor leading to the side of the compound facing the road. At the end of the corridor, he opened the door and stepped outside. Immediately, his sense of hearing was assaulted by screams and growls. He narrowed his eyes and examined the travelers. In the rear of the cart, one of the local wild men, a large man in yellow-and-green stripes and a short, fat man in purple, screamed and growled at each other. Off to one side, a quiet old man, also in purple, seemed to be nodding off. Shart rubbed his hands together. "Excellent!"

The cart pulled to a stop in front of the doctor, and the huge lizard that provided the vehicle's motive power sat down and held out its right front foot, palm up. "Anow here. Payup."

The wild man jumped from the cart, then caught a sack thrown to him by the large man in green and yellow. The sack was handed to the lizard, and Shart watched as the lizard reached into the sack and began stuffing fat cobit roots into its mouth. The wild man kicked the lizard. "Look, you wait. Understand?"

The lizard nodded without looking up from the sack. "'Stand."

The wild man walked around the lizard and came to a stop in front of the Vorilian. "Doctor? I understand that you will treat patients for a fee."

Shart looked from the wild man to the pair screaming and growling in the cart, then back to the wild man. "What seems to be their trouble?"

The wild man looked confused, then he laughed. "There is nothing wrong with them, doctor. They practice their acts. Your patient is the old one. His name is Pulsit. The two in the back are Durki and Raster, and I am Azongo of the Mbwebwe wild men, also headman of that village."

Shart frowned, then nodded. "What is the old one's trouble?"

Azongo whirled a finger next to his head. "He sees things."

Shart waved a hand at the cart. "Bring him down from there, and let me look at him."

Azongo held up a hand. "One moment, doctor. What is your charge? We were told by the villagers at the base of the plateau that you desire plants and animals."

Shart shrugged. "I have no need of such things now. But, I will look at him all the same."

Azongo frowned. "You mean you will treat him for *nothing*?"

Shart remembered that, in the curious reaches of the Moman mind, a service not charged for is worthless. If he charged nothing, he would lose his patient—and, possibly, his head. "Of course not. I must have money—those little copper things."

"How many?"

Shart rubbed his narrow chin. "Twenty-five."

On the cart, the one called Durki reached into the old

one's robe and withdrew a small sack. He turned to Azongo. "Pulsit has only twenty-three coppers on him."

Shart nodded. "That will do."

Azongo backed up and rubbed his own chin. "Well, Doctor, what *is* your price? I expect such haggling in the market, but from a doctor, I expect a firm price for a specific service."

Shart sighed. "Of course. My price is twenty-five, but surely between the three of you, another two coppers can be produced."

Azongo shook his head. "Buying roots for the lizard cleaned us out. Can Pulsit owe you the remaining two coppers?"

"Of course."

"At what rate of interest?"

"N-n-n . . ." Shart stopped himself from saying "none."

"What was that, Doctor?"

"Nine."

"Nine! Nine percent!" Azongo pulled on his lower lip, then shrugged. "Very well." The wild man motioned to the others in the cart. "Lower him down."

Shart and the wild man steadied Pulsit as he came down, and immediately the doctor began examining Pulsit's head. Well above the old man's hairline, he found a large, dark bruise. Azongo folded his arms. "How long will it take? Should we wait?"

"No. It will take some time. You and your friends go back. I'll send him along when he is well."

Azongo shook his head. "How will he pay for the return trip?"

Shart's black eyes bugged. "By the spirits!" He turned toward Azongo. "By then he will be well enough to negotiate his own loan!"

The wild man nodded and held out his hand. "Here."

"What's that?"

"Your coppers."

Shart held out his hand, took the coppers and watched while the wild man climbed back up into the cart, picked up a plank, and swatted the lizard. "On to Mbwebwe!"

The lizard lifted an eyebrow, checked the sack to make sure it was empty, then tossed it aside and began moving the cart around. As the cart pulled out of sight, Shart threw the twenty-three coppers into the grass, then led the old man into the corridor.

Pulsit awakened and found himself in a small room containing only a cot and a small table cluttered with medical-looking things. Images of pirates, cannibals, and dragons flashed through his mind, but he could distinguish them from the world of fact. He assigned the images to his story mill, sighed at his new feeling of well-being, then swung his legs to the floor and sat up.

"Ah! I see you are awake."

Pulsit's eyes widened as he looked around at the empty room. *The ghost of Harvey Marpole leered at the new victim, seated helpless, alone—trapped. Cold, rotting, unseen hands reached for William's throat. Fingers of ice closed around vessels of pulsing blood, stemming their flow. They pressed against the path that air must take to feed William's lungs—ending it . . .*

Pulsit jumped as the door opened and Doctor Shart entered. "It is good that you are better. Come, we have much work to do."

Pulsit frowned. "Eh?"

Shart pushed seven-fingered hands into the pockets of his lab coat and looked down his pointed nose at the Moman. "It is my fee for making you well. You are to work for me."

"Work for you? I agreed to this?"

"Yes."

The storyteller frowned, then nodded. "Well, if I agreed." He looked up at the Vorilian. "What kind of work is it?"

Shart pulled a hand from his pocket and motioned toward the door. "Come."

After being brought to the laboratory, Pulsit was introduced to his tasks, which consisted of operating the automatic glassware cleanser, changing and cleaning the complex's air filters, monitoring the vector-escape alarm system, laundry, and assorted tasks from filing to emptying the trash. Pulsit observed, listened, then nodded at the Vorilian. "Doctor, I can see that you are a great scientist with many important responsibilities. How is it that you have no assistants to perform these insignificant tasks?"

Shart shook his head, then nodded. "Even a Moman can understand, where the Warlords do not." The Vorilian sighed. "You must understand, Pulsit, that no one is more loyal to the Warlords of the Tenth Quadrant than I. But . . ." Shart shrugged, then held out his hands to indicate his laboratory. "This is the work of a lifetime—a lifetime of too little appreciated struggle and privation." The Vorilian walked to a rack of clear tubes that towered from the floor to the overhead. The tubes were coiled with dark wires and were filled with a pink, cloudy vapor. "Do you know what this is?"

Pulsit walked to the rack, stopped next to it, and shook his head. "I know not, Doctor."

Shart placed a hand on one of the braces supporting the tubes, and caressed it as he answered. "This . . . this is the work of thirty years—much of it financed out of my own meager resources. No one had my insight—my *vision!* As only a mere student at the Vorilian Academy of Total Warfare, I formed the theories that made all this possible." Shart made two fists and shook them. "But it took all these years to acquire for my effort the limited attention I now have. This station and myself for an assistant!"

Pulsit frowned and nodded. "Excellent."

Shart raised his brows. "Excellent?"

"I mean, your life—its circumstances—make excellent material for a storyteller."

"A what?"

Pulsit bowed. "I am Pulsit of the Sina storytellers." The old man stood up and rubbed his bearded chin. "I also do biographies." The storyteller held out a hand toward the rack. "What is this? To do your life and play it before the crowds on Momus, I should be familiar with your work."

Shart smiled, exposing his triple rows of pointed teeth. "My life?"

"Certainly. The lives of great heroes are very popular. Your struggle, your achievement—these are the things of heroics."

Shart looked at the rack, then placed a hand on his cheek. "That's true, old Moman. A hero. Yes, that *is* true!" The Vorilian held out his hands toward the rack. "This is my work—a virus, each one for the infection of a different life form." Shart rubbed his hands together. "Once a life form is infected I can control it—make it do what I want, or go anywhere I choose. And, once a life form is infected, it will spread the virus among others of its kind. By directing the movements of just a few infected creatures, in time I will be able to control all the life forms on this planet—with the exception of the humans."

Pulsit raised his brows. "Quite an accomplishment! Indeed, yes. Quite an accomplishment. But, what could you do with such a power?"

Shart held out his hands. "If one controls the animal life on a planet, one controls the planet. Plagues can be directed to any part of the globe's surface, ecological balances disrupted, causing crop failures, great masses of predatory creatures can be used as an army to lay waste vast populations—Just think of the weapon it would make!"

Pulsit nodded. "It would have even more uses of a peaceful nature, Doctor."

Shart shrugged. "Yes, I suppose so, but the Warlords are interested in my work only as a weapon. Still, its success as a weapon will make my name. Then, perhaps, it can be incorporated into plans of a peaceful nature."

Pulsit held out his hands. "Doctor, as important and impressive as this work is, why do you not have at least one assistant?"

"Hah! The Warlords have no idea of the complications. This is why my work does not include the control of humans—the complications are too vast to untangle by myself. Each strain of the virus must be suited to each life form, which is difficult even for the simple creatures. My experiments take time, and the Warlords want results now." Shart shook his head. "They are skeptical of my work, and plan to cut off my funds if I can't show them . . . well, you understand."

Pulsit nodded. "Doctor Shart, I would like to tell the story of your life to the people along the roadside fires. To do this, I must know all about you."

Shart rubbed his hands together. "No one knows more than I that my story needs telling, Pulsit, but there is so much to do, and the Warlords—"

"Tut, tut, Doctor. These few tasks I am to do to work off my debt will not take up all of my time. I can work on your biography in my spare time."

Shart nodded, then grinned. "I have kept a daily journal

since the Academy, and I have my old yearbooks—would they be of any assistance?"

Pulsit clapped his hands together. "Wonderful! Do you have them here?"

"Yes. One moment, and I'll get them." Shart turned and all but ran from the laboratory.

Pulsit walked once around the lab, his mind trying out bits and snatches of narrative. *Almost from his first day, the young Shart knew he was destined for greatness. What the brilliant Vorilian scientist did not know was how he would have to fight, claw, and struggle to achieve his due . . .* Pulsit nodded as he decided that the bio would find many willing listeners at the fires. "It will definitely play."

Pulsit stopped before a bank of dials, readouts, meters, and switches. The console had a swept panel that enabled an operator seated before it to reach and see all the controls easily. Mounted above the console was a large screen. "Hmmm." Pulsit stepped before the chair and lowered himself to the seat. *Captain Nova seated himself before the ship's controls, set his square-cut jaw, then placed a thick-knuckled hand on the override switches to the ship's reactors. He waited until the enemy formation swung, presenting its side to his ship, then he jammed the switches, throwing power to his engines. "Now, you'll see this possum come to life!" His hand flew among the controls, turning dials, flicking switches, forcing the ship to seek and destroy the enemy ships. Smoke filled the cockpit, and Captain Nova saw, almost too late, the enemy ship that had opened fire on him. Flicking another row of switches, Nova launched a salvo of torpedoes at the enemy, held his breath, then laughed as the rogue ship vaporized . . .*

"Wha . . . what are you doing?"

Pulsit turned to see Shart standing in a doorway with his arms loaded with books. The Vorilian was looking around at the laboratory, which Pulsit noticed was filled with a grey-yellow haze of smoke. The storyteller turned back to the console, then removed his fingers from it as though they had been burned. "I apologize, Doctor. I must have been carried away with a new kind of story I was thinking—"

Shart dropped the journals and yearbooks with a crash. "You . . . you tripped the vector purge!" He walked to the rack of tubes. The vapor inside was no longer pink; it was now grey. Shart shook his head, placed a hand on the rack brace, then leaned his weight against it. "The work of thirty years . . . gone. All gone."

Pulsit stood, walked over to the rack and placed a gentle hand upon Shart's shoulder. "I am very sorry, Doctor. Had I the coppers, I would lay a handsome apology in your hand."

"Gone. All gone."

"But, Doctor—" Pulsit rubbed his hands together, then-slapped Shart's back. "Just think how this will help your biography."

Shart looked at Pulsit, a dazed expression on his face. "Help?"

"Indeed!" Pulsit held out his hands. "So close to success, only to have victory snatched from you. The determined scientist, however, is not defeated. He gathers himself together and begins again the task." Pulsit patted the Vorilian on the back. "It does much to strengthen the hero's character, don't you think?"

Shart pushed himself away from the rack, stared at Pulsit with ever-widening eyes, then began patting his pockets. "My gun! Where is it? Where's my gun?"

Pulsit looked around the laboratory. "I don't know, Doctor. Where did you have it last?" The storyteller turned and began looking in the vicinity of the swept control console. "When we have a spare moment, Doctor, I have a new kind of story I'd like to discuss with you. As a scientist, your opinion would be very useful." Pulsit took a last look, shrugged, then turned around. "I don't see your gun over here, Doc—" The old man saw Shart, gun in hand, taking aim between the storyteller's eyes.

"All gone. All my work—*gone*!"

Pulsit held up his hands. "Now, Doctor . . ."

Shart fired, but anger shook the hand that held the gun, causing the weapon to ignite the magnesium front panel on the control console. The thick white smoke, intense heat, and blinding light—more than the gun—caused Pulsit to pull up his robe and head for the nearest door. "I'll *kill* you, you old maniac!"

Pulsed beams deflected off the walls and deck as the old storyteller sped through the door, then closed it behind him. Pulsit leaned against the door, took several deep breaths, then noticed that he was in one of the animal compounds. Through the door, he heard Shart crashing in his direction.

The old man pushed himself away from the door, then ran for the fence. Squawks, hisses and growls assaulted his hearing as feathered, furred and scaled creatures ran to get out of his way. The fence around the compound was double his own height, and he knew he could never climb it. He heard a snoring, looked in the direction of the sound, and saw one of the great lizards of Arcadia sleeping next to the fence. He ran over to it, stopped and kicked the huge lizard in the shoulder. "Wake up!"

The lizard opened one slitted eye and observed the human. "Uf?"

More squawks and growls told Pulsit that Shart was close on his heels. "Quick. Lift me over the fence."

The lizard sat up. "'Ow much?"

"Two sacks of roots, and another of tung berry cakes."

The lizard smiled and held out his palm. "Payup."

Pulsit looked around the lizard's shoulder and saw Shart dashing around the compound, weapon in hand. He pointed at the Vorilian. "He'll pay for both of us."

The lizard nodded, grabbed Pulsit by the back of his robe, and hoisted him over the fence. The storyteller's feet were running before they touched the ground.

The lizard turned and looked back into the compound at Shart. "Doc'or." Shart looked at the lizard, then looked to where the reptile was pointing. Through the fence he could see Pulsit running down the road. He turned to head toward a gate, but stopped short as a great green foot grabbed his shoulder.

"Wawk! What are you doing? Let me go!"

The lizard shook its head. "You payup. Two sack roots, sack tungarry cake."

Pulsit came to a turn in the road, slowed, then stopped. "This . . . too much . . . old man." He saw a rock, sat down and took several deep breaths. When his vision cleared, Pulsit looked back toward the station. The lizard had Shart by both ankles and was shaking the Vorilian. He could barely make out the lizard demanding "You payup! Payup!"

The storyteller nodded. "As well he should, too!" Still puffing, Pulsit pushed himself to his feet and began the long trek back to Mbwebwe.

Four days later, Pulsit sat at Azongo's table, waiting for his companions' reaction to his tale. Raster shook his head.

"The doctor doesn't seemed to have helped much."

Azongo nodded. "Pulsit, I don't know if you'll ever chase the devils from your mind."

Pulsit frowned, then held up his hands. "Wait! I am not seeing things—"

"Oh!" Raster smiled, then laughed. "Then, it was a fine story, Pulsit. A fine story."

Azongo nodded. "It is good that you are well." The wild man shrugged. "But, as a story . . ." He shook his head.

Pulsit turned toward Durki. "What do you think?"

Durki grimaced, then shook his head. "It was a terrible story, Pulsit. Just terrible!"

The old storyteller's eyebrows went up a notch. "And, just what is so terrible about it?"

The apprentice shook his head. "Such a tale; it's awful. First, its too . . . technical—all those knobs, tubes, coils, and such. Then, a being from another planet! That's story fare for the likes of Raster."

Pulsit frowned. "Doctor Shart *is* from another planet!"

Durki shook his head. "Which still doesn't make it a story worth telling." Durki clasped his hands together and spoke as though he were the master lecturing a none-too-bright apprentice. "The people only want to hear the classic tales: the circus, fights between white and black magic, great fortune tellers solving mysteries. This kind of stuff—this technical fantasy story—will never be popular."

Pulsit rubbed his chin, then shrugged. "Nevertheless, Durki, this is the story I shall tell when we get back to the fires."

Durki looked down. "Then, that decides me, Pulsit."

"In what?"

"My screaming and growling are coming along so well that Raster and Azongo have asked me to join their act. Azongo will be the wild man, Raster the hero, and I shall be the victim."

Pulsit thought a moment, then nodded. "I suppose you are all ready to head back to Sina."

Durki shrugged. "I have had enough adventure, and we are anxious to take our act on the road. Will you devise a story for our act?"

Pulsit nodded. "Certainly."

"How much?"

Pulsit stood, walked to the door, and turned back. "We

can discuss that later. I would be alone for a while."

Raster stood. "Pulsit?"

"Yes?"

"I thought it was a fine story."

Pulsit nodded. "Thank you."

"Even though you had no pretty girls in it. Perhaps, next time, you could add one or two?"

"Perhaps." The old storyteller lifted the door curtain and left.

It is, of course, well-known that the new act of Azongo, Raster and Durki became an overnight success in Tarzak, where it first played the Great Square, and was then commissioned to play the Great Ring as part of the circus there.

Less known is the old storyteller who brought a new kind of tale to the fires along the road from Kuumic to Tarzak. He spoke his tales of space, strange beings and high adventure, and all listened in wonder. Few appreciated his tales at the beginning, but soon a following began to grow—small, but enough to keep the old fellow in coppers. It is said that he told his stories as though he actually lived them, but little heed should be paid to such things, for that is only part of the storyteller's art. And, Pulsit of the Sina storytellers was an artist.

Priest Of The Baraboo

ARNHEIM & BOON'S CIRCUS
For Over 3 (Standard) Centuries
The Longest Continuing Performing Circus In The Galaxy
—NOW ON PYROEL—
with
THE GREATEST 116 MULTI-SPECIES ACTS IN THE UNIVERSE
and
THE BIGGEST MIDWAY ANYWHERE

★ ★ ★ ★

DO NOT BE CONFUSED! Arnheim & Boon's Circus is the first and oldest Show of Shows, not to be confused with the poor imitation from Momus, Allenby's Greater Shows, which has never seen an off-Momus performance...

"Bah!" Bunsome crumpled up the rat sheet distributed by the quick agents of the competing circus, dropped it on the dusty soil of the planet Pyroel and kicked it into the road where it was soon flattened by the heavy canvas-laden sledges pulled by the lizards. The great reptiles of Momus, their lovely green scales hidden under layers of grey dust, puffed and strained against handmade harnesses, while handlers and roustabouts pushed the sledges or pulled with the lizards. A handler pointed toward his lizard's destination, and the lizard stopped and muttered an obscenity at the handler, who shouted more obscenities back at the huge beast.

The scene reflected too well his own mood, and Bunsome turned his back, pulled up his robe, stitched with the black and white diamonds of the priests, and sat cross-legged on a crate. A few squat Pyroelian nestlings, bored watching the lizard and the human argue, waddled off to where other humans and lizards pushed and pulled the huge timbers that would support the big top. Bunsome shook his head, then let it drop into his palms, his elbows resting on his knees.

As the junior Moman priest on the *City of Baraboo II,* he had been assigned to collect information on the competing circus, and that he had done.

While Allenby's Greater Shows used lizard power and human muscle to move canvas, timbers and heavy equipment, Arnheim & Boon was fully mechanized, with quiet, powerful tractors and cranes to use against the heavy Pyroelian gravity. Instead of hectares of painfully hand-woven, hand-stitched canvas, Arnheim & Boon sported a huge, light fabric dome inflated by compressed air that, because it was clear as glass, needed little additional lighting at night, and none in the daytime. While Allenby's lizards and humans vented their frustrations on each other, Arnheim & Boon's company was finished setting up and was preparing for its great free parade through Cukyu, Pyroel's principle population center.

There is more, thought Bunsome, always more. Even though the *Baraboo* has spun to provide increased gravity the entire three weeks from Momus to allow the performers to adjust their acts, few of them seemed confident about working at the heavier weights. The Arnheim & Boon unit on Pyroel, only one of twenty-four such companies, did nothing but play the heavier gravities, and even had a number of Pyroelians in its acts. Pyroel had been picked because it was the closest planet to Momus that could be booked, and Allenby's Greater Shows couldn't afford to fuel the *Baraboo* any further. Who could have known that Arnheim & Boon would be there?

"Hey you!" Bunsome turned toward the voice and saw a figure standing in the hatch of the *Baraboo*'s decrepit cargo van. "You waiting to go back to the ship?"

Bunsome nodded. "Yes."

The figure waved. "Let's go, then. We're empty as Allenby's purse."

The priest climbed down from the crate and shuffled through the dust, recalling the five brightly painted shuttles that put Arnheim & Boon's Circus on the surface. With no shuttles in working condition, the *Baraboo* itself had put down outside of Cukyu using up the remainder of its fuel in the landing. The artwork on the ship had burned off in the atmosphere, leaving the *Baraboo* black and mottled. As he stepped up and entered the hatch, Bunsome bumped into a Montagne wearing the roustabout's black-and-tan robes.

"Why don't you watch where you're going?"

Bunsome reached into his purse and dropped five copper beads into the roustabout's hand. "My apologies."

The roustabout pocketed the coppers and pointed with his thumb at the seats along the side bulkhead, then returned to his task of securing the van's cargo straps. When he was finished, he moved to the front and joined the Arvanian driver.

Bunsome strapped himself into the unpadded seat and wished he was back on Momus. If the original *City Of Baraboo* hadn't stranded its company on Momus two centuries ago, thought Bunsome, bless my coppers if we wouldn't show Arnheim & Boon a show. But, the necessities of survival on an uninhabited planet and two centuries without an audience had taken a toll.

The van lurched, banging Bunsome's head against the bulkhead. As the cargo compartment filled with fine, choking dust, the priest glared at the earless Arvanian driver, prepared to demand coppers for the poor ride. Bunsome saw the Montagne staring indifferently through a side port, seemingly unbothered by the dust, noise and bouncing. The priest shrugged and turned his growing hostility on his own occupation.

"Priests," he muttered. "What good are we, except to collect our facts and write our little histories?" Bunsome recalled the Dovinite missionary he had met on Pyroel. "Now, *that* was a priest!" He remembered the clean lines of the altar and the gleaming gold and purple of the windows. But, most of all, the Dovinites had gods to worship, that would do things for them if they asked properly. But the gods would not hire out to a circus; Bunsome had asked the missionary. It seemed that the Dovinites had an exclusive contract, and the contract was not up for sale. Whether it was a case of too little or too much business sense on the part of the Dovinites, Bunsome wasn't sure. He dozed, wishing he had followed his original hunch years before and had apprenticed as a mason or carpenter. Priesting was an easy life, and he liked the books, but there was no money in it, nothing else of importance either.

The priest came fully awake as the van lurched to a halt. He turned and looked through the dust-covered side port behind his head. The ugly, patched hulk of the *Baraboo*, it's superstructure, vanes and fins sagging against the gravity, looked back. Bunsome snorted. Threads of his dream, of the Dovinite minister's service, still ran through his mind—the congregation uplifted by the Dovinite's story, and by the promises the Dovinite had made. Bunsome sighed, turned from the port and released his straps.

As he stepped down from the hatch and walked around the van, Bunsome saw the next load of lizard-drawn equipment waiting to pile on the vehicle. Against the open door to the *Baraboo*'s cargo bay stood Nusset, the apprentice to the ship's senior priest, Shelem. Nusset picked his teeth with a fingernail and watched Bunsome approach through half-closed eyes. The apprentice priest wagged a finger at Bunsome. "You'd best get cleaned up. Shelem wants to see you."

Bunsome reached into his purse. "What about, Nusset?" The apprentice shrugged and turned into the ship's bay door, leaving Bunsome with his coppers.

Nusset looked over his shoulder. "Will you recite your notes for me to copy right away?"

"No. I shall have to see what Shelem wants of me first."

"I'll be at level six, then, watching the flyers practice, if they'll let me."

Bunsome nodded. "I'll be in the scriptorium."

Nusset laughed. "Where else?" The apprentice turned off the main corridor leaving Bunsome to himself.

Bunsome walked quickly, his nose wrinkling at the lizard stench. *If we do manage to get some customers into the big top, despite Arnheim & Boon, the smell will probably drive them out again!* He shrugged, remembering it was mostly the closeness of the ship. On Pyroel's surface, the lizards would be able to wash themselves. *A chip of consolation,* Bunsome snorted to himself, *floating in a sea of disaster.*

As his path took him deeper into the bowels of the *Baraboo*, others passed him in the corridor, or stood in small groups—clowns, freaks, magicians, roustabouts—either arguing or talking sadly in low voices. Even the usually emotionless Arvanians in the company were shouting and fist-shaking. Bunsome shook his head, sighed, and turned right into a narrow corridor.

As he approached the door of the scriptorium, at the end of the dimly lit, deserted corridor, Bunsome hesitated as he recognized Allenby decked in gold cape and black slouch hat, pacing in front of the door. Allenby looked up at the sound of Bunsome's footsteps.

"Ah! I hoped you would be back soon."

Bunsome halted in front of Allenby and nodded. "What may I do for the Great Allenby?" He held out his hand and Allenby dropped several copper movills into it.

"Arnheim & Boon—are they ready for their parade?"

"Yes." Bunsome couldn't meet Allenby's eyes. "They will march before the sun sets."

"What do they have for great beasts, Bunsome?"

The priest pulled at his lip, then dropped his hand. "Nine acts, Great Allenby, from as many planets—"

"Do they have elephants?"

Bunsome nodded. "Twenty. They're magnificent animals. Before, I had only seen pictures—"

"Yes, yes." Allenby waved his hand for silence, his pale blue eyes staring into an ocean of poor options for the unknown thing that would save the *Baraboo*'s bacon.

"Great Allenby, at least we have the lizards. Arnheim & Boon has nothing like our lizards," Bunsome tried to encourage.

"Humph!" Allenby shook his head. "Stoop, the head lizard, only this morning demanded more pay for the reptiles." Allenby waved his hand, then dropped it. "Because of the gravity. I thought we could beat the gravity. I must be seven kinds of a fool! At least you don't have to pay elephants." Allenby looked into Bunsome's eyes. "What of their clowns, magicians?"

"I saw none of their acts, but surely ours are the best, Great Allenby."

Allenby shook his head. "Perhaps. I would feel better had we not left our best on Momus."

"They are too old, Great Allenby, too old to make the trip."

"Shelem made the voyage."

Bunsome shrugged and held out his hands. "A priest doesn't have to perform, and, besides, Shelem hasn't been feeling well."

Allenby frowned. "Is it anything serious?"

Bunsome dropped his hands to his sides. "I'm no physician, but it's probably nothing more than age."

"Age." Allenby repeated, then looked at the corridor deck. "I understand age to be a terminal affliction." Bunsome shrugged and nodded. "I wish him well, Bunsome.

I may need his services before long." Allenby nodded, then walked around Bunsome, heading with deliberate steps toward the main corridor. Bunsome turned to the scriptorium door and opened it, exposing the manuscript-piled interior. The built-in metal desk, Shelem's customary working place, was unoccupied.

Bunsome entered and closed the door, grateful that the smells of ink, leather and aged paper drowned the unwashed lizard smell that creeped throughout the ship. The compartment was empty, and Bunsome poked around, waiting for Shelem. On the large copy table in the center of the room, he noticed that Nusset had fallen behind copying Shelem's latest manuscript, which would never do. Many priests back on Momus would want copies—Bunsome laughed to himself. *If we ever get back to Momus. The last of our fuel was used to put the company planetside without enough to spare to relocate elsewhere on Pyroel, away from Arnheim & Boon.* Allenby's had been at it two days, setting up, with the raising of the big top still to be done. Seeing the weak competition, Arnheim & Boon put down their show in the same city eight hours before, and they were ready to parade.

Bunsome turned his eyes toward the volume-crammed shelves, and ran his fingers along the glossy leather bindings until he came to *One: The Book Of Baraboo*. Half the book was filled with tales and reminiscences of ancient Earth, before the circus began to cross the void, but the second half told of the voyages of the *City Of Baraboo*, and O'Hara's Greatest Shows, the finest collection of artists and games in the entire Ninth Quadrant. *The old company*, thought Bunsome, *now, that would have been something to see*. The old *Baraboo* would begin its parade four hours after achieving orbit, with combination function ship's compartments detaching and acting as their own shuttles.

Bunsome shook his head, thinking of the salvaged Arvanian battle cruiser that served as the *Baraboo II* with only two of its original twenty combat landing shuttles remaining, and both of those broken down on Pyroel with no hope of repair without money for parts. He let his fingers slide down the binding, then drop to his side.

"SCRIPTORIUM."

"Aaaahhh!" Bunsome clamped a hand over his racing heart, and quickly looked around the compartment, relaxing only when he saw the intercom set in the bulkhead above Shelem's desk. *I never will get used to that.*

"SCRIPTORIUM, THIS IS THE SICK BAY."

Bunsome went to the desk and touched the call button. "Yes?"

"BUNSOME?"

"Yes."

"THIS IS DOCTOR VOR. CAN YOU COME DOWN TO THE SICK BAY?"

Bunsome disliked the Arvanian physician. He disliked all Arvanians as a rule, but disliked Vor in particular. "What's the problem, Vor. I'm very busy."

"SHELEM IS DEAD. I HAVE ALREADY NOTIFIED ALLENBY. SHELEM LEFT A MESSAGE FOR YOU."

Bunsome lowered himself to Shelem's chair. "I'll be down . . . I'll be down as soon as I can."

"PLEASE ACCEPT MY CONDOLENCES."

Bunsome was nodding as the intercom clicked off.

Returning from the sick bay, Bunsome stopped at the wardroom as he had been instructed by the barker sent by Allenby. As he entered, Bunsome looked at Allenby seated behind a large bowl of sapwine, rubbing his eyes. Allenby looked up and dropped some coppers on the table. "Here, Bunsome. We haven't much time." Allenby pointed at a couch to his left at the table. Bunsome pocketed the coppers and sat. "Are you well, Bunsome? You look terrible."

Bunsome nodded. "It's only this on top of everything else . . ." He weakly waved a hand, then dropped it in his lap.

Allenby sighed, and both sat for a moment in silence. "Bunsome, I need your help."

"Of course; whatever I can do, Great Allenby."

Allenby nodded, his jaw set, his eyes unblinking. "I don't suppose it's any secret that the show is in trouble."

"Someone in the universe might not know, although I doubt it, Great Allenby."

Allenby drank from his bowl, then placed it on the table. He pointed at the bowl. "Care for some?"

"Please."

Allenby reached behind his couch to a shelf and picked up a bowl and a fresh jug of sapwine. As he poured, he continued. "The only secret left, Bunsome, is just how much trouble we're really in." He plugged the jug and pushed Bunsome the bowl. The priest dropped some coppers on the table and picked up the bowl. "Before we left Momus, even before we formed the company, the fortune tellers saw this coming. If something cannot be done, I doubt that we will even be able to open, or, if we do open, it will be a complete farce."

"What is it?"

Allenby leaned forward and rubbed beneath his nose with the thumb-side of his hand. "The performers—they are afraid to go on—"

Bunsome let out an involuntary burst of laughter. "My apologies, Great Allenby," he tossed two movills on the table. "Please excuse me, but nothing could be harder for me to imagine. They are all master performers, with many years in ring and midway behind them. Afraid?"

"It's true, all the same. How many practices have you seen?"

Bunsome sipped from his bowl, then shrugged. "Quite a few soon after we left Momus, but none for more than a week. Even the clowns stopped letting spectators watch, even if they paid."

"You see? Does your imagination stretch to the point of that? Clowns refusing to perform for coppers?"

Bunsome nodded. "I see what you mean. It happened so gradually, I never suspected . . . but why? They are no less the performers they were on Momus."

Allenby rubbed his chin, then leaned back on his couch, bowl in hand. "This ship, Pyroel, both are strange grounds. The Pyroelians are a strange audience, and now, with Arnheim & Boon as competition . . . Doctor Vor treated Rulyum the juggler today for a broken toe. Rulyum dropped his clubs during a practice."

"Rulyum!?" Bunsome's mouth hung open. "Not Rulyum!"

"Are you beginning to understand, now?"

"Yes." Bunsome shook his head. "Yes and no. Why are we plagued in this manner? Can't something go right for us?"

"We knew we were taking a big chance putting the show on the road so soon, but we had to go when we could get the coppers. If we had waited any longer, the backers would have begun withdrawing their funds." Allenby shrugged.

"It was go when we did, or not go at all."

Bunsome recalled his feelings after observing the Arnheim & Boon preparations. "That may have been the better choice—not going at all."

"It is academic; we are here, and here we stay unless we can put on enough of a show to meet our expenses." Allenby put his elbows on the table and clasped his hands. "I am convinced that this company can draw a paying crowd. What we lack in numbers and glitter we more than make up in skill and polish. I have our parade scheduled for the sixth post meridian hour this day—a full hour before Arnheim & Boon takes to the road."

"The big top isn't even up."

"Nevertheless. Right now every spare pair of hands and every reptile, including Stoop, is out there getting ready. I think the equipment will be ready on time, but this will do us little good unless the company hits the streets of Cukyu, not as a shambling, dispirited mob, but as a circus."

"Great Allenby, you asked me if I would help." Bunsome raised his eyebrows and shrugged. "But, what can I do? I am only a priest—a mere historian."

"Shelem worked with the fortune tellers before we left Momus. He had an answer."

"What was it?"

Allenby shook his head. "I was hoping he had told you."

"No."

"He discussed nothing about it with you?"

Bunsome shrugged. "He discussed nothing about anything with me starting from when we left Momus. He spent all his time buried in his manuscripts writing . . ." The priest reached into his robe and withdrew the slip of paper Doctor Vor had given him.

"What's that?"

"Vor copied it. He said it was Shelem's message to me." Bunsome unfolded the paper, then let loose a disappointed sigh. "It's nothing."

"What does it say?"

"Forty-seven: thirty-four. Read this."

"That's all? What do the numbers mean?"

"You must understand, Great Allenby, Shelem was very old, and his mind . . . well, this is a perfect example. It's obviously a book and chapter index number, but Shelem's histories for the Tarzak priests begin with book forty-one and end with forty-six. There is no book forty-seven."

"Bunsome, perhaps that was what he was writing."

"No doubt, but no priest could perform in recital material that has not been passed on by the rest of the Tarzak priesthood. Perhaps they do things that way in Ikona, but..."

"What period does that chapter cover?"

"I don't know. Young Nusset—Shelem's apprentice—would know. He's been copying the manuscript."

Allenby pressed a panel in the table top and called the scriptorium. Nusset answered. "This is Allenby, Nusset."

"YES, GREAT ALLENBY?"

"In Shelem's new book, what period is covered by chapter thirty-four?"

"ER, I'M NOT SURE. ONE MOMENT."

Allenby raised his eyebrows at Bunsome who only shrugged. "Apprentices aren't what they used to be."

"GREAT ALLENBY?"

"Yes, Nusset?"

"I HAVE IT. NOW, THIRTY-FOUR... HMMM. THAT CHAPTER COVERS THE WAR. IT SEEMS TO BE COMPLETE."

"Nusset, bring it to the wardroom." Allenby looked up to see Bunsome frowning. "What is it?"

The priest shook his head. "Shelem would have me read *that* to the ship's company? The blackest period in the history of Momus? If the company's frame of mind is as uncertain as you describe it, Great Allenby, that chapter should easily put them over the edge."

"Perhaps."

"Perhaps? I do know something of priesting."

Allenby nodded. "I meant no offense, Bunsome, but Shelem's office as senior priest of the *Baraboo* leads me to believe that he, too, knew something of his trade."

Bunsome blushed. "Of course. But where is the inspiration for this company in death, defeat and despair? Wouldn't a few passages from the older works—perhaps the voyages of the original *Baraboo*—wouldn't something such as that be better?"

"Perhaps." They waited a few moments in silence, then turned toward the wardroom door as Nusset entered holding a sheaf of papers. Allenby took them and handed the apprentice several coppers. before Nusset had left the room, Allenby was reading the papers, motionless save for his darting blue eyes. As he reached the end of a page, he would place it in back of the remaining sheets. Bunsome thought again of the Dovinite missionary as he watched Allenby giggle, then frown, then sniff back a tear as he nodded, turning to the next page. *I'm not too old,* thought Bunsome. *I could apprentice again as a mason. There are many similarities between priesting and newstelling—story-telling, too. If I ever get back to Momus.* He sighed and looked up to see Allenby, a strange look on his face, holding out the papers. After Bunsome took the chapter, Allenby stood and walked to the door, then stopped.

"Bunsome, you will address the company with that chapter at the fourth hour. Be ready." He turned and left.

The priest sat staring at the empty door for a few moments, then looked at the papers in his hand. Shelem's familiar scrawl covered the unlined sheets. Shaking his head, Bunsome began reading.

At the fourth hour, Bunsome stood on a packing crate in the *Baraboo*'s cargo hold with the assembled ship's company surrounding him. Humans, Arvanians and lizards—all in parade costume—stood silently, waiting for the priest to begin. Bunsome cleared his throat and began:

It was the two hundred and fourth year of the Baraboo *disaster, and the fifth year of Lord Allenby's office as Great Statesman of Momus. The protection of the Ninth Quadrant Federation of Habitable Planets, which Allenby once represented as ambassador, had been withdrawn under orders of the Ninth Quadrant's Council of Seven to strengthen the defenses near the center of population which had come under the scrutiny of the Tenth Quadrant's warlords. All that remained were a scattering of Montagne soldiers who had taken retirements or discharges on Momus, and the assurances of the United Quadrants that it would come to Momus's defense in the event the planet suffered an invasion.*

As Bunsome read Shelem's words, the months of struggle, pain and suffering melted until both priest and performers were carried back to that dark hour.

At the same time the last Ninth Quadrant ship abandoned the skies of Momus, Lord Allenby invited the great masters of the planet to meet. They gathered in Allenby's quarters in the ιown of Tarzak and met with representatives of the Montagne soldiers who had been left behind...

Lord Allenby, seated cross-legged behind his table, let his eyes drift over the gloomy faces in his quarters. "Any suggestions?" He stopped on the face of a young man dressed in roustabout's black-and-tan. "Painter? You're the senior Montagne left on the planet."

Standing behind those seated around Allenby's table, his back against the wall, the former infantry lieutenant shrugged. "If the intelligence projections General Kahn supplied you are accurate, the Tenth Quadrant will pile in mercenaries—Arvans probably—under some pretext that will give the United Quadrants a loophole through which the UQ can refuse intervention. When is the question, but we can count on it being soon."

Allenby rubbed his chin. "The size of the Arvanian force?"

"No more than a battalion. The UQ would have to notice anything larger. But—" Painter dropped his glance. "It should be enough to do the job. They'll be carrying sustained burst beamers for light weapons and probably pulse beamers and disruptors for their heavy weapons company. In addition, the Arvans are tough."

"What about our Montagnes? Aren't there around two hundred on Momus?"

Painter nodded. "About half of them are technical personnel—mechanics, medics, electrical and computer types—no more combat qualified than clowns..." Painter noticed Great Kamera, Master of the Tarzak clowns, raising an eyebrow in his direction. "No offense, Great Kamera." The lieutenant turned back to Allenby. "Subtract them, and the ones who are unfit because of age, we have, perhaps, a dozen combat soldiers equipped with nothing but their bare hands."

"And?"

"And, if this were a problem back at officer's school, I'd pick the better part of valor and I wouldn't be marked wrong."

"Impossible."

"I know."

"What's the alternative, then, Painter?"

"Guerrilla warfare. Avoid direct confrontations, hit-and-run, wear them down . . . make life on Momus Hell for the Arvans . . ." Painter looked down and shook his head.

"What is it? What were you about to say?"

Painter pursed his lips, then looked up. "To make it Hell for the Arvans, we will necessarily make it Hell for ourselves as well. A war such as that is a contest of spirits—guts. To increase the price of conquest to the Arvans, the people of Momus will have to pay a price. It might take years. They may wear us out first—"

"Hah!" Everyone in the room turned toward Dorum, strongman and Master of the Tarzak freaks. "Painter. You suggest that Momans lack spirit?" Others in the room nodded their approval.

Painter rubbed his eyes, then dropped his hand. "I have seen such a war before, Dorum. It was used against the Montagnes six years ago on Hessif as part of the rebellion. I saw my company commander blown to pieces by a small child wired as a walking bomb . . . she asked him for water." He stood away from the wall. "Do you have the spirit to wire yourself as a bomb, Dorum? Or, to wire your daughter or wife? That's what the Hessifs had for spirit, Dorum, and it wasn't enough. We cracked them. The Montagnes broke the rebellion."

Allenby looked at the lines deepening on the faces in the death-silent room. "Are there any other suggestions?" No one moved. "Very well, Painter, where do we begin?"

Oblivious to his battle cruiser, *Sword*, hurtling toward the planet Momus, Naavon Dor, commander of the Arvanian mercenaries, sat in his couch playing his stylus against the screen that covered one of the bulkheads to his quarters. With rapid, sure strokes, images of Arvan's bleak mountains and harsh winds bending the filmy vegetation appeared on the screen. Naavon's screen could have shown his drawing in motion, the grey clouds slipping beyond the mountains, the dia trees whipping back and forth, but he preferred to draw in still and achieve the same effect. In the foreground appeared the edge of a cliff, and upon the cliff appeared a whirl of lines and shades that soon became a likeness of himself—tall, smooth head held erect, night black eyes staring from under protruding brows at the distant mountains. Naavon hesitated a moment and observed the likeness. The figure wore the old style, high collar and crossed belts of the land mercenaries. Naavon frowned, then recognized the figure. *My father, why am I thinking of you now?*

"Naavon?" The field officer turned from the screen to the compartment hatch to see his second in command leaning half through the opening.

Naavon deenergized the screen, erasing the image, and tossed the stylus on the couch's armrest table. "What is it, Goss?"

"Fingers shuttled over from his command ship and wants to see you."

"By that racial slur, Goss, I assume you mean Admiral Sadiss."

"The same."

"It may interest you to know, Goss, that Sadiss, as a Vorilian, can no more help having fourteen fingers than we Arvanians can help having ten."

"Yes, Naavon." Goss, old soldier and the field officer's faithful friend, cast his eyes down in mock shame, the hint of mischief at the corners of his mouth. "I bet he can tickle up a storm, though."

Naavon shook his head. "What does our patron's agent want?"

Goss grinned. "He wishes to bring charges against one of the men."

The field officer raised his brows, then nodded. "Very well, Goss. Please show the admiral in."

Goss turned from the compartment and shouted over his shoulder. "You! In here!" Goss stepped into the compartment, took a seat facing Naavon and awaited the appearance of the Vorilian admiral.

Sadiss entered, and the Arvanian commander observed the squat humanoid, clad in black cape and suit, looking around the compartment for a place to sit. Naavon pointed to a stool. "It's the best I can offer, Admiral."

Sadiss glared at Goss's seated figure, then turned to Naavon. "I shall remain standing."

"As you wish." Goss lifted one booted foot, dropped its heel on the stool, then crossed it with his other boot. Naavon wondered if he should point out to the Vorilian that Goss acted the same with Arvanian officers. He shook his head and turned back to Sadiss. "And, your business, Admiral?"

"A soldier in your third company: "T'Dulna. I am bringing formal charges of treason against him."

Naavon nodded. "I see. What did he do?"

"Defeatism. He spoke disparagingly of our glorious mission."

"Hmmm. That is serious. What did he say?"

"He called our mission of liberation an invasion, and he implied that it was an act of cowardice to bring modern armed force against what he called 'an innocent society of clowns and jugglers.'"

Naavon nodded. "And you heard T'Dulna say this?"

Sadiss turned to the open door and waved his arm. "Emis, Yust, in here!" Two Arvanian soldiers entered the compartment and stood at attention next to the admiral. "These two heard him and reported his treason to me."

Naavon leaned back in his couch and clasped his fingers over his belly. "I see." The field officer studied soldier Emis, then soldier Yust. Nodding, he turned to Goss. "Have these two mustered out of the unit and get them off my ship. If the Admiral won't take them on his ship, throw them outside and let them walk."

Goss stood and rubbed his hands together. "Yes Naavon, my pleasure." Goss walked between the soldiers, grabbing each by the arm, and dragged them backwards out of the compartment. The one called Emis looked pleadingly at Sadiss before he left the room.

Sadiss fixed his eyes on Naavon. "What is the meaning of this, field officer?"

"The invasion of Momus is an act of cowardice, Sadiss, and speaking truth is not treason on my ship."

"It exhibits a lack of loyalty to the Tenth Quadrant!"

"True." Naavon nodded. "Very true. But, neither is that a crime on my ship. The men of this battalion owe their loyalty to me and to each other. No other loyalty is required, which is why you can have your two spies back. I won't have them causing mistrust in the ranks."

"What am I supposed to do with them?"

"Add them to that collection of criminals you call the Moman Liberation Army."

"Criminals? Field officer Dor, they are representatives of the oppressed peoples of Momus who have requested the aid of the Tenth Quadrant to overthrow—"

"Be still, Sadiss! Feed your fiction to the United Quadrants, and not to me. Your liberation army is nothing more than murderers, thieves and cheats exiled from Moman society, and your excuse to land troops on Momus without interference from the UQ. That is right, isn't it?"

Goss entered the compartment and resumed his seat. "Naavon, I stuffed them into Sadiss's shuttle."

The field officer nodded, then turned back to the admiral. "I imagine that concludes our business, Sadiss."

"Not quite, Dor. Your soldiers are sworn to—"

"*My* soldiers are sworn to follow *my* orders. Your superiors hired me to secure Momus for the Tenth Quadrant, cash on delivery, which we will do—" Naavon grinned. "Unless we get a better offer. Meanwhile, we don't have to like what we are doing; be content that we are doing it. That will be all."

Sadiss turned his glare from Naavon to Goss, then back to Naavon. "This isn't the end, Dor. I am the appointed commander of this mission—"

"That *will* be all, Sadiss. Now, do you wish to have Goss escort you to your shuttle?"

Sadiss turned abruptly and marched from the compartment. Goss shook his head. "Naavon, he will make trouble for us. The warlords of the Tenth may listen to his prattle."

Naavon laughed. "Goss, old friend, you really don't see, do you?"

"See what?"

"Admiral Sadiss is an incurable romantic. I'm sure he thinks of himself as a liberator and our mission as one of liberation. The Tenth's warlords, however, are not at all the dreamy fellows Sadiss would like them to be."

Goss scratched his nose. "If I didn't see before, Naavon, I see even less now."

Naavon reached, picked up his stylus and energized his drawing screen. As he talked he stroked in a grotesque representation of Sadiss. "Goss, you must understand the philosophy behind the Tenth Quadrant. It's interesting, if you don't get in its way. They feel that the Vorilians are destined to rule the universe."

Goss shrugged. "Sadiss feels no differently."

"Ah, but there is a difference, Goss. The present warlords, and all the warlords before them, are serving an idea. Sadiss is serving himself. The warlords see the Vorilians as the eventual rulers of all that exists. Sadiss sees himself as *the* ruler. The warlords are content to push until resistance is met, then back off and wait, letting the next generation of warlords make the actual kill. It is a ruthlessly slow, plodding plan of conquest, not enough to upset the races that surround them, but enough to eventually succeed. Take our own little mission, for example. Here we are, an insignificant military force being sent to secure an insignificant planet for the Tenth—in scale with the universe, scraps of dust, too little to be concerned about. 'It is nothing to us,' say the quadrants, 'let the Tenth have it.' And the Tenth will take it, my friend, and add it to all the other scraps of dust it's gathered, because enough of those scraps of dust . . ."

"Make up the universe." Goss frowned, then raised his brows. "Sadiss?"

Naavon shrugged. "It is a plan that must take a thousand generations to work; Sadiss doesn't have the time. He serves his ego, while the warlords serve a destiny."

Goss pulled a small wooden flute from his blouse, put it to his lips and ran a few scales. "Where should we be in this, Naavon? If what you say is true, the warlords will level their sights on Arvan someday."

Naavon leaned back and pressed the animation program for the screen. "We will be long gone, by then." The field officer shrugged as the image of Sadiss jerked and stumbled on the screen. "Even though Arvan will be absorbed, think of the grandness of the plan, Goss. The ghosts of an army of warlords will be able to look back at what they have done."

Goss tweeted out a short comic phrase in time to the screen figure's stumble, then took the flute down and slapped it against his hand. "I wouldn't want to live under the Tenth."

"That's not the point, Goss." Naavon held out his hands. "You and I, Goss, what have we that will remain centuries from now? As soldiers, perhaps we have set certain events in motion, but they can be easily countered by other events. I draw my pictures and erase them and you play your excellent little tunes that disappear into the air. But, the warlords of the Tenth are changing the universe, whatever that change might be."

Goss put his flute to his lips, then lowered it a bit. "You approve?"

Naavon shrugged. "Compared to the event, what does the approval of a mere soldier amount to?"

"Nothing, I suppose. And that applies to Sadiss as well, which is why he can't make trouble for us?"

"Exactly. The warlords hired us to do a job. As long as we do that job, they will be satisfied."

Goss played another short phrase, then frowned. "Naavon, what if Sadiss could accomplish, in his lifetime, the plan of the warlords?"

Naavon turned from Goss and studied the screen. "If I thought he could accomplish the plan—or defeat it—I would serve him, I think, to be a part of it. I would like to be responsible for some kind of permanence, even if it's negative, but . . ." The field officer shrugged.

"But, Naavon, you'll settle for two meals a day and the company of eight hundred sorry soldiers."

Naavon laughed. "The ones who live long enough." He picked up his stylus, stopped the animation and flicked in more lines, aging the figure of Sadiss by eighty years. As he animated the figure, Goss trilled off into a halting, ragged melody, "The Last Of Us To Die."

Squatting at the edge of the forest north of Arcadia, Oswald Painter, former Montagne lieutenant, scanned the desert and sky and found them clear. *They will not always be so. Allenby has high hopes for his magicians and fortune tellers,* he thought, *that they will fuddle the Arvans and foresee their plans.* Painter snorted and stood. *They will need more than that.*

He turned into the forest and pushed his way through the thick underbrush until he came to a small clearing. There he stopped and eyed his rag-tag collection of roustabouts, freaks, clowns, tumblers . . . *and, at least, one knife-thrower. Perhaps he will be of some use.* Painter held up his hands. "All right, people, listen up." He motioned them into the center of the clearing. As they shambled in and formed a half-circle around him, Painter looked at their faces seeing boredom on one, excitement on another and mischief on still another. *Children playing soldier. Whatever it takes to make a guerrilla fighter, these people don't have.* "We have a lot of work to do and not much time—"

"Painter." A ragged fellow in black-and-scarlet held up his hand and Painter nodded. "Painter, I am Roos of the Anoki magicians."

"Yes?"

"There is still the matter of payment to be settled."

"Payment?" *Great Juju, what am I doing here?"*

"Of course. Our being here is of value to you, is it not?"

That is the question, isn't it? Painter shook his head. "This is different."

"Different? Different how?"

"We're here to learn how to defend your homes—your planet!"

Roos half closed his eyes and held up his head. "Is our being here of value to you?"

"Of course!"

Roos shrugged. "Then it is of value to us."

Shaking his head, Painter reached under his robe to find an empty purse. "it seems that I am a little short."

A woman in a white short robe held up her hand. "I am Fayda of the Sina cashiers. If I might advance the instructor a small loan?"

Painter looked at his charges, then smacked his right fist into his left hand. "You silly people are staring a bloodbath square in the face, and you're standing here trying to turn coppers on it!" *They are insane; absolutely yang-yang!* Painter let out his breath. "All right! How much?"

The recruits haggled among themselves for endless minutes, then a fellow in clown's orange stepped forward. "Two movills each."

The cashier from Sina counted the house, then reached within her robe and produced forty-four of the copper beads. As she handed them to Painter, she grinned. "There is, of course, the small matter of interest."

Painter took the coppers and glared at Fayda. "Of course! And, how much would that be?"

"Ten percent."

"Ten . . . that's robbery!"

Fayda shrugged and waved her hand at her companions. "You must admit the risk I take is considerable."

Painter nodded, then passed out the coppers. *She sees it, too. If an unlearned copper counter sees it, what am I doing here?* After dropping the last two coppers into the last outstretched hand, Painter resumed his place in the center of the half-circle, remembering exile to be the penalty for failing to pay debts within a reasonable length of time. He looked down, scratching the back of his neck. *A few more sessions like this and I'll be in hock up to my ears.*

He nodded once, then looked up. "Before we begin, there is the small matter of the payment for my services."

Roos looked at his companions, then back at Painter. "How much does the instructor charge?"

Painter folded his arms. "Three coppers apiece."

"Thief!" cried a freak from the back. "We only charged two!"

Painter shrugged. "A war is about to leap square in the middle of your chests, and you have no idea what to do about it. I do. Is this knowledge of value to you?"

As the recruits grumbled, Painter heard footsteps coming up from behind. He turned to see Allenby smiling and shaking his head.

"Lord Allenby."

"I see things are progressing well, Painter."

Painter snorted. "May I ask what brings you here?"

Allenby nodded. "I have come to congratulate you, Painter. By my appointment, you are now the official military commander of the Moman Armed Forces." Painter stared at the Great Statesman while several comments competed for expression. Allenby turned and spoke over his shoulder as he left. "War is Hell, Painter. War is Hell."

Painter turned back to face his charges. Roos, a black frown on his face, held out Painter's coppers and dropped them into his outstretched palm. "Do you want to count them?"

Painter nodded. "Of course." Painter counted out the forty-four coppers, plus interest, handed them to the cashier and pocketed the balance. Fayda, the cashier, bowed.

"The instructor may depend upon a lower rate of interest in the future from Fayda. I see he is a man of means."

Painter nodded as an image of himself leading the Moman Armed Forces against Arvanian mercenaries flashed through his mind. *I must remember to ask Allenby how much the job pays. I don't think it will be enough.*

Koolis, Master of the Great Ring of Tarzak, stood in the center of the darkened amphitheater, his gaze caressing the starlit cut-stone tiers. The circus, loaded into lizard- and horse-drawn wagons, had departed hours before. They had begged him to come, but Koolis remained behind. *My place is here, with the Ring. My obligations to the circus are met; the circus is safe.*

"Father?"

Koolis turned toward the spectator's entrance and squinted as a figure approached. "Lissa?"

"Yes, father." The slender young woman crossed the sawdust, stopped and lowered her pack. "You must leave. The invaders will be here soon."

Koolis turned his head away and crossed his arms. "We have nothing to discuss."

"You are angry with me still?"

Koolis snorted. "My daughter the soldier."

"I did not want to disobey you, Father."

"But you did all the same."

"We must fight—"

"Bah! We are keepers of the Ring, Lissa, not killers. And, if Momus would field an army, where is it? Why does it leave Tarzak to the enemy? Why does it not stand and fight?"

"Father, if we did face the Arvanians as an army, it would be all over for us. We must use different tactics."

"Skulking behind trees, slipping a knife into a back when no one is looking." Koolis spat on the ground. "Why are you here in Tarzak instead of hiding in the hills along with the rest of our brave soldiers?"

Lissa stooped over and lifted her pack, putting the strap over her shoulder. "I was sent to pick up the fireballs." She reached into the pack and held out an object the size of a small plum. "It is the magician's trick of intense fire. The case is made of raw cobit dough which forms two chambers inside. Each chamber contains a substance, and when the ball is crushed, the substances mix. You've seen the trick before and know how hot the fire is. These are special ones—three times larger than the ones the magicians use."

Koolis shook his head. "This is a fine day; magicians giving up their secrets—a fine day, indeed!"

Lissa placed the fireball into the pack, then turned and faced Koolis. "We are all giving up something, father—"

Koolis placed a hand over Lissa's mouth. "Hush!" he whispered. "Quick, to the north entrance!"

They ran quietly across the sawdust, stopping as they came to the opening in the tiers. As torch light flickered from the spectator's entrance, they flattened themselves against the entrance wall. Peering around the edge, Koolis began recognizing faces as they entered the Ring. Kardik the murderer, judged and exiled by the town of Tarzak, laughed and slapped another on the back. His companion, Haroman the arsonist, held up his torch and waved it over his head.

This Ring was my father's, and his father's before him.

Mysor—thief, murderer and gang chieftain—walking next to a squat, black-clad Vorilian, laughed and jabbed the alien in the arm. The alien smiled.

This Ring has seen the finest art of Momus.

A squad of the earless Arvanian mercenaries, armed with rifles, were followed by a drunken gang of exiles, the blue marks of their judgments still on their foreheads.

In this Ring were born our two great laws.

Dazzul, thief.

Jokosin, thief and murderer.

Vaserat, murderer, and many more unfamiliar to Koolis, but all bearing the blue marks of judgment.

"Hail, Mysor! Hail, Mysor!"

In the center of the Ring, Mysor held up his hands for silence. The gang of cutthroats quieted. "Who would the Great Ring have for its king?"

"Mysor!" shouted the small crowd. "Great Mysor, King of Momus!"

Koolis turned and saw the horror in Lissa's eyes. "Lissa, you must tell Allenby."

"Come with me, father."

Koolis looked down into Lissa's face and kissed her on the forehead. "I must stay. You see what they do to my Ring?" Lissa closed her eyes and nodded. "Go, then, but leave me a handful of those doughballs." Koolis reached into Lissa's pack and filled the pocket of his robe with magician's fire. Looking up, he saw Lissa crying. "Have strength, little soldier. There will be many such moments before Momus is free of the invaders. Now, go!" The girl turned and ran quickly through the tunnel, out into the dark dusty street. When she stopped and looked back, her father was gone from the entrance.

The Arvanian squad leader climbed the low hill overlooking the road to Tieras, signaled his identification, then dropped into a hole occupied by three other mercenaries, two of them still alive. "All quiet, Ias?"

The Arvanian squatting before the portable sensor looked

up and nodded. "For more than two hours, squad leader. Think they'll hit us again?" The night air was still.

"No. But keep a sharp eye." He cocked his head toward the dead mercenary. "How did T'Dulna get it?"

The soldier peering over the edge of the hole pulled something from his belt and held it back toward the squad leader. It was a guardless, thin-bladed knife. As the squad leader took the blade, the soldier nodded toward a tree next to the road. "That one down there, next to the tree. He threw it." The crumpled figure lay motionless.

"Threw it? That must be fifty paces, and an uphill throw."

"I make it closer to sixty paces."

The squad leader let out a low whistle. "You two hear about what went on in Tarzak?"

"What?"

"You know that Moman, Mysor?"

The soldier standing at the rim turned his head and spat. "What of him?"

"Fingers and his liberation army were staging a little ceremony to crown Mysor King of Momus when a local patriot took the opportunity to throw some kind of firebombs all over the place."

The soldier laughed. "This is the truth?"

"I swear it."

"Fingers and Mysor?"

The squad leader shrugged. "A little scorched, but still alive."

The soldier turned back to watching the area in front of his position. "Too bad. What of the bomb thrower?"

"No one will ever find the pieces." He climbed to the rim. "Keep alert, unless you want one of those bombs knocking on your palace door." He stood. "I'll have your relief here before morning."

The sensor operator pointed at the dead mercenary. "What about him?"

"He bothering you?"

"No."

"We'll be moving out in the morning. Grab his papers and turn them in to the company clerk before you fill in the hole."

The squad leader disappeared into the night and the two soldiers on guard avoided each other's eyes. The one on the rim sighted down his rifle at the fallen knife thrower. During the raid the fellow had stepped out from behind the tree and lobbed the blade into the hole catching T'Dulna in the chest. Before he was cut down, the knife thrower simply stood, looking shocked, making no attempt at escape. The soldier shook his head, turned his gaze from the dead knife thrower and studied the shadows.

The fortune teller shook her head. "It is no use, Allenby. The Arvanians are not human; their futures are unclear. I cannot see them."

The magician nodded his agreement. "It is as she says, Allenby. They are not human; their minds are closed to my powers."

Allenby looked at the two shadows, then turned to a third. "Well, Painter?"

The figure shrugged. "At the rate we're going, we'll be finished inside of a month. More are joining up—especially after what happened in Tarzak—but we have no time to train them and no equipment." Painter sighed. "All I can suggest is to follow the circus to the Westlands and begin training all over again."

The fortune teller spoke. "What of our prisoner, Painter? With a prisoner, perhaps we can learn enough about the Arvanians—"

"No!" Painter turned from the fortune teller and faced Allenby. "The Arvans have fought this kind of war before, and our two attempts to get prisoners have cost us over twenty men and women. . . . We no longer have the time if anything is to be saved."

The Arvanian mercenaries under the command of Naa-von Dor, moments after achieving orbit around Momus, put down shuttles near Tarzak, Arcadia, Kuumic, Miira and Ris, the main population and road network centers. Against no resistance, all five towns were occupied, with Admiral Sadiss installing a puppet regime in Tarzak and declaring it the legitimate government of Momus. A sixth force of Arvanians, mounted in swift moving hovercrafts, and in higher flying fighters, began sweeps of the countryside, routing out the Moman guerrilla bands. In the short span of nine days, the remains of the Moman Armed Forces—less than a third of its original strength—managed to flee to Anoki and escape by taking to the fishing boats under cover of a storm. The morning of the tenth day saw Naavon Dor declare the central continent secure . . .

High above the vee formation of hovercraft streaking across the calm blue waters of the Western Sea, Naavon's command vehicle—one of the *Sword*'s shuttles—banked to get a sensor reading on one of the islands that had begun appearing as the force approached the almost uninhabited land mass called Westlands by the Momans. Naavon looked down at the unspoiled jungle, then left the cockpit and returned to the cargo bay. The large compartment contained his command center, medical unit and communications. The command center staff sat glumly behind their consoles making indifferent adjustments to already adjusted controls. From the back of the compartment Goss's flute wailed a song of mourning. Naavon walked to the screen that separated his and Goss's quarters from the cargo bay and looked through the door. Goss was stretched out on his cot playing his flute with a large brown jug nestled in the crook of his arm.

"Goss!"

The huge officer lowered his instrument and turned a bleary eye toward the door. "Hail, conqueror." Goss lifted his head and put his mouth to the jug, now upraised. He wiped his mouth on his uniform sleeve after he finished, then belched. "Have we found the elusive foe yet, mighty leader?"

"Goss, have you lost your mind? I could have you executed for this. What is that stuff?"

Goss shook the jug. "This? It's a local remedy for a troublesome conscience. It's called 'sapwine.'" He took another swallow, then held it out. "Care for a blow?"

Naavon took the jug and sniffed at it. "Goss, this will kill you before I have a chance to prop your carcass up in front of a firing squad."

Goss sat up, retrieved his jug, and took another gulp. "Good stuff. Helps you forget the work we've done these past ten days. Too bad the whole battalion can't go on a blind; it needs it."

Naavon sat on his own cot facing Goss. "Speak. What demon has its claw in you this time?"

"Sadiss. The creature could make mud out of diamonds."

Naavon dropped his glance. "Yes, Naavon, you know what I'm saying. Every soldier in your command is saying the same thing. You saw what Sadiss's glorious liberation army did to that town? Porse, was it?"

"I don't know. I think so."

Goss drank again. "Doesn't matter, now, does it? All that looting and killing—just part of the warlords' magnificent plan, right? In the scale of things, just a few scraps of dust destroying a few more scraps?"

"Field officer?" Naavon looked up to see an orderly standing in the door.

"What?"

"We've made landfall. Sensors are picking up something at the base of that small plateau a few minutes inland."

Goss laughed. "By the loving gods, Naavon, we've got them now! Hurry and give the orders. This is as much fun as shooting babies in a schoolyard—"

"That will be enough, Goss!" Naavon turned to the orderly. "I'll be out in a moment." The orderly nodded and left. He turned back to see Goss stretched out again on his cot emptying the jug. Goss lowered the jug to the floor, closed his eyes and began snoring.

"Goss, you fool." Naavon whispered. "A mercenary is never on the right side nor wrong side of a war. A mercenary is just on a side—the side with the pay voucher." Naavon hung his head and looked at the deck. *I am telling this professional soldier the standard fare fed to raw recruits, and I don't even believe it myself.*

The Momans had fought with courage, if not with skill. The few modern weapons they possessed had been taken from the bodies of fallen mercenaries. The rest fought with whatever they had: firebombs, knives . . . Naavon smiled as he remembered that night outside the town called Ris. Arrows began falling into the Arvanian positions. *Arrows!* The first impulse was to laugh, and they all did, save the five mercenaries who died, wooden shafts protruding from their bodies.

Naavon shook his head. The orders from Sadiss were clear: slaughter every last defender. No quarter. He wanted no competition for his liberation army left on the planet. One heavy weapons sweep would probably do it—two at the most—if the terrain were clear. But, the Westlands, with its rugged mountains and dense jungles, would require the time consuming process of rooting the Momans out one at a time. It would require much from the battalion, and the men were long past looking upon this particular job as a war bearing even a shred of dignity.

Naavon looked at Goss. *The men have seen what Sadiss and Mysor are doing with their gang of criminals, and they have seen the desperation, the courage . . . the honor of the Moman defenders.* Naavon shook his head and left the compartment to step into the cargo bay, coming to a halt next to his communications operator. "Get me Sadiss."

The operator coded in the signal and turned to Naavon. "Admiral Sadiss, field officer. Do you want the admiral on visual?"

Naavon shook his head. "Admiral?" he called to the blank screen.

"FIELD OFFICER DOR? HAVE YOU FOUND THEM?"

"Yes, Admiral. I plan to put down my force soon and attempt to make contact with the Momans by—"

"I REMIND YOU AGAIN: THEY ARE NOT MOMANS; THEY ARE REBELS AND TRAITORS. I ALSO REMIND YOU THAT I AM THE COMMANDER OF THIS MISSION, AND THAT YOUR ORDERS ARE TO SLAUGHTER EVERY—"

"Arvanians do not make good butchers, Sadiss. If I can bring them to the point of surrender, I will accept—"

"NAAVON DOR, YOU WILL ACCEPT NOTHING! DO I HAVE TO REMIND YOU, AS WELL, THAT I HAVE A MILITARY FORCE OF MY OWN?"

"You threaten me with a gang of thugs?"

"AND MY BATTLE CRUISER. I HAVE GIVEN YOU YOUR ORDERS, AND IF YOU DO NOT OBEY THEM, I WILL HAVE YOU HUNTED DOWN AS I WOULD ANY ANIMAL!"

"I advise against that, Sadiss. That's a fight over which my men could work up some enthusiasm." Naavon nodded at the operator. "Break contact, then order the hovercraft force to prepare to put down." Naavon frowned, then nodded. "Better notify the *Sword* to go to full alert."

"Yes, field officer."

"What are you grinning at?"

"Nothing, field officer. Nothing at all."

Jeda of the Miira riders, temporary road boss of the Tarzak Circus, followed the juggler named Puga into the dank cave at the base of the plateau. The entrance was hidden behind a thick cover of brush and overhanging trees. He could see no guards, but he knew they were there.

The juggler held up his hand. "Wait here, Jeda." Puga disappeared around a bend leaving Jeda alone with his thoughts. He looked toward the mouth of the cave at the jungle green. In the six days since the Arvanians had landed in the Westlands, the Moman defenders had begun holding their own. The invaders would strike, but their target would melt into the jungle before the Arvanians hit. At the cost of many lives, more Arvanian weapons had fallen into Moman hands, and the experienced seasoned fighters were trading lives with the mercenaries one-for-one. *While we sit safe in the jungle, doing nothing!* Jeda turned as he heard footsteps.

Puga's head appeared around the bend in the tunnel. "Come, Jeda. Allenby will see you."

Jeda followed the juggler around twists and turns until they entered a low, torch-lit chamber. Allenby sat cross-legged before a low table littered with hand-drawn maps. Allenby looked up. "Jeda. What brings you? Is all well with the circus?"

Jeda crossed his arms. "As well as can be expected."

"Meaning?"

"Meaning, we would join the fighting, Allenby. The entire company agrees; that's why I was sent."

Allenby nodded. "I see." He shook his head. "No."

"No? Do you have so many fighters that you can afford to ignore almost two hundred more?"

"Don't be a fool, Jeda."

"A fool?"

"Yes, a fool. Those men and women fighting out there—don't you know what the circus has become to them? It is their reason to keep going, their symbol, their banner. Do you understand?"

"I understand that we sit by letting others do our fighting for us. Momus has been without a circus before—many times."

Allenby rubbed his eyes, then placed his hands together on the table. "Jeda, the circus *is* Momus right now. Before the war, it was different—everything was different. But now, every freak, clown and roustabout crouching in the jungle out there needs to know that the circus is intact, safe. If I allowed the circus to break up and join the fighting ranks, I would be serving the Tenth Quadrant's cause, not ours. Our spirit would crumble."

Jeda looked at the floor of the chamber. "Great Allenby . . . it is hard. It is a hard thing you ask of us."

Allenby nodded. "I know. Go and explain it to the company and make them understand. I am depending on you."

Painter entered the chamber and stood next to Jeda. "Lord Allenby, the Arvans are beginning the hovercraft sweeps again."

"Is the net ready?"

Painter nodded. "And the rockets."

"Will the rockets work?"

Painter shrugged. "We couldn't exactly test them without giving our positions away. The paper and bark tubes seem strong enough to handle the fireballs, but . . ."

Allenby nodded and stood. "We should be going, then."

Painter frowned. "I don't think you should be there, Lord Allenby. If things go wrong, which is highly probable, you shouldn't be in the area."

Allenby pursed his lips, then looked at Jeda. "You're right, Painter. Keep me informed."

Painter nodded, turned and left the chamber. Jeda shrugged. "I should be getting back to the company."

Allenby walked around the table and escorted Jeda through the tunnel. At the mouth of the cave, he placed his hand on the rider's shoulder. "Good luck to you, Jeda."

"And to you."

Allenby watched Puga lead the rider into the jungle until they were both out of sight. He waited another full minute, then turned to his right and ran through the brush to catch up with Painter.

In the hovercraft cockpit, Naavon pulled back on the wheel slightly and banked to the right. "See anything?"

Goss looked up from his sensor panel. "Nothing." The four armed mercenaries in back watched through the bubble canopy at the jungle below. Goss shook his head. "It was a mistake to split up and scatter the force, Naavon."

Naavon nodded and swung the hovercraft on a shallow arc to the left. "Probably, but this way we can cover the same amount of territory in one-tenth the time. If Sadiss would have let us use the shuttles from his ship, it wouldn't be necessary."

Goss laughed. "Naavon, if that piece of slime had kept his gang in check on the central continent, we would have enough of our own shuttles."

Naavon grimaced. The central continent had been secure, but Mysor's bully boys had stirred things up. Sabotage had left all but two of the shuttles from the *Sword* useless. "Goss, have you heard anything further from the second company."

Goss shook his head and returned his gaze to the sensor screen. "My guess is that the resistance on the central continent isn't organized and isn't directed from here. I think it's simply a popular response to Mysor's political acumen—wait!" Goss adjusted the screen, then looked up and out through the canopy. "Eighteen degrees to the right, in that valley. I picked up motion readings, but they're gone now."

Naavon banked the craft to the right. "Let's take a look. We'll come in high first." Naavon guided the craft down the length of the valley, turned and hovered at the opposite end. "Readings?"

Goss shook his head. "Nothing on motion or electromagnetic fields. Try it low and slow and I'll look for some heat."

Naavon pushed the wheel forward, into the valley, and leveled the craft a few meters from the treetops. "Anything?"

Goss studied the screen. "Not yet." Bits and flecks of red appeared on the screen showing the rich animal life below, but none of the traces were large enough to be men. "Wait . . . no, the way it moved off it must have been an animal." Twin red streaks went up the sides of the screen. "Naavon—"

"I see it!"

Goss looked up to see two rockets pulling skyward, lifting a huge net. The craft lurched as Naavon attempted to avoid the trap, but the bottom of the net held to the jungle floor causing the rockets to swing over, letting the net fall over the craft. Naavon struggled to land the craft upright, but it pulled sideways and slammed into a tree, then into a vine-covered rock wall. Naavon opened his eyes to see the craft on its side, the canopy shattered open and himself staring into the business end of a beamer. At the other end of the rifle was someone he recognized from the intelligence briefings: Oswald Painter. The young fellow grinned. "Well, well, Naavon Dor. Look at you."

In the light of a single torch, Naavon walked around the small cave-prison examining the wall while Goss played a dreamy melody on his flute. The field officer halted his search for an escape route and looked down at his second-in-command sitting cross-legged on the cave floor.

"Seeing that four of our comrades are dead, Goss, wouldn't a serious tune be more appropriate?"

Goss lowered the flute and looked up. "In scale with the universe, Naavon, what are the deaths of four mercenaries? Next to the rock that is the plan of the Tenth Quadrant's warlords, we are but splashes of fluid, a hiss of vapor—"

"You twist my words with skill, Goss." Naavon crossed his arms and leaned against the cave wall. "Very well, old friend, let's hear it."

"Hear what?"

"Whatever it is you've been wanting to say ever since the *Sword* went into orbit."

Goss shrugged, played a short phrase and stopped halfway through a repeat. "We've been together a long time, Naavon." He smiled. "If you want, I know you can outtalk me with theories and ideas. I am a soldier and I do not think in terms of universes, thousand century schemes, not the kinds of thoughts you have. Am I making sense?"

"Go on."

"Naavon, perhaps we are—as you say—scraps of dust, too unimportant to bother with. But, I bother with them, because I *am* one of those scraps. If I could see and know the entire universe at once . . . But, I don't. I see this cave around us; I see you standing there. In battle, I see enemies bleed, friends die."

Naavon squatted in front of Goss. "We are mercenaries, Goss."

Goss rubbed his chin, then tapped his flute against his knee. "These things I see, Naavon, are the important things to me. We are different. You see the destiny of the warlords shaping the universe; I see Arvan falling someday to an armed force—I see this filth, Mysor and Sadiss, serving the warlords by destroying a way of life . . ."

"Mercenaries have no sides, Goss, except—"

"Except the pay voucher, I know. We can have no cause,

Naavon, but I find myself in a strange position. I am in a war where I want . . . no, where I have to take sides, and I find myself on the wrong one."

Naavon stood. "Goss, in time this planet won't even exist. How can you lend yourself to this uncertain, minuscule corner of the present, when before you stretches unlimited future?"

"I will never see it."

"Aah!" Naavon turned his back. "What's the use talking to you?"

"Probably none."

The field officer looked at Goss. "Tell me, then, Goss. If this is how you feel, why do you not desert? Why do you not join the sorry forces of Momus? Why are you still here with me?"

Goss lifted his flute and studied it. "In the scale of things, Naavon, my reason is nothing—less than nothing: the oath of one soldier to serve another. As I said, it is nothing, but it is important to me." Goss resumed his playing.

Naavon looked up as a red and purple clad figure carrying a torch entered the chamber. "Come with me. You two are to dine with Allenby."

The wood fire in the center of the large underground chamber hissed and popped, casting against the walls large shadows of those seated around its warmth. Allenby glanced to his right at Gens the fortune teller, trying to catch her eye. Gens, however, was occupied studying the two Arvanian officers seated across the fire from her. Allenby looked at the troubled face of Naavon Dor and couldn't believe the Arvanian's concern to be rooted in the fact of his capture. The one called Goss watched Dishnu, a minor clown from Dirak, do a comic pantomime of a man building a house with rubber tools. The clown finished and bowed.

Allenby clapped. "Excellent, Dishnu." He reached into his purse and withdrew several coppers. "Here."

The fortune teller handed the clown coppers, as did the roustabout named Painter. Then Dishnu faced the Arvanian called Goss. Goss reached into his uniform blouse and withdrew a wallet. "A fine performance, clown. Are Tenth Quadrant credits acceptable?"

Dishnu frowned. "Have you no coppers?"

Goss shrugged. "I would think this money to be a promising currency, considering everything."

Allenby laughed and tossed Goss a small purse. "There, I'll exchange your paper."

Goss handed the clown several coppers, then handed the purse to Naavon. The other Arvanian seemed startled, then took several coppers and put them into Dishnu's hand. Allenby rubbed his hands together. "And now, perhaps a little magic?"

Dishnu sat down and nodded. "Yes, Great Allenby, I would see your illusion of the night flower."

Painter laughed. "Perhaps our guests would like to perform?"

Goss pulled out his flute. "My pleasure."

Painter shook his head. "Yes, but our suffering."

Goss pointed his flute at Painter. "If I am not mistaken, Painter, you wear the garb of a laborer—"

"Roustabout."

Goss nodded. "Yes, then can we see your act? Perhaps you would give us a demonstration of lifting, loading and hauling?" As Painter blushed, Goss put the flute to his lips and blew a complicated exercise. Upon its completion, he trailed off into a sad, haunting tune. Others in the chamber, at other fires, halted their chatter to listen. Allenby felt tears well inside of his chest at the images of pain, loneliness and empty existence Goss's flute created in his mind. Before the war, it would have been just another tune. But, as he listened, he knew it to be a soldier's song speaking of life risked, worlds conquered and lost, death achieved, an existence overflowing with events, yet devoid of meaning. Allenby looked up, surprised the song had ended. Painter leaned forward and dropped coppers into the Arvanian's hand, nodding.

Gens the fortune teller placed her hand on Allenby's arm as Naavon got to his feet, bent over and pulled a smoking brand from the fire. He turned, stepped outside the ring behind Dishnu and began drawing the charcoal across the wall of the cave. Allenby could make little sense of the scrawl of lines and curves, but all the time Naavon drew, he felt Gens's hand tightening on his arm. She turned and whispered into his ear. "I have it! I can read them now!"

While the Arvanian officer drew, Gens motioned to a barker, slipped him a few movills and whispered into his ear. The barker nodded and crept back to his fire. The fortune teller turned back to Allenby. "I have already sent a message to Jeda to prepare the circus for performance."

"Why?"

"Great Allenby, you must suggest a truce to the Arvanian."

Allenby frowned. "Are you sure?"

Gens frowned back. "Am I a fortune teller, or not?"

"You are indeed a fortune teller," Allenby whispered, "but Naavon Dor will want to know the reason for the truce."

"Tell him you must have a truce in order to hold a performance."

"A performance—"

"Excuse me," interrupted Goss. "is it customary to maintain this chatter during another's performance?"

Allenby raised his eyebrows and shrugged. "My apologies, Goss. No offense to your commander was intended."

Goss nodded and turned his glance toward the drawing taking shape at the end of Naavon's stick. "Remember that when it comes time to pay my commander's fee for his art."

Two days later, Allenby stood on the edge of a large clearing watching the two companies of armed Arvanian mercenaries mingling with three hundred of his own armed Moman defenders. Both groups were gathered around the clearing waiting for the parade to begin. *It is enough to test one's faith in fortune tellers.* A blowing shriek from the steam calliope signaled the start, and from the far edge of the clearing, the crowd parted letting in a lead of costumed clowns followed by a string of performing lizards, horses, jugglers, tumblers, a float carrying the flyers, then the calliope itself bellowing out a march that could be heard for the distance of a two day's walk against a strong wind.

Arvanians and Momans, for the most part, avoided each other. But, in several small gatherings, Momans pointed out the various stars and acts, explaining them to curious mercenaries. By the time the sun began setting, halfway through the show, the torches illuminating the perimeter showed Momans and Arvanians passing jugs of sapwine, discussing the merits of the various acts and . . . laughing.

Allenby felt a presence at his side and turned to see Naavon Dor looking back at him. "Field officer Dor."

Naavon nodded. "Lord Allenby. Could I ask a question?"

"Of course, although I can't guarantee an answer."

"This truce, this circus, why did you propose them?"

Allenby shrugged. "Do you know of our fortune tellers, field officer?"

Naavon frowned, then nodded. "The one called Gens, she saw much in my drawing, did she not?"

"And in Goss's song."

Naavon looked down, then shook his head. "Gens saw in me something that would not let this circus be destroyed. How does she see where I do not?"

"It is her training."

Naavon nodded. "And, does she see if this truce can be made into a peace?"

"Not everything is clear to a fortune teller's eyes, Naavon Dor. What is clear is that we do not serve anyone's destiny save our own, that of the circus."

"Where did Gens see this in me?"

Allenby shrugged. "It's hard to explain, and I don't understand it myself. I doubt if Gens understands it. She saw in your drawing, many meanings, yet many contradictions." Allenby shrugged. "I saw neither. I saw a great hand with a hundred tiny galaxies in its palm, another sad face and a lone fist." Allenby rubbed his chin. "Will peace come?"

Naavon looked up, his eyes widening in horror. "Sadiss!"

Allenby looked up and saw the streaks of shuttles in the sky. "What is it? What kind of treachery is this, Dor?"

But Naavon was already running into the clearing, shouting for the torches to be extinguished and for everyone to take cover. He disappeared from Allenby's view just as a wall of flame erupted from the clearing.

Before the Arvanian commander died, he ordered his second-in-command to join the Arvanian forces with those of Momus to destroy Sadiss and the puppet government of Mysor. To Allenby he said: "Take the circus and spread it throughout the galaxy—the universe. We all follow gods; mine was destiny—an empty spirit. Follow your god; it is the circus; it is your strength."

Within four months Mysor and his followers were dead and Admiral Sadiss had escaped on his command ship, but not before inflicting serious damage to the Sword. *Damaged as well was the circus, which took nearly a year to replace its acts and equipment. During the same year, the home looms of Momus turned out the canvas, loggers brought down the timbers and the mines of Kuumic turned out the fittings to raise the big top. Arvanians and Montagnes brought the* Sword *to full readiness, and renamed it the* City of Baraboo II. *After two centuries, the circus was back on the star road.*

Bunsome put down the last sheet of Shelem's chapter and looked up at the assembled company. Lissa, ringmaster, blew her whistle and Goss, the Arvanian, landed on the keys of the calliope. The sounds echoed in the vast cargo hold as the company cheered, then moved out into the night, toward the streets of Cukyu.

After they were gone, Bunsome nodded. *We will succeed; we cannot fail.* He looked toward the open door of the hold. *And, I shall be a priest. Thank you, Shelem.*

EXTRA! EXTRA!

LONGYEAR WINS TRIPLE CROWN!

Exciting news for science fiction fans—Barry B. Longyear was awarded both the Hugo and the Nebula for his novella, "Enemy Mine," as well as winning the John W. Campbell Award for Best New Writer of 1979. These spectacular achievements have established Longyear as the hottest writer around. Berkley is proud to offer these Longyear selections:

CIRCUS WORLD 04709-1/$2.25
MANIFEST DESTINY 04530-7/$2.25
(includes "Enemy Mine")

Available at your local bookstore or return this form to:

Berkley Book Mailing Service
P.O. Box 690
Rockville Centre, NY 11570

Please send me the above titles. I am enclosing $________
(Please add 75¢ per copy to cover postage and handling). Send check or money order—no cash or C.O.D.'s. Allow six weeks for delivery.

NAME________

ADDRESS________

CITY________ STATE/ZIP________

86

MS READ-a-thon— a simple way to start youngsters reading

Boys and girls between 6 and 14 can join the MS READ-a-thon and help find a cure for Multiple Sclerosis by reading books. And they get two rewards—the enjoyment of reading, and the great feeling that comes from helping others.

Parents and educators: For complete information call your local MS chapter. Or mail the coupon below.

Kids can help, too!

Mail to:
National Multiple Sclerosis Society
205 East 42nd Street
New York, N.Y. 10017

I would like more information about the MS READ-a-thon and how it can work in my area.

Name ______________________________
(please print)

Address ______________________________

City ______________ State __________ Zip __________

Organization ______________________________

78JA